CW00551659

Other non f

LOOKING FOR LULU

Four decades ago she died for her country …
now it's time for redemption

A NOVEL by

JEFF CONNOR

2QT Limited (Publishing)

First Edition published 2015
2QT Limited (Publishing)
Unit 5 Commercial Courtyard
Duke Street
Settle
North Yorkshire
BD24 9RH

Cover Image: Gerhard Gronefeld. Paris, 1940

Back cover image used under license from Shutterstock.com
Image copyright: Stiftung Deutsches Historisches Museum
Unter den Linden 2, D - 10117 Berlin

Printed in the UK by Lightning Source UK Limited

ISBN 978-1-910077-69-6

Best wishes
— Jeff !

AUTHOR'S NOTES

Looking for Lulu stands between fact and invention. Here are the facts:

Thirteen female agents of the Special Operations Executive (SOE) died during the Second World War. Some were held and tortured by the Gestapo at 11, Rue de Saussaies in the 8th arrondissement of Paris and others were later murdered. All, without exception, were French speakers with fictional names.

After Palestinian terrorists killed eleven Israeli athletes at the Munich Olympics of 1972 at least one British competitor shared accommodation with others close to the Israelis in the Olympic Village and was later interviewed by West German authorities.

The botched rescue attempt at Munich Airport persuaded Bonn to establish an elite anti-terrorist group (GSG 9) under the leadership of Colonel Ulrich K 'Ricky' Wegener. Colonel Wegener and GSG 9's first operation was the rescue of eighty-six crew and passengers in Lufthansa Flight 181 in October, 1977.

Operation Fire Magic, as it was called, is still regarded as one of the most successful rescue operations in the history of counter terrorism. Two British members of the Special Air Service were also involved in this operation, notably the shoot-out at Mogadishu Airport.

The hijackers had tried to secure the release of members of the West German terrorist group Red Army Faction (RAF), but a day after the rescue three of the RAF leaders died in Stuttgart's Stammheim prison. Another RAF member, Ulrike Meinhof, had hanged herself in the same jail five months previously. Some say all four committed suicide, while others insist these were murders formulated by a combination of Bonn and the prison authorities. I have used the names of the four RAF leaders – Andreas Baader, Meinhof, Gudrun Ensslin and Jan-Carl Raspe – here.

Lieutenant Colonel Colin Mitchell – 'Mad Mitch' of Aden and Argyll and Sutherland Highlanders fame – was MP for Aberdeenshire West from 1970 to 1974 and Braemar, on the edge of the Cairngorms, was part of his jurisdiction. Lieutenant Colonel Mitchell's low opinion of Whitehall officialdom is well known.

Finally, a national newspaper was once based in Albion Street, Glasgow, although it was not called *The Inquirer.* The pub next door is still the Press Bar.

THE AUTHOR

JEFF CONNOR was born in Manchester, went to school in Bury and spent most of his career in national newspapers including the *Daily Mirror, Daily Express, Daily Star, Scottish Sun and Scotland on Sunday.* He is the author of twelve sports books, among them *Wide-Eyed and Legless,* the classic account of the 1987 Tour de France and *The Lost Babes*, the story of the Munich air disaster of 1958.

He lives in Lytham. *Looking for Lulu* is his first novel.

Acknowledgements

I thank Colour Sergeant Anthony Wilson, formerly of 2 Rifles, for advice on military matters, and Annegret Schottmayer's work of German translation was priceless. As was Tracey Lawson's advice and support.

I am obliged to *Stiftung Deutsches Historisches Museum* archive in Berlin for allowing me to use their image for the cover. I emphasise: *Looking for Lulu* is a work of fiction and the people in the cover image, taken by official Wehrmacht photographer Gerhard Gronefeld, bear no relation to the characters in the book. Finally, I owe much to the staff of 2QT Publishing, particularly Catherine Cousins, Karen Holmes, Joanne Harrington and Hilary Pitt.

CONTENTS

PROLOGUE

FAO All Staff

This is the first of what I hope will be weekly Editor's Notes to Staff. I hope you find it useful.

After my first six months in the hot seat at Albion Street I can now resolve some aspects of The Glasgow Inquirer *in editorial terms.*

As everyone will be aware, the latest ABC figures were not the best. They showed a tenth successive fall in circulation, and while the newspaper has not yet reached a critical stage the patient is definitely in need of medication.

There will be some changes.

After meetings with the management and the owners (and a detailed analysis by a market research team) it has been decided that from Monday, September 20, The Glasgow Inquirer *will be known as* The Inquirer.

As I told staff two weeks ago, I have always hoped this would be seen as a cosmopolitan rather than a parochial newspaper. As it stands, news, sport and features are devoted to Glasgow and the West Coast and little else.

In my view a hard news story is a hard news story anywhere, whether it is about Glasgow or Gloucester (even Germany, if you forgive the alliteration).

The new masthead will appear on September 20. There will be two editorial conferences a day rather than four, as in the past: morning at 10.30 a.m. and evening at 6.30 p.m. I will be meeting staff individually over the next few weeks.

In the meantime, it will not be necessary for staff to wear suits and ties for work, unless covering court or council. I am bringing back bylines (the first in twenty-two years, I am told) and I look forward to seeing the names on the lead stories of the first edition of Monday, September 20! I remind all reporters that they MUST have a workable home telephone and an up-to-date passport.

Finally, I am sure you will join me in congratulating Mrs Lucienne Batch, who is to take over a new role as editorial administrator of Inquirer Newspapers Ltd.

Harold Bloom, Editor.
September 15, 1982.

CHAPTER 1.

Sunday, September 26. Ten at night, three hours into his shift, and prison officer Gert Friedmann was already falling asleep.

Friedmann, twenty-four, grew up in Heidelberg, the country's oldest institute for higher education, and had once imagined a more agreeable calling than this. A night shift at Stammheim Supermax had to be as tedious as being an inmate: move forward one way, back another; eat and drink at this time, go to bed at that time. Colleagues said one could expect drama on day shifts; perhaps catch a prisoner with drugs or break up a fight. So far he hadn't even had to foil a suicide – once a regular occurrence, and almost always after midnight.

Friedmann could sense his eyes closing so he stood up, took several deep breaths, slapped both cheeks hard and looked around for something, anything, that might fight off the tedium. Whatever else, a guard who was only five months into his probationary period must not nod off during his watch.

He first checked the banks of CCTV monitors that watched all seven floors: quiet, quiet as a grave. He filled the kettle, reinforced the first-aid kit on the wall shelf and made sure the telephone was still working.

Friedmann knew he should not complain. The money and food were good: he had his own living accommodation within the complex and a free uniform. There was a large staff library, a small film theatre and regular seminars on the use of firearms and how to deal with difficult inmates. True, it was a male/female environment but with a couple of exceptions the female guards, and the female prisoners, were as ugly as sin anyway. There was little he could do about that.

There was, of course, Gerber, the senior officer, lying asleep on a makeshift mattress in the corner of the guards' cubicle.

Night shift guards – usually single, or divorced, or too old to handle the heavy stuff – worked in pairs, and Friedmann had been unlucky with this one. The first things he had learned about Gerber (after being told he was fifty-four, a grandfather and from some Frankfurt am Main hellhole) were that he was work-shy; a moaner: his pay, his pension, the food, the football results and everything else. But Friedmann also knew that when the time came for the governors to check a probationer's suitability, or lack of it, senior guards were always asked for their views. Friedmann was certainly not going to complain about Gerber, much though he would like to.

His superior officer broke wind and began to snore, loudly.

'Thanks for that,' Friedman called out, but not quite loudly enough. 'You … are … a fat lazy pig … and you stink … like a polecat.' Thus emboldened, Friedman flicked a cigarette stub with his right index finger so accurately it hit Gerber on the side of his head. Gerber made a funny sound, turned over and slept on.

Friedmann reached down with thumb and first finger and squeezed the nostrils tight, covering his mouth with the other hand at the same time. After a few seconds Gerber started to splutter and choke. That seemed to do the trick.

Friedmann's little victory had brought him to life and made him quite industrious so he pulled the clipboard down from the wall behind Gerber and, whistling happily to himself, started on the first encounter sheet of the night:

Stammheim Supermax, Sunday, September 26, 1982, submitted by night duty officer Gert Friedmann.

Then in large letters below:

8.45 p.m., male Cell 109 requests new toilet rolls. Floor guard supplies.

9 p.m., check on all floors. Male in Cell 451 given prescribed sleeping tablets; two Zolpidem. All quiet.

9.12 p.m., female in Cell 212f visited by lawyer. Discussion held in Interview Room 2. Two female guards overview from distance.

9.46 p.m., lawyer leaves after discussion with female in Cell 212f. Female prisoner returns to cell. Full search on return by two female guards. All clear.

10 p.m., checks on all floors. All quiet. Cell and corridor lights off.

11.12 p.m., male in Cell 511 asks for cough mixture. Prospan supplied by corridor guard.

12 p.m., checks on all floors. All quiet.

Friedmann took his time to read it through and check his spelling. Quite erudite, he thought. The deputy governor always liked short words and sentences when the time came to check a guard's notes.

Given the history of Stammheim Supermax, the new encounter sheet system made sense to most. When Chancellor Erhard opened the building in 1964 the boast had been that this was 'one of the most secure prisons in Europe'. That no longer applied. After four young prisoners were found dead in their seventh-floor cells, three of them on the same night, Stammheim did not seem secure at all. Death Night, the newspapers had dubbed the events of May 21, 1975, a description that had stuck. Improvements in security inside and out followed; there were more guards and a new CCTV system. The nightly encounter sheets, too.

If a coroner, a Federal Prosecutor, the press and the public then asked why Prisoner A had been found hanging in his cell or Prisoner B failed to recover from a sudden bout of pneumonia the answer was there in black and white. In effect, encounter sheets were written witnesses for the state. Of course, old-timers like Gerber objected. They were like pet dogs: they didn't like changes in their little routines, and half of them could probably not write anyway.

Who and why they were named 'encounter' sheets was a different matter, thought Friedmann. A non-encounter sheet was more like it, particularly on night shifts. He giggled at his wit and moved to a second sheet.

Monday, September 27.

1.50 a.m., male in Cell 367 complains of headache. Two tablets Dolviran.

2 a.m., all quiet.

2.10 a.m., female prisoner in Cell 212 complains of insomnia. Sedatives refused on advice of night duty doctor.

4.02 a.m., female prisoner Cell 212 demands to see prison governor, bangs loudly on cell door, but calms down after an

hour. Check on cell; prisoner asleep.
6 a.m., checks all floors. All quiet.
6.45 p.m., telephone call…?

That strange telephone call and the rumpus in Cell 212 apart, it had been a peaceful night. All that remained was the 7 p.m. encounter sheet, a sign-off by both guards and home to a well-deserved sleep.

Friedmann thumped his colleague hard on the shoulder to wake him.

'Is it that time already?' said Gerber. Then, without the slightest sense of guilt, 'Has anything happened, *junge*?'

Friedmann thought it best to tell him.

'The last section of the encounter sheet?' he said. 'I've left it open for now, because I wasn't sure. It was a call from one of the office staff.'

Gerber yawned and stretched and climbed slowly to his feet.

'Don't tell me, *junge*,' he said. 'Let me guess. Lukas Rückeran telephoned to tell you he's not coming in today. Am I right?'

'About ten minutes ago,' agreed Friedmann. 'Is he always crying off work?'

'We are *always* filling in for that swine. I bet I know the reason this time.'

Friedmann was tired of Gerber's old school homilies, so he sweated him a bit.

'I think this one might surprise you,' he said.

'I doubt it, *junge*,' said Gerber grandly. 'I've known Rückeran for over twenty years, so nothing surprises me. Did you know his wife died of cancer two months ago? His father has been killed in a road accident at least twice, to my knowledge. Before you ask, he never married and *both* his parents died in the Allied bombings. He'll be off on one of his benders. Out of interest, what did he say?'

Friedmann gave a wooden smile and told him, as slowly and as quietly as he could, 'He said … he was going … to die today.'

Gerber did shake his head in what might have been disbelief but carried on adjusting his white *Gefängniswärter* hat and dark blue uniform.

'Did he say what he was going to die of?'

'No. He didn't elaborate.'

'He didn't *what*?'

'He didn't give me any details. All he said was that he was going to die.'

Gerber thought for a few moments and then decided,

'Don't worry about it, *junge*; the original boy who cried wolf is our Rückeran. He'll be back at work in a couple of days. Did he sound upset?'

Friedmann admitted he had not been the slightest bit concerned, just drunk.

'That's it then,' said Gerber triumphantly. 'Believe me, no one will take any notice.'

Friedmann wanted to know how a guard who was drunk before seven in the morning managed to keep his job. Gerber folded his *Stuttgart-Zeitung* newspaper, shoved it in an inside pocket and unlocked the door from the cubicle to the corridor.

'He was drunk because he is an alcoholic, and has been for years,' he said. 'As for exactly *why* he keeps his job, your guess is as good as mine. Now come on, let's finish off. The day shift will be here soon. Give me a hand to carry these mattresses back to Cell 602.'

'I will, but what do I say in the report?'

Gerber sighed and impatiently banged the door with

his heavy key ring.

'Were I you I would just put it down as "sick". I don't think the deputy governor will be amused if he reads "*Rückeran said going to die today*". That's my advice, at any rate. See the weather forecast in the newspaper? Snow, they say. See you later. *Grüß Gott.*'

Friedmann did as suggested:

6.45 p.m., telephone call … Prison Officer Lukas Rückeran, 3b Münchingerstraße. Sick and will miss work today.

He made a copy with the Xerox, left the original on its clipboard and marked the copy 'for the attention of the secretary to the deputy governor'. Then he signed off, too.

There was a walk of some 800 metres from the main complex to the single men's quarters. It was still dark and so cold he shivered, in spite of his winter uniform, so he set his feet walking faster. Waves of cirrostratus were thickening the skies above the hills to the south-east. Snow. Gerber had been right about one thing.

Friedmann had just keyed in his access code at the entrance to the block when he stopped and remembered something else Gerber had said: Rückeran, the drunken prison guard, who was always crying wolf. Thinking back to his days at primary school, which were not too long ago, he was certain that the shepherd boy had not been crying wolf on the day he was attacked and eaten by the beast.

There again, it was only a fable.

CHAPTER 2.

Stammheim-Mitte. Wednesday, September 29.

Bux's mood shifted from everyday grumpiness to out-and-out foul temper the moment he saw the number plates of the cars, all badly kerb-parked in the manner of police everywhere.

The Volkswagen belonged to Dietrich, a police doctor who was not entitled to a company vehicle. The nearest green and white Mercedes was that of a photographer, Krause, and an almost identical car next to that was shared by two of the *Kriminalpolizei* (*Kripo*) ballistics and forensics team, Luft and Neumann, who always worked together. The third Mercedes, ghost-white and far larger than the others, was parked as close to the front door of 3 Münchingerstraße as possible and belonged to the public prosecutor of the city of Stuttgart.

'*Scheisse*,' said Kommissar Markus Bux, to no one in particular.

A small crowd, absorbed by the drama in this quiet neighbourhood, had gathered outside the police cordon. Among them was a crime reporter from *Stuttgarter-Zeitung* who Bux knew and a photographer he did not.

'How on earth did they know about this?' asked Lang,

Bux's young deputy.

'Those two journalists?' said Bux. 'I suspect they were tipped off.'

Then, in case Lang had not understood first time, which was often the case, 'One of our blabbermouth colleagues at Hahnemannstraße—'

Lang wanted an explanation, but the reporter had already interrupted.

'A quick word, Kommissar?' he said as the two detectives walked past.

Bux despised newspapermen. They worked in a business that thrived on inexactitude and occasional malevolence, but he stopped, looked down at the ground and scratched his head as if in deep thought.

'Jesse Owens,' he said. 'Two quick words for you. Will that do?'

The reporter, thin-faced and scruffy, gave a sardonic smirk.

'Thank you, Herr Bux, so gracious of you,' he said. He waited until Bux was out of earshot before he added, 'Miserable old pig. Hope you rot in hell.'

The photographer, a boy in his teens who was struggling to grow a moustache, knew little about Kommissar Bux and nothing at all of Jesse Owens, but he asked anyway, 'Who the hell is Jesse Owens?'

The reporter sighed and tut-tutted. *Stuttgarter-Zeitung* seemed to be employing all sorts of idiots these days.

'An athlete,' he said. 'The Berlin Olympics of '36. American. Black. Very fast.'

'A bit before my time,' said the boy photographer. He yawned, scratched an ear and vaguely pointed his camera in the direction of Kommissar Bux's backside.

Dietrich the police doctor was on his way out – 'Hello,

Herr Bux, and how you are today … and how is the lovely Silke?' like a barman greeting a regular customer – and stopped to talk further. They had known each other for some twenty years and Dietrich knew Bux would not approach the body until the forensic and ballistic teams had finished, so he filled in what he had seen already. Bux, in his turn, listened intently, for he had great respect for medical people.

The victim had been dead for approximately forty-eight hours, said Doctor Dietrich. The cold weather had taken the edge off the usual noxious smell, although it was bad enough. Congealed blood from a hole in the front of the forehead down to the stomach and bleeding from the mouth, ears and nose as well as effusions of blood the size of fists that hid both eyes. More blood and a shard of bone on the wall just behind the victim. Rigor mortis had set in and the skin was purple and waxen. Age: probably the early sixties.

'Oh, and he appeared to be smiling at something.'

'Something … or was it someone?' asked Bux.

'Perhaps both; it could have been the tightening of facial nerves. The skin of corpses can often look like that. Or someone had just told him a funny story.'

Bux thought it was a doctor's notion of truth in jest, but Dietrich wasn't smiling.

'We should find out more when the pathologist has had a look,' he said. 'By the way, Markus, there's no lighting in there. Someone failed to pay the electricity bill and all he had were candles. The telephone was disconnected, too. Good luck.'

Bux plodded up the steep concrete stairs like an ageing sumo wrestler following the two *Schutzpolizei* who had raised the alarm originally. The closer they got the more they could smell the blood and excrement for the first time. Then the youngest of the policemen piped up.

'The man has been deceased for some time,' said the boy showily. 'A single shot to the head killed him; obviously the Red Army Faction again.'

The other man, his hair as grey as Bux's, rolled his eyes in dismay.

Bux rounded on the boy at once. 'What's your name, *junge*?'

'I am *Schutzpolizei* Andreas Richter from Klingenbach, Stuttgart-Ost, Kommissar,' said the boy, almost standing to attention.

'Well, Andreas Richter from Stuttgart-Ost, here is your thought for the day: there is no such thing as "obvious" in detective work. It is not your job to tell me how this man died and who killed him. I do not require "expert opinions" from a *Schutzpolizei* juvenile. I think I can also work out for myself that a single gunshot to the head is likely to kill someone. Agreed, Herr Richter?'

The boy's face crumpled and his elderly colleague came to the rescue.

'Kommissar Bux, the name of the victim is Rückeran. Lukas Rückeran. He was fifty-nine and lived alone. He worked at the Supermax.'

'*A prison guard?*'

'Yes, Herr Kommissar, another one.'

Bux took off his homburg and used his black leather trench coat for a cushion on the stone stairway. He lit his fifth Lucky of the morning and prepared to wait. Below, on the ground floor, an elderly couple stared back, with what looked – to Bux – like cheerful expectation.

'Tired, Kommissar?' said a voice from behind. 'You should try giving up those cancer sticks. You might live a little longer.'

'Drescher,' said Bux without looking round, and with what most would describe as contempt. 'How rare to find our public prosecutor at a murder scene – and so quickly, too. One of your contacts at Hahnemannstraße? Perhaps that journalist waiting outside, or was it just coincidence?'

Drescher reddened and tried to think of a suitable response.

'I am the public prosecutor of Stuttgart in the state of Baden-Württemberg,' he said, as if reading from an old inventory. 'One of my many jobs is to cooperate with members of the state's police force. Let me remind you that the *Kripo* may be the first agency in the criminal justice process, but statute obliges me to take action when a crime is brought to my attention. The state demands a swift resolution to this case, and justice must be merciless.'

'The state demands, Drescher?' said Bux derisively. 'You're here to lick the arse of our new Chancellor.' He blew some cigarette smoke in the direction of Drescher, who spluttered and coughed dramatically.

'You are a disgrace, Bux,' he said. 'I am here to do a job. I even thought I could help with this case.'

Bux turned to look round at a man in his fifties, well dressed and with a neatly-cut Vandyke beard. 'And what help would that be, Herr Drescher?' he asked.

'How long before we can celebrate the retirement of the great Kommissar Bux?' asked Drescher with a sardonic little cackle.

'Fourteen days,' said Bux who was counting every day. 'Why do you ask?'

'Well, here we are: a nice easy one to finish with.'

'Go on,' Bux said cautiously.

'A Stammheim prison guard, isn't that obvious? It was another murder by members of the Red Army Faction.'

Bux didn't think so, though he had guessed Drescher would say that. This was a man who blamed the RAF for everything, from murder to bad weather – an obsession dating back to 1977, when he was first appointed public prosecutor. After the three leaders of the RAF committed suicide in Stammheim Drescher had started a campaign to have them buried in some unmarked forest graves.

'We do not want this becoming a pilgrimage point for radical lefties,' Drescher had told the media, his favourite choice of discussion groups.

Manfred Rommel, the Mayor of Stuttgart, disagreed, Drescher lost, and all three were buried in Waldfriedhof Cemetery south of the city. When 200 of the *Landespolizei* were needed to keep peace at the funerals, it was the last straw for Drescher. From then on, Mayor Rommel had an enemy for life.

Bux didn't believe in wasting time on brainless bureaucrats like Drescher, but did offer him some advice. 'It was not the RAF,' he said decisively. 'Nothing here pertains. This was a single gunshot, and the RAF have never been into solo assassinations.'

Drescher was unable to think of a suitable response for that, either, so he changed the subject.

'If you are interested, the victim's neighbours phoned the local police station just after 9 a.m. They claimed that they hadn't seen him for two days. He wasn't answering his door – or his telephone.'

'The old couple on the ground floor?'

'Jan and Doreen Huber, aged seventy-four and seventy-two. They own all three apartments and did the identification. Apparently they have had the misfortune of having to live in Stammheim-Mitte for over thirty years, and the victim was their tenant. They had a pass key, but the door was unlocked. No forced entry.'

Bux went heavy with his sarcasm.

'So a prison guard at Stammheim left the door open for the RAF to march in? A bit foolish of him, don't you think? Your RAF theory is falling apart already. Is there anyone in the third-floor flat?'

'Empty for over a year. I will leave the rest of it to you. Incidentally, Bux, it may be a good idea if I discuss this with you at some stage.'

'For what?'

'Perhaps Sunday, 3 p.m?'

'Too busy. Try me next year.'

Drescher gave up and manoeuvred past Bux's bulk and down the stairs, checking hair and tie on the way. There was the sound of a clicking camera and Drescher and the reporter in conversation, though too far away to catch the detail.

Slowly Bux climbed to his feet and looked inside apartment 3b for the first time.

The blinds had been pulled up and the window opened but it was still so dark the *Kripo* team had to use large flashlights, and so cold it was hard to distinguish between the men's breath and their cigarette smoke.

The victim had been sitting on a chair close to the window, and the light from outside showed one half of the head while the other remained in darkness. He did appear to be smiling. There was something Gothic about the whole thing: the blackness, the maniacal grin, the torchlights and the cold breath.

In an effort to speed things up Luft, the ballistics specialist, pointed out the bullet he was bagging into a plastic case. With thumb and two fingers he mimicked the shooting of a pistol and made a clicking sound, like a child pretending to be a gunman, but just the once. Neumann was talking into a Dictaphone when Bux heard the words he had known all along, 'Person or persons unknown, forty to forty-eight hours, a 9mm Parabellum, victim was seated, no sign of forced entry.'

Bux blew a smoke ring so flawless it was still O-shaped when it reached the top-floor flat. He sat down on his leather coat and continued warming his backside.

CHAPTER 3.

After an hour of smoking and wondering about the black-eyed body waiting for him inside, Bux dimped the last of his cigarette and put it in his pocket.

'*Scheisse*,' he repeated, this time more liverishly.

Lang cracked his knuckles and said, 'What was that, boss?'

Bux did not think it worth repeating, so instead he muttered, 'I have told you before, Lang, I am Kommissar Bux, Herr Bux or even Bux. You do not call me "boss". And please stop cracking your knuckles.'

Lang shrugged and clicked his fingers.

'How much longer to wait out here?' he asked.

Bux looked Lang up and down and thought, No, there's nothing for you, junge, unless you suddenly fall downstairs and break your neck.

Almerich Lang was Old High German for 'work power', and Bux had seen little of either. Lang was one of the Hahnemannstraße 'Hairy Chesters': young, strapping non-smokers, herbal tea drinkers ... and rather stupid.

Lang had proved to be a good marksman at Münster's Police University, but little else. His examination results were poor, with low marks in psychology, criminology and law. It had baffled many when he scraped through his

28

preliminaries to start a three-year *Kripo* apprenticeship. Some were convinced that Lang's father, a senior director of Bosch Electronics at Gerlingen, had pulled some strings. Almost everyone mentioned Lang's role in his second murder inquiry: the stabbing by a Ravensbury garage proprietor of the wife caught in an affair with a young car cleaner. Lang – stupidly – handled the knife, and it was only an astute state prosecutor who secured a guilty verdict. Bux would have had little difficulty in relegating Lang to the ranks of *Schupo* … but he didn't. He had other tasks for Lang.

'If you want something to do,' Bux said with a real touch of malice, 'go down and ask the old couple if you can borrow their telephone. Then persuade the local electricity company to turn on some lights in here. If you manage that, search the upstairs flat.'

Lang furrowed his brows and thought for a few seconds.

'The *Schupo* have already done that,' he said. 'They found nothing.'

'Go and have another look. You might find something they missed.'

It was unnecessary. Bux would have to check up there himself, but he was running out of patience. He wanted Lang and his cracking fingers out of the way … or there would soon be a second murder in Münchingerstraße.

Lang was back within thirty minutes, just as the forensic and ballistic teams announced that it was safe to go in.

'Gloves on then, Lang,' Bux ordered. 'Take notes of all I say, and *don't* touch anything.'

The squalor in the flat shocked both of them.

There was a curdled quality about the place, like a West Berlin squat. Ashtrays were overloaded; spent matches and old newspapers were piled six feet high in a corner.

Empty bottles of wine and whisky lay on a grubby nylon carpet.

It would take a couple of days for a full analysis, but Neumann had found several fingerprints, all identical and probably those of Rückeran. The only 'clue' was the bullet casing. It would be examined in detail at Hahnemannstraße, but a 9mm Parabellum slug could be used in a variety of firearms, from a Luger to a Walther – even a Uzi sub-machine gun, so this was no clue at all.

'Notes, Lang,' Bux said as he circled the victim and his chair. 'Door unlocked, so the victim let the killer in or the killer had his own key. Gun fired from six feet, approximately.'

Bux moved within kissing distance of the victim and sniffed. 'No powder marks, broken veins on face so possibly a boozer, a fierce cigarette habit. No sign of a struggle, so nothing spontaneous about this killing at all.'

Bux made another slow circle of the body and pointed his flashlight.

'That entry wound, Lang. Anything odd?'

Lang could think of nothing.

'Try this, then,' ordered Bux. 'Stand in front of the corpse, but six feet away. Imagine you are aiming at that entry wound.'

'Left hand or right?'

'Either,' said Bux. '*A finger will do, Lang, so put your pistol away*. Now kneel slightly until it is level with the entry wound.'

Lang did as he was told.

'Now sit on the floor and point your finger at the victim.'

Lang sat down as ordered. 'Lower, lower,' said Bux impatiently.

Finally, Lang did it to the Kommissar's satisfaction and was allowed to stand.

'The bullet passed through the middle of the forehead,' said Bux. 'Very neat, that, but you will notice the exit wound is at least two inches higher.'

'Meaning what, Herr Bux?'

'Meaning what you have just demonstrated: the killer was sitting in front of Herr Rückeran, though it might have been a small child, or even a dwarf.'

People did not expect humour from Bux so the joke was wasted, and Lang moved on. 'But why sit on the floor to shoot someone?'

'I don't know, Lang, but if you look around there is only one seat and the dead man is still using it. Our mystery man was sitting six feet away on the floor, so I assume there was some sort of conversation before the shot was fired.'

'Herr Drescher and the forensic team are convinced it is a RAF murder.'

'All are entitled to an opinion, even Drescher,' said Bux and he was neither agreeing nor disagreeing.

With difficulty he squatted so his backside almost touched the floor. He tut-tutted,

'I don't have a crystal ball, but I would bet all the money I have against the RAF being involved. They always work in teams, Lang, and use as many weapons as they can carry: a pack mentality without the marksmanship, if you like. If we were looking for a vaguely similar RAF murder we'd have to go back a few years. Way before your time, but I'm thinking of the president of the Supreme Court of Justice—'

Lang held up a hand like a schoolboy showing off to a teacher and interrupted,

'Günter von Drenkmann, Neu-Westend, West Berlin, shot dead on his sixty-fourth birthday, November 10, 1974. Yes, I *did* learn one or two things at Münster Police

31

University.'

Bux did not expect sarcasm from juniors, but he made do with a scowl.

'Von Drenkmann was also alone,' Bux continued. 'The door was not locked, but that is where the similarities end. A RAF commando unit charged in and von Drenkmann was shot three times – *pop, pop, pop* – with three different weapons. In such circumstances it is hard to get a murder conviction because no one knows who was using which weapon. One other point, Lang: the RAF has always claimed responsibility within half a day. It is forty-eight hours since the shooting of Rückeran and so far … nothing.'

'There must be a motive in killing a prison officer, Kommissar.'

Bux thought that unworthy of response so he pulled out another Lucky, only to think better of it. He was close to Silke's 'allowance' so he scrounged a pack of chewing gum from Lang, who nodded and smiled, like a care worker applauding a crabby old pensioner for pouring his own tea.

Bux rose slowly to his feet and his knees made a loud clicking noise just as Lang cracked his knuckles again. Lang guffawed loudly and said,

'That was funny, Herr Bux. That sounded just like castanets in an orchestra's percussion section!'

Then Lang realised. Kommissar Bux had not found that funny at all.

CHAPTER 4.

Bux pointed his flashlight up and down and around three rooms, all windowless cubicles except the lounge, where a small window overlooked the street.

Rückeran had not employed a housekeeper or even made an effort himself. The single bedroom, a small bathroom and an even smaller kitchenette alcove hadn't been cleaned for some time. The kitchen sink was fenced by dirty crockery: quite typical of many single men, who always left the washing-up as long as possible.

A dozen empty bottles of wine and spirits stood on top of a tiny fridge. Bux remembered driving past the grocery shop on the corner of Gelbrandstraße, and he reminded himself that they must interview the owners. He opened the fridge: half a bottle of sour milk, some half-eaten cooked meat and an empty foil of Cambozola cheese.

'Not much of a houseman, our Rückeran,' said Lang. 'What a stink in here.'

The clothing inside the bedroom closet was basic, too: a spare prison guard's uniform, a pair of hiking boots and two white shirts and a black suit and tie – the dress of a funeral mourner. The sheets hadn't been changed for some time and the pillows had no covers. Three bricks and a Baedeker guide to Stuttgart propped up one corner of the bed, and there were four well-used paperbacks on the bedside table.

'A bizarre choice,' said Lang, who, as well as his annoying habit of turning to look at his passenger when driving, moved his lips when reading.

Bux watched fascinated as Lang spoke.

'Kafka's *The Trial*, Remarque's *All Quiet on the Western Front*, a picture book about birds and insects … and what is this? *Trouble Shooter* by a French writer, Louis L'Amour.'

'An American writer,' Bux sighed. 'Louis L'Amour was American. If you take the trouble to look at the book cover you might see that the man pointing a pistol is wearing a cowboy hat.'

The bathroom toilet and a one-tap basin were filthy and smelled of old man's urine. A small shower had been used not to wash, but to hold more old newspapers, which were piled as high as your chin. Bux took a cursory look and left.

Some coins – maybe twenty Deutschmarks in all – had been left on top of an IKEA sideboard, and on the wall above that was an expensive Sunburst golden resin wall clock, which seemed innocuous amid the squalor. An ancient gramophone was within reaching distance of the chair, one that could be rotated 360 degrees. The stylus was stuck at the end of a single-track vinyl record. Another, a long player, had been left on the floor.

'*Song of the Earth*', by Gustav Mahler,' said Bux pointing at the LP. 'This was a man with taste.'

Lang pulled a derisive face but then said, 'What is the single track, Kommissar?'

Bux pointed his flashlight and squeezed his eyes tight. '"*Prix de Beauté*", and the singer is Hélène Regelly. An old French song, all squeeze box and fiddles, but popular with the Wehrmacht during the war.'

'Surely the Wehrmacht preferred German music?'

'*Not* if you were serving in Paris,' Bux said thoughtfully. 'If they told the truth many soldiers would prefer 'La Vie en rose' to 'The Horst Wessel Song': far more romantic.'

Bux took the stylus off the record, closed the turntable and moved back to the sideboard.

He pointed his flashlight again: a wooden carving of the Virgin Mary and a collection of the sort of faded black-and-white photographs found in every home – a mother and father alongside a smiling boy, about ten years old, and all three on the top of a hill looking down over Stuttgart and the Neckar River.

The final photograph was in colour and probably taken by a Wehrmacht publicist. The same boy, now a handsome soldier with dark eyes and stark blond hair, was wearing a full dress *Heer* uniform. An Eastern Front campaign medal was on his chest with the collar insignias of an *Obersoldat*. The Y with three dots told Bux this was the 7th Panzer, the first division of *Generalfeldmarschall* Erwin Johannes Eugen Rommel, the father of the current Mayor of Stuttgart. The young private first class, soon to be lying on a slab in a Stuttgart mortuary, also had a Knight's Cross of the Iron Cross on his neck.

Rückeran's life, or the life he wanted others to know about, ended there, for there were no more family photographs and no personal letters.

'This is odd, Kommissar,' Lang said, pointing his flashlight at a small, clean area amid all the dust on the sideboard. 'It appears there was another frame here and someone has removed it. Maybe this was a robbery after all. Maybe the killer had been caught in the act.'

'Think again, Lang. The money is still on the sideboard. There is a vintage clock on the wall; probably the most expensive piece in here. A robber who took an old snap but left an expensive clock and money? There must be another reason.'

Bux let Lang attempt to work that out for himself and, when he could not, called his *Kripo* team back in and set them to work.

'I want everything in here bagged, but I want those photographs left for now. All the material, including the books and those newspapers and all his clothing can go. All the ashtrays and cigarette stubs, too.'

Lang and the other *Kripo* operators concurred.

'One more thing, Lang: when their tenant has left the building, go and tell the old couple downstairs to come up here.'

CHAPTER 5.

An ambulance team of three pushed and pulled and squeezed the body into a rubber cadaver pouch and were halfway down the stairs when the Hubers brushed past on the way up.

'Poor Herr Rückeran, murdered in his own home,' shouted Frau Huber to anyone who was listening.

'Another tenant lost,' bellowed Herr Huber. Then to Bux, 'How long will this take?'

'Why do you ask?' said Bux, raising his voice when he saw the hearing aids.

'We have a train ticket for Mannheim this afternoon,' said the old man petulantly.

'To see my daughter and her husband,' said his wife.

'*How long?*' said Bux.

'A week or perhaps more; it all depends on the weather.'

Bux had no objection. Münchingerstraße would be closed for some time, and the old couple were best out of the way. But he sighed and pretended to be annoyed.

'If you must, you must. Leave an address and a phone number with my colleague here when we go. Now tell me, have you seen any strangers here recently? And what about his friends?'

'Herr Rückeran was a good tenant,' Frau Huber said.

'That's your opinion, Doris,' said her husband. Then to Bux again, 'Did you know this lush was a Stammheim prison officer?'

'Hush, Munchkin, that is not fair,' said Doris. 'The officer will know all of this. They wish to know if Herr Rückeran had guests. The simple answer, Kommissar, is "No". Did you see a guest, Munchkin? No, he was a very lonely man. I don't think he had *any* friends. Were you aware his parents died during the war?'

'The Stuttgart bombings?' said Lang. The Hubers spun around as if they had just realised Lang was there.

'August 1940, *junge*,' said Herr Huber. 'It was the first of the Allied attacks, though not the last. Rückeran was away so someone else had to look after the burials.' Munchkin didn't get a response so he tried again. 'There was not much left of them. His parents were the real casualties of war in that family.'

Bux didn't like history lessons about the war so he changed the subject.

'Did you ever visit Herr Rückeran? Collect his rent; repair his goods; anything like that?'

'*Piss Kunstler*,' said Herr Huber, outraged again. 'I don't like lushes.'

'Come, Jan, behave yourself. That is just not fair!'

'It's all right, Doreen, we can say anything we like about Rückeran now,' said Herr Huber who was enjoying his role of police collaborator. 'I often wondered why a prison officer had the need to drink so much. I would have thrown him out.'

'So you saw him quite frequently?'

'Oh, no. We kept away. He invited us the once for a drink and, believe me, once was enough. He was stewed to the gills by the time we arrived and it was only nine o'clock. Totally out of it, he was. I had to tell him to behave in the end.'

Herr Huber paused to await approval of such determination.

'Has it always been in this state?' said Bux instead and pointed towards the grubby floor and the filthy front window. The Hubers followed his eyes, like owners checking the damage from a house fire for the first time.

'No. Oh, no. He certainly made an effort for us.'

'Did you have to stand? There's only one chair in here.'

'We had to carry up two of our collapsible stools,' said Frau Huber. 'Can you believe that? It was most uncomfortable.'

Herr Huber wanted to tell more about his tenant's unworthiness, and wasn't the type to worry about being thought of as nosy neighbours. 'We are not drinkers,' he said. 'Rückeran carried on as if it was his hobby.'

'*Herr Stagger!*' shouted Frau Huber.

'That's right,' said her husband. 'It was what the couple who own the grocery shop on the corner called him: "*Herr Stagger*". They even took bets on whether he was going to buy two – or three – bottles. It became a joke for the locals. The Müllers said they knew what he would buy by the time of month.'

'The time of month? How is that?'

Herr Huber pulled a face as if he had just smelled something nasty and said,

'His Scotch time. If it was the end of the month – payday, obviously – he preferred Scotch. He was on that stuff the night we arrived. A celebration, I think.'

'Celebrating what?'

'He never told us. If you are a piss artist you will find any excuse for a celebration, will you not? Rückeran would have celebrated the arrival of a winter sun.'

'Can you recall the exact day?'

The Hubers didn't hesitate and spoke together. 'February 28 this year.'

The old man took it on from there. 'Obviously his payday, but it also happened to be our wedding anniversary. It was a disaster. He spent the night weeping and joining in with that damn French music.'

'He offered us some whisky, but nothing to eat,' said Frau Huber.

'He obviously didn't have anything in the fridge,' said her husband, as if this was part of a well-rehearsed double act. 'My wife thinks a lot of people in authority, but not me. *Piss Kunstler*! That was how I remember our Rückeran.'

What a party that must have been, thought Bux: the party from hell.

'Did you know he was decorated during the war?' he asked.

The Hubers didn't look impressed and simply nodded, so Bux continued.

'You saw his photographs, then?'

More nods.

'Did he say anything about the Wehrmacht? What about Stammheim?'

'He never mentioned the war to us, but he seemed very proud of his guard duties. He looked after some of that RAF gang. At least that is what he claimed. I asked the usual questions: Did they top themselves? Or was it murder? The newspaper rumour was that all their conversations were bugged. Rückeran just grinned; that stupid grin of all drinkers.'

'Was that here, then?' said Bux and pointed his flashlight at the wall clock.

'First time I've seen that. Some sort of present? I have seen that cheap IKEA furniture before; also the telephone and the phonograph.'

Frau Huber started to weep, this time in earnest, or so it seemed. 'Whatever you think about Herr Rückeran I admired him; his friends, too.'

'His friends?' said Bux. 'I thought you said he had no friends.'

'Well he certainly had Wehrmacht friends. He had a photograph of all three of them in their uniforms. Two were soldiers and one served in tanks – all black uniforms, you see. One of the first things we noticed, wasn't it, Jan? Herr Rückeran was very young and quite handsome and the others were a similar age.'

'What were they doing?'

'They didn't look very happy, I must say – not the usual Wehrmacht in Paris photographs – and none were looking at the camera. I don't think they knew they were being watched. A "snatch", don't they call it? I do know it was Paris but there was something odd about it.'

'Odd, Frau Huber?'

'It had been snowing heavily.'

'And the French girl,' he husband reminded her. 'Don't forget the French girl.'

'That's right! I forgot; a girl with one of those berets the French always wore—'

'How do you know it was Paris?' said Lang, having managed to interrupt the flow. Frau Huber turned on him just before Bux did.

'Young man, I may be an old woman and I may never have been to Paris, but I do recognise the Eiffel Tower when I see it. All four of them were talking together with the Tower in the background.'

'Were there any names on that photograph?' said Bux.

'The only one I saw was on the front. "Lulu and Friends" was all it said. Yes, that girl must have been called Lulu.'

Just then, someone in a distant electricity company

restored the power. The lights dazzled for a few seconds.

Bux pointed at the sideboard and said, 'The picture that was there?'

'My God,' cried Frau Huber. 'Someone has stolen Herr Rückeran's photograph!'

Chapter 6.

By midday the city cleaning and clearing squads had done their best, although many streets were still veined by the remains of the melting snow.

Bux had the use of a company Mercedes, but disliked driving in the wet or in the dark, or in the city. He thought most drivers were too fast and others too slow and he had never mastered Stuttgart's new one-way system. Silke called him the worst passenger in the state of Baden-Württemberg, if not the world.

'Have you got your handbrake on?' he demanded brusquely of Lang as they approached Relenberg, on the way north towards Stammheim. Lang looked uncomprehending and checked his handbrake.

Bux lit up, knowing it always upset non-smokers.

'Can't you go any faster?' he asked. 'You're no Fangio, are you?'

'Fangio?' asked Lang.

Close by the end of the K9501 and the turn on to Siegelbergstraße they were cut up by an impatient motorcyclist on a BMW. Lang braked and cut his own speed. Bux, his face white with rage, wound down his window and bellowed at the biker, who retaliated by giving him the fingers. Bux pulled out a notebook and started to take the number.

'Calm, Kommissar,' said Lang, who was quite concerned. 'You will give yourself a heart attack. Light up if that helps. I won't object.'

Bux's heart was beating madly and this was not the behaviour of a senior Kripo detective, so Lang was right. He breathed deeply and thought of apologising, but didn't. By the time they moved out of the heavy traffic he was as calm as he ever would be.

Lang opened all four windows and asked,

'Do you think this was a professional execution, Kommissar?'

Bux thought for a few seconds and decided,

'I pray not. If someone was paid for this killing we do have problems.'

'The theft of that photograph … do you think the killer wanted a memento?'

'Mementos are usually the work of serial killers and—' Bux stopped himself there. He was beginning to sound like those world-weary senior officers he met when he first joined the force. They always spoke in homilies, and Bux thought that was the certain sign of approaching old age.

Lang was persistent. 'Prison officers? The fifth in the last few years, and four of those were RAF executions.'

Bux tried to avoid a sermon, but Lang was heading in the wrong direction and he told him so.

'Those were different, Lang. Two were murdered in West Berlin inside vehicles on the way to work, and several shooters were involved. Sub-machine guns killed one guard out shopping in Hamburg, and another four years ago in Heidelberg.'

Bux needed another cigarette but waited for the next set

of lights because he had already burned a hole in Lang's new carpet.

'There is another reason why I will never believe it was a RAF assassination,' he said. 'Do you read the local newspapers, Lang?'

Lang admitted he did not.

'You should do, if only for the photographs,' Bux told him. 'A year ago I saw a picture – in Stuttgart-Zeitung, admittedly – of a young woman handcuffed to a prison guard. It had been taken outside Stammheim and they were obviously on the way to court. It was definitely a quiet day for newspapers because it was an inside page, and was a poor-quality print snapped from a distance. I did not recognise the girl, but the white hair of the prison officer was unmistakeable.'

'Rückeran?' said Lang. 'You recognised Rückeran?'

'It was certainly Rückeran: the same uniform, the same white hair and under-nourished body. My point is this: the photograph of a prison guard had managed to find its way into a local newspaper.'

'I do not see the significance,' said Lang.

'Stammheim governors always insisted that prison officers photographed for newspapers had to have their faces blurred. I have seen several other images of guards with prisoners, but all with their faces blanked. The reasoning was obvious and editors always complied, but equally obviously did not apply to Rückeran.'

Lang whistled, but then asked, 'If the RAF saw that photograph it would make their job easy, surely.'

Bux allowed himself a little pontification.

'I agree, Lang. If the RAF were after him they must have known what he looked like and where he worked. At some stage, too, they must have found out where he lived. My question is this, Lang: if it was the RAF, why has it

45

taken a year to kill a rather minor prison guard? And why have they not claimed responsibility?'

Lang parked some distance from the main entrance.

'At least the weather has improved,' he said to the sky. 'No snow now.' He reached for his briefcase in the back seat of the car, took off his trench coat and put it in the boot.

Bux's eyes widened.

'What did you say? Just repeat that.'

'I said the weather has improved. No snow.'

'*Scheisse*,' cried Bux. 'I had forgotten. Didn't Frau Huber mention snow in Paris? That photograph of three Wehrmacht men and a French girl with the Eiffel Tower in the background. Heavy snow on the ground in Paris.'

Bux grabbed Lang's briefcase from him, threw it back into the car, handed him his trench coat and even opened the front door for him.

'Back to the office, quick as you can,' he said. 'You have phone calls to make.'

'Where do I start, Kommissar?'

'Try starting with the Federal Archive in Koblenz,' Bux said impatiently. 'There are numbers on my wall. I want details of the 7th Panzer Division and their leaves in Paris. The likeliest time will be the winter of 1940 or early 1941. Once you have a time and a date contact Wetterdienst at Offenbach am Main and ask about the weather in Paris in the same period. We are looking for heavy snows, don't forget, and we need the exact days. I'm sorry, but this may take you some time.'

Lang tried not to sound smug when he replied,

'It should not take long at all, Kommissar. I do not need to use the telephone, either. Wetterdienst are connected to our network, as are the Federal Archives. I should get replies within an hour.'

Bux remembered then why Lang was still a Kripo detective and was not a traffic cop. Lang was incompetent at many things, but he was an expert in the new word processor system and Bux was not.

He had recognised the virtue of a machine that gave officers details of cars and their owners with the press of a finger: they could now follow plane flights in and out of cities and discover who was living where and with whom. It was simple to cover border crossings and every passport in the Federal Republic. If that way inclined, detectives could even check individual bank accounts.

Not Bux. After six months the Commodore 64, which was as devious and autocratic as it sounded, was still a mystery to a man who had trouble in changing a light bulb. He decided then it was far too late in a distinguished career to learn how to play with a damn machine. He would leave it to subordinates like Lang and his Commodore 64, a pair for whom it had been love at first sight. Lang could almost make it speak and would probably go to bed with it, given the chance.

Bux tried to sound approving when he told him,

'Very good, Lang. And records of all 7th Panzer Division troops born in Stuttgart? There will be a number of them.'

'That should not take long, either,' Lang replied matter-of-factly.

Bux thought Lang's high-speed reverse was totally unnecessary, and the cheery wave as he left laced in irony. He didn't think he was going to like this new, holier-than-thou Lang. The boy was becoming far too clever for his own good.

CHAPTER 7.

Outside the main entrance a guard went through Bux's papers, a second photographed him and a third told him to check his weapon, a Walther P4. The security men on the roofs pointed sub-machine guns in his vague direction.

This was only Bux's second visit to Stammheim Supermax, but he had never forgotten the first.

On May 21, 1975, he sat in the spectators' gallery and heard the opening of the state's 'trial of the century'. A specially constructed courtroom had been built there and there was tight security then, though none of that could stop the trial from descending into chaos. On that first day one of four RAF defendants called the presiding judge a 'fascist arsehole', and it went downhill from there. The defendants were thrown out of court on several occasions, as were their attorneys. After two years the three surviving defendants (mother of twins, Ulrike Meinhof, had been found hanged in her cell on May 9, 1976) boycotted the trial before the presiding judge announced the life sentences.

Seven months later, and on the same morning, Andreas Baader, Gudrun Ensslin and Jan-Carl Raspe were also found dead in their cells. The coroner decided Ensslin hanged herself and Baader and Raspe shot themselves with weapons supplied by 'persons unknown'. The suicides left Bux, among others, with too many question marks. The trials were supposed to epitomise the battle between good (the state) and evil (the RAF defendants) but at times Bux had difficulty deciding which was which. He condemned the RAF as left-wing Marxist killers … but knew that two of the trial judges were former Nazis. It was Old Germany against Young Germany, and Old Germany had won.

Bux was guided down a succession of long corridors and locked doors. He could hear deranged chanting from one cell and a female with a good voice singing '*Muss Ich den*' from another. There were shouts and arguments, which could have been prisoners, but may have been guards. Bux saw little difference.

A male secretary in his thirties with a boxer's face waited by the final double doors next to a large sign that read: *Herr Mario Koch, Deputy Governor*.

'Herr Koch will be with you directly,' said the boy. 'You will not mind waiting?'

'Is he expecting me?'

'Herr Koch is on the telephone.'

Bux sat down to wait and asked for the sound on the small wall TV to be turned up, which the secretary did, rather begrudgingly.

The Rückeran shooting was the main item on *Heute-Journal*, but it was obvious that the director of the TV news programme was struggling. The 'witnesses' were the newspaper reporter who had so annoyed Bux in Münchingerstraße and Drescher, of course. Bux knew what came next: 'The killer is still at large in our streets', so someone had to be blamed. Bux also knew who that 'someone' would be even before the usual, unflattering image appeared on screen. *Heute-Journal* had moved on

49

to the second item, the bad weather or 'The Day of Death and Disaster' as it had been titled. Then a buzzer sounded from next door.

'Herr Koch will see you now,' said the secretary.

The deputy governor of Stammheim Supermax was sitting behind a large corner desk in a room the size of a basketball court. There was a flag of the country on one wall and some Dürer reproductions on another, along with the faces of Chancellor Helmut Schmidt and the Mayor of Stuttgart. Some would describe the room as ambassadorial but all the windows were barred, and even here there was the smell of disinfectant that Bux always associated with prisons.

Koch may once have fitted the Aryan stereotype of blond hair, blue eyes and a slim appearance, but no longer. He was now in his early sixties, his hair was grey and years of good living had taken its toll. He was as heavy as Bux, but Bux's heaviness was that of a former shot-putter, which he was.

He was a former Nazi, of course: 11th SS Panzer. Bux had few problems with that. Life had to go on in post-war Germany, and 11th SS Panzer was slightly more acceptable than one of the SS death squads at Auschwitz or such places. It would also have been difficult to charge eight million Germans with the crime of being members of the National Socialist Party. If some had their way West Germany's favourite opera diva (and former member of the Nazi party) Elisabeth Schwarzkopf would be on trial, and every piece by Wagner banned.

Bux always associated damp hands during a handshake as a weakness, or guilt, and he was usually right. Koch's hands were as wet as a bathroom tap. His eyes were bloodshot and he had cut himself shaving. His fingers were yellow and his voice hoarse, like an infrequent smoker forced to become a frequent smoker. Bux did not think it would take long to get these lips to wag.

First he must soften him up and he tried to sound concerned when he asked, 'Have you been unwell, Herr Koch?'

'I have been unable to sleep,' Koch said plaintively. 'I blame this Rückeran thing. A sad loss to the service.'

Koch pointed to a sheet of writing paper on his desk and said, almost proudly this time,

'In fact I am working on an obituary for the local newspapers.'

'And what will it say?'

'Family, school days, the war, his time as a prison officer and his—'

'Popularity with his colleagues?' said Bux.

'It does say that,' said Koch with a watery smile. 'But doesn't it always?'

The secretary brought in two glasses of Dallmayr coffee and Koch waited until he got to the door before calling him back.

'Gottlieb, bring in the files on Rückeran. At once.'

When Gottlieb trotted back, like an obedient puppy, Bux lit up without asking and began to read the small file.

It wasn't much of a CV and Bux knew most of it already, thanks to the Hubers. There had been some expeditious office work because it had 'Lukas Rückeran, senior officer, Supermax-Stammheim (deceased)' on the front cover. A single piece of paper attached to that mentioned 'disciplinary action' and that Rückeran had moved out of the main jail to the administration wing in October, 1980. This was signed by Koch, but there were no other details.

Bux questioned that by pointing a finger at the file and Koch replied,

'I'm sorry, Kommissar, that's all we have on Rückeran.'

'In that case you will fill in the gaps,' said Bux, leaning back in his chair. 'Put it all in words for me.'

Koch gave a pained expression and took time to light a huge Cuban cigar before he began.

'Rückeran joined the prison service in 1950,' he said. 'His first job was at Landsberg prison in Bavaria and he moved to Stammheim in 1964.

'Rückeran spent much of his time in a state of sodden despair,' Koch said disapprovingly. 'He had never married, had no friends – nothing that people would regard as normality.' Koch was so taken with the phrase he used it again. 'Normality for Rückeran was wine and Scotch.'

At work he was a melancholic who spoke only when necessary, dipped his head for 'Yes' or shook it for 'No'. He probably knew that his fellow officers despised him, and vice versa, although possibly not as much as he despised himself.

'That is only my opinion,' said Koch. 'But I think many here would agree.'

'If Rückeran was such a good officer, why was he taken off guard duty? Your notes say he was moved to an office job.'

It was not warm in the room, but sweat began to run from Koch's forehead. Some landed on his cigar so he had to relight it before he continued.

'Rückeran served the prison service reasonably well. I think we ran a very precise and functional operation, but the RAF affair made it even more difficult. Some people could not cope. It was well known Rückeran liked a drink, but he had always controlled himself. Something made him flip, sometime near the end of the RAF trials. He began to fortify himself here.'

'You mean he got drunk at work?'

'It got so bad we thought he should move to one of the

52

offices.'

'What exactly was the job?'

'He did paperwork, looked after arrivals and transfers and detailed their useless little life stories. It was nine to five, but he kept his uniform and from then on what he did at home was his own business.'

Bux raised his voice a key.

'Why not sack him, or grant him early retirement? By the sound of it he would have been happy to leave.'

'I could have done that, but the general opinion was that if sacked he would sit at home all day and drink himself to death.'

'The general opinion among whom?'

Koch had problems and hummed and hawed.

'Just say it,' said Bux, even louder. 'I haven't got all day.'

'His colleagues, his friends, some of the management here.'

'So Rückeran *did* have friends?'

Koch blustered. 'We all had friends in the Wehrmacht, didn't we?'

'A simple "Yes" or "No" would do.'

'Yes,' said Koch.

'His landlady mentioned Wehrmacht colleagues. Did he mention them to you?'

'No.'

'Two friends from the 7th Panzer Division, perhaps?'

'I knew he was in the 7th Panzer, but he never mentioned companions to me.'

'What about a girl – a French girl he met in Paris?'

Koch was adamant. 'Certainly not. Who is this French girl?'

Bux leaned forward and wagged the file at the deputy governor like a weapon.

'It says here he won a Knight's Cross of the Iron Cross "for special services to the Reich". That is *all* it says, which seems rather odd for someone who earned one of the Reich's most distinguished war medals. As far as I can recall, "special services to the Reich" in the old days involved taking Jews to the gas chambers.'

'I did not receive full details,' insisted Koch 'He was just a Wehrmacht private and was never involved in "special services", as you call it.'

'But the Wehrmacht made extensive military records, particularly the awarding of medals. We Germans have always been obsessed by paperwork, have we not? But there is nothing mentioned here. Odd, Herr Koch?'

'The records may have been destroyed. It happens during wars.'

Bux looked at Koch with what was close to a sneer.

'Did you manage to keep the records about his move to Münchingerstraße?'

'I cannot say I like the way you are addressing me, Kommissar,' said Koch peevishly.

'Do not concern yourself,' said Bux. 'I talk that way to everyone. Now ... the records of Rückeran's move, please.'

'It is a long story.'

'I have the time, if you have.'

There was another long sigh, and Koch checked his watch.

'Very well, Kommissar. I will be as brief as possible. As you know, the RAF trials lasted two years,' he continued. 'There was a special courtroom built here, but obviously the accused had to be taken from the seventh floor to the courtroom every day. It was thought the officers involved should live in – if they agreed, of course. The suicides changed things and safe enough for guards to move into housing outside the complex, Rückeran among them. I did not agree with that, by the way.'

'The suicides were in '77: Rückeran moved out a year ago.'

'I found that odd, too, Kommissar. He always struck me as the type who would have trouble looking after himself. The accommodation here was ideal: single rooms for unmarried men inside the complex and a communal eating area. I tried to dissuade him, naturally.'

'Tell me about that.'

'I remember it well,' said Koch warming to his task. 'I did my best. "Do not be silly, Rückeran," says I when he announced that he was "breaking out", as he put it. I warned him: "You will become an easy target for the RAF within a week or so".'

'But the leaders were dead,' Bux pointed out. 'The others were in disarray. Why would a minor prison guard be a target?'

'I never believed the RAF were finished,' Koch insisted. 'There are always lunatics around. I was concerned. "It will be simple for them to find you", I told him. "That white hair of yours and the *Gefängniswärter* uniform are unmistakeable. If you insist on moving, try a different route to work. Buy yourself a car. Or use public transport".'

'And he took no notice?'

'He never took the advice of others. "Do not worry about me," says Rückeran to me. "The RAF will not show their faces round here again". He spoke nonsense: "It's as bad as being a prisoner," he said. He compared his own "imprisonment" with being an inmate: "This is a life governed by officials with guns. Everyone here is chained to iron bars". He decided that was enough.'

'Did anyone else take up the offer to live outside after the RAF suicides?'

'Several.'

'I assume they all moved back into Stammheim after Rückeran's murder?'

'No. I don't think so.'

Bux stared at him in disbelief, which forced Koch to look away.

'Forgive me,' said Bux in his best sarcastic tone. 'You just told me you thought the RAF were finished, but several of your guards are now living outside the complex. Was Rückeran the only one in danger?'

'Some thought the RAF were finished by '81.'

'You obviously did not agree?'

'Of course not, Kommissar. True, the RAF appeared to be falling apart. They failed with that rocket-propelled grenade attack at Heidelberg and the US Army nuclear storage site at Nuremberg. Several instigators are in prison awaiting trial, but the RAF has always managed to rebuild itself. There are always dangerous lunatics willing to carry on. I thought prison guards were still a target.'

Koch paused and leaned closer, as if about to give away a state secret.

'Strictly between ourselves, Kommissar, I thought Schmidt and Bonn were trying to save money. Persuading guards to move out was one way, because then they have to find their own food and heating.'

Another check of his watch and then,

'Anything else, Kommissar?'

Bux had not finished and asked, though he knew the answer.

'Shouldn't Rückeran have been at work on September 27, the day he was murdered?'

Koch had to think carefully.

'You must be aware, Herr Bux, that Rückeran often cried off work and he always found different excuses. It would always be an illness, stomach ache or headache –

even family funerals. Rückeran, of course, had no living relatives.'

'What happened?'

'He phoned the night duty officer and told him he was going to die.'

'Well, he was right about that, was he not?' Bux asked sardonically. 'No one did anything about it?'

'No one ever took him seriously, Herr Bux. If you tell enough fibs no one ever believes you. He must have run out of excuses so he came up with this one.'

Bux pulled open his notebook and checked.

'The night duty officer's record says here, "*6.45 p.m., telephone call … Prison Officer Lukas Rückeran, 3b Münchingerstraße. Sick and will miss work today.*" Those were the exact words. I think if I heard someone say he was about to die I would have made sure it was written down.'

'Herr Bux, that guard is a young man on one of his first night duty shifts. He has been reprimanded, of course. They both have. If I were honest, I think no one would have batted an eyelid if Rückeran had never showed up for work again.'

'Well they got their wish, did they not? He obviously had enemies here.'

'Most guards have enemies. It is part of the job. Rückeran was an odd fellow. I don't think he was particularly liked among staff, but most people put up with him. Even those RAF criminals tolerated him.'

'He had worked on the seventh floor, then? He was there on Death Night?'

Koch wouldn't look at Bux, and took his time in lighting another cigar.

'We selected certain officers for the seventh floor,' he said. 'It wasn't necessarily the toughest guards, though

I knew prisoners like Baader could be very difficult. Rückeran was there because they tolerated him.'

'What do you mean by "tolerated"?'

'Prisoners hate all guards, you know that, but some are different from others and have to be treated that way. Rückeran, for example, preferred the ice cream to the stick, and that worked with thugs like Baader. They never spoke, of course, because the RAF policy was not to talk to anyone official. I always thought, too, that Rückeran and Baader were similar: people with the self-loathing of the defeated. As for the suicides – Death Night, as you call it – I am fairly certain he was off work sick that night, too. As I said, that often happened with him.'

Bux reached into his briefcase for another piece of paper.

'Have you seen this newspaper photograph before?'

Koch glanced briefly.

'I may have. It's certainly Rückeran.'

Bux pushed the photograph to within a few inches of Koch's face and said,

'I also noticed it was Rückeran. I just wonder why his face is not blanked out, like every other prison guard I have seen in newspapers.'

Koch leaned back in his chair and gave another long sigh of resignation.

'Rückeran told them *not* to cover his features,' he said. 'That is the reason.'

The only sound was the ticking of the large clock in the corner of the room. Even the shouting outside seemed to have stopped, as if all in the prison were listening to the same conversation.

'Did this man have a death wish?' asked Bux incredulously.

'I believe so,' said Koch.

'But he never attempted suicide – easily done for an armed prison guard?'

'Are you a Catholic, Herr Bux?'

'Lapsed.'

'But you may recall the Catholic Church regards self-murders like divorces: both mortal sins. So Rückeran wouldn't have had the guts. There are other ways, of course.'

'An assisted suicide … that is what you imply?'

'You could call it that,' said Koch, more confident by the second. 'I thought he was like one of those ducks in a carnival shooting gallery: all he needed was a marksman. Making sure your picture appeared in a newspaper would also help, don't you agree, Herr Bux? As I pointed out he always wore his uniform, never his hat, and walked to and from work. For the record, Kommissar, I telephoned the editor to complain. He alleged that Rückeran had insisted on "a picture as a memento for his family", and those idiots never bothered to find out if he had a damn family. I was furious, but the paper was out by then.'

'Did it never occur to you that this man's mind had been seriously damaged? No one tried to stop him, even after that telephone call to the prison on the day he died? There are doctors and psychologists who can help people like this.'

'I was not his nursemaid,' said Koch huffily. 'It is hard enough to look after a prison like Stammheim. Now, is there anything else? I have a meeting with the governors in a few minutes.'

Bux ignored that and carried on.

'It says here there was a disciplinary matter. Disciplined for what? There is no mention of his drinking here.'

Koch bought time by calling in his secretary and demanding another coffee, though he did not offer Bux a refill.

'The disciplinary action?' said Bux.

'As I have said, Rückeran had no friends here. He did his work and then went home. But life in Stammheim can be very lonely for officers. Even for Rückeran. He became quite close to one of the females here.'

'A female guard?'

'A female prisoner,' said Koch – this in a stage whisper. Bux was so taken aback he almost dropped his cigarette.

'It wasn't in a sexual sense, Herr Bux. They chatted if Rückeran was walking from the offices to the prison laundry where she worked. I turned a blind eye at first, but then a few others noticed and I decided it was time for me to step in.'

'Was it the girl in that photograph? Tell me!'

Koch replied sheepishly,

'It was a young woman called Birgita Springer.'

Bux was outraged.

'Birgita Springer? A Stammheim guard was screwing a RAF terrorist?'

'I take great exception to that, Kommissar! That is wicked talk. I told you before: sex was *not* involved. She was a very minor member of the gang, anyway.'

'*Do* tell me more!'

'She earned some remission from the authorities in 1977. She had been a sort of spy for the state – a stool pigeon, if you like. She gave details about the RAF leaders, those radios someone had smuggled in, and their notes to each other.'

'What was she doing in that photograph?'

'There was an appeal on her sentence: ten years for possessing firearms and stealing a vehicle, but that was reduced. In fact, she should be out soon. For obvious reasons we keep snitches in solitary, but once Baader and the rest of them topped themselves she moved into the main part of the jail.'

'Where she met Rückeran?'

'By then she'd be desperate to talk to anyone. Informers start to depend on people, and it doesn't really matter who that other person is. I decided on a warning and there was a small mention on his file. Up to the time of his murder I don't think they had spoken for some time.'

'I need to talk to this girl,' said Bux. 'I need to talk to her today.'

'I will make sure of that,' said Koch who was suddenly anticipating his own discharge. 'You can talk to her now if that will help. Fraulein Springer has much time on her hands.'

Bux finished his drink and pocketed his notes and cigarettes. Koch found the right internal number and told the voice at the other end,

'This is Deputy Governor Koch. I have a gentleman from Stuttgart Kripo here who would like to talk to Birgita Springer from Cell 212. She will be in the laundry room, so take her to the library. She won't need a guard there.'

There was a short silence. Koch's eyes widened in disbelief and he shouted – so loudly his secretary galloped in from next door.

'WHAT? *SCHEISSE*! I told you I must be informed at once of any such incidents. I will come down immediately.'

He slammed down the phone and hurried towards the door.

'That bitch!' he snarled. 'She attempted to kill herself. She is alive and apparently in no danger. But you will *not* be interviewing her for now, Kommissar.

CHAPTER 8.

The wretched deputy governor of Stammheim Supermax had been right about one thing: Bux would have to wait for his interview with Birgita Springer.

When Bux phoned on the Thursday for an update (in the words of Koch) the girl had used a kitchen fork to stab herself in the stomach, and hadn't made much of a job of it. Koch made that sound like a personal affront, as if she had done this to annoy him.

'In my opinion she was just trying to get attention,' Koch insisted. 'She is always looking for attention. But you know the routine, Kommissar.'

Bux did know the routine. Bonn wanted this kept out of the newspapers and away from the public. No one wanted an imbroglio like the RAF suicides of '77.

'For now she is in the US Army Hospital at Bad Cannstadt,' Koch said. 'She is unlikely to attract attention there. She will be examined by doctors and a psychiatrist. She will be under strict surveillance, of course. The girl will not be allowed visitors until she is fully recovered.' The visitors in question included Bux, of course.

Kommissar Bux kept what he called a daybook of notes in a large pad inside his desk. He used to think it demonstrated a German's devotion to detail; now he wrote everything down, lest he forgot.

It had a title: *Kommissar Markus Bux, Stuttgart* Kripo, *Thursday, September 30, Murder of Rückeran, Stammheim prison officer,* but little else. Most of it read like a housewife's shopping list:

Update new members of staff.
7th Panzer, 1939 to 1945, Federal Archive (Lang to follow).
Snow in Paris 1941 to1945, Wetterdienst, Offenbach am Main (Lang).
Rückeran and his Iron Cross? (Federal History Archive).
Coroner's inquest and Rückeran funeral (dates and times needed).
Status of Fraulein Springer, US Army Hospital, Bad Cannstadt.
Progress of house-to-house searches.
Data on active RAF members.
Flowers for Silke.

In the parsimonious manner of the state the President of Police had assigned him only two extra detectives.

Bux thought the mixture was good: Baum was in his fifties – a former lecturer at the University of Freiburg before he joined the force. In crime cases a historian could be as useful as a marksman or a forensic expert.

Hertzog was in his mid twenties and rather fond of himself. He made a bad start when he arrived for work in a black polo neck and was sent home to change into shirt and tie. But Hertzog, unlike Lang, had passed *all* his grades at police academy and, like Lang, loved his Commodore 64. Bux always believed that competition among police officers never did any harm.

For the sake of the newcomers, Bux backtracked to the

day of the murder and began thus,

'According to the deputy governor of Stammheim Lukas Rückeran moved to his apartment at 3 Münchingerstraße a year ago. Why he chose this I will not go into now, but you can read about it in my notes. This street, as you will see, is one-way, narrow and poorly lit. The majority of residents are quite old and not the best of potential witnesses—'

Hertzog interrupted. 'An ideal place for a murder, then, Herr Kommissar?'

'Correct, Hertzog, but do not interrupt. You can have your say later.'

Hertzog's face reddened. Lang chortled. Bux continued,

'At 6.45 a.m. on the Monday, Rückeran phoned Stammheim Supermax and told the night duty officer he would not be at work that day. The exact words he used are included in the transcript of my interview with Stammheim's deputy governor. Unfortunately, someone leaked the night duty officer's exact words to the local press: I gather STAMMHEIM GUARD FORSAW HIS MURDER is one of the headlines. Whether Rückeran expected to be murdered that day remains to be seen.

'What we do know is that the victim died between 8 p.m. and 10 p.m. that evening and the alarm was raised on the Wednesday. There was nothing untoward about that. According to his landlord, Rückeran was often not seen for days at a time. The killer had some help from the bad weather. Many potential witnesses would have been hiding under umbrellas or dashing for cover. It went dark early that day, too.'

'At 2 p.m. Rückeran walked to the grocery shop on Gelbrandstraße and bought three bottles of Baden Riesling, some Cambozola cheese and sixty Lux cigarettes. This was Rückeran's regular order, according to the shop owners. I should add that our victim always wore his *Gefängniswärter* uniform, so was easy to spot for a killer.'

The only 'witness', said Bux, was the Salvatore Catholic *Kirche* priest who had been leading a funeral cortège towards the waiting vehicles. The victim was arriving from the opposite direction and was carrying a large paper bag.

'His supply of wine, obviously,' Bux explained. 'The odd thing is that, according to the priest, Rückeran felt he had to hide his bag of booze.'

Baum raised his hand for permission to speak.

'That is not unusual for heavy drinkers, Kommissar. They are always trying to hide their guilt.'

Bux sipped at his glass of water, cleared his throat and concluded with precise details of the missing photograph: the 9mm bullet, the phonograph and the phone calls. Then he stared balefully at his three colleagues and said,

'The forensic team found no striations on the 9mm, so it looks as though we are not going to identify the gun. It goes without saying we have to look in other directions. Has anyone anything to offer?'

Hertzog was still keen to impress and his hand went up first.

'It sounds like a professional murder to me,' he said.

Bux resisted a reprimand and told him instead,

'Hertzog, you are new here, so I will forgive you for stating the damn obvious. I also believe the killer found his way into the apartment while Rückeran was either on his way to the shop or while he was outside watching the funeral cortège. In effect someone had been waiting for him inside his apartment. The Hubers, the elderly couple on the ground floor, have hearing difficulties so did not heed a gunshot. In any case the victim's phonograph was at the loudest level. There is no one living on the third floor. The other possibility is that the two men may have

65

known each other. There was no sign of a forced entry and no evidence of a struggle, you see.'

Hertzog tried again, this time with better luck.

'Is it possible that the killer was one of the mourners, Kommissar?'

'A good question, Hertzog, but they have all been interviewed. Right, Lang?'

Lang's eyes were fixed on something inside his new toy and he didn't reply.

'Are you tired, Lang?' Bux demanded. 'Are we keeping you awake?'

Hertzog and Baum sniggered, but Lang was prepared.

'I have details of the 7th Panzer Division on screen,' he said.

'So quickly?' said Baum, who was still at computer lessons, grade one.

'Computers are a great help,' said Lang and then, without looking away from his screen, 'I contacted the Federal History Archive and this is their response:

A total of 4,357 men born in Stuttgart joined the Wehrmacht between 1935 and 1945. Half of those enlisted in Der Heer (army), and of those 108 joined the 7th Panzer Division. Forty-two of them were killed on the Russian Front, seventeen during the invasion of France and ten during the Battle for Berlin. Nine have since died of natural causes. That leaves us thirty men for interview. I have the relevant names and addresses here.'

'Snow in Paris?' said Bux. 'Anything from Wetterdienst?'

'I'm sorry to tell you this, Kommissar, but it snowed in Paris every winter between 1940 and 1945. The heaviest falls were in February, 1944, from the 25th to the 28th. But that is irrelevant: the 7th Panzers certainly had leaves in Paris, but only in the summer of 1940.'

'Damn it, Lang,' cried Bux, banging his desk with a fist.

'Have you no good news for us?'

Lang was not going to be fazed.

'The cigarettes and the ashtrays?' he asked. 'There were two spent cigarettes different from the others: just two. I took the opportunity of telephoning one of his prison colleagues, and Rückeran always smoked Lux filters. The others were English cigarettes: Capstan Full Strength. One stub had been left on the victim's ashtray and the other on the floor six feet away. What do you think that means, Kommissar?'

'It means,' Bux said quietly, 'that someone with a taste for English cigarettes needed a smoke. I think we can also say that whoever killed Rückeran was male. Capstan Full Strength is a somewhat toxic brand, and not the type ladies would choose. It appears Rückeran had accepted one offered by his guest.'

'A last smoke before facing the firing squad?' said Baum.

'Very good, Baum. So poetic,' said Bux and lit up one of his own cigarettes.

'For all you non-smokers,' he said, 'here is a little demonstration: a cigarette lasts around three to four minutes and devotees often share the pleasure, lighting up and finishing at the same time. This is called the camaraderie of smokers.'

The other three, all non-smokers, looked at each other but said nothing.

'So Rückeran and his friend had at least three minutes together before the shot was fired. I don't think they would just sit there and pass the time of day in total silence. I don't think they were there just to listen to old French music on a phonograph, either. There must have been a discussion, like all chums together, until the killer decided enough was enough. Now what about the phone calls, Lang?'

67

'I checked with the Stuttgart telephone service and they have found five calls from Rückeran's line in the week before it was disconnected, which was the Monday he died. There would probably be others, but calls are automatically deleted after seven days. Three of Rückeran's calls were to the same number, the Daimler-Benz factory at Untertürkheim. The address is Mercedesstraße, 70327 Stuttgart.'

'I *do* know the address of the Daimler-Benz factory,' said Bux truculently.

Lang carried on regardless.

'Those three calls were on the same day, Friday, September 24, and within four hours of each other. None of the calls lasted longer than twenty seconds. Unfortunately they were to the main switchboard.'

'It should be simple to find who took the calls,' said Baum. 'The switchboard operator should know who Rückeran had asked for.'

Lang took his time to reach for his glass of water before he continued.

'The duty guard at Stammheim also notes that he took a call there at 6.45 a.m. on the Monday which, as we all know now, that was when he announced he would not be in work that day. The really interesting one is this: a call made a week before that to a number in the United Kingdom. It lasted just over two minutes, according to the telephone company. It was an English code number in Glasgow.'

Got you, thought Bux. He had been waiting for this one.

'A *Scottish code number*, Lang. Glasgow is a large city north of the English border. Were there any other details?'

'It was to a direct line in a building in Albion Street, Glasgow, G1 1RU. It was at 2.01 a.m. on Tuesday, September 21.'

'Someone was working late,' said Bux. 'The name of the company?'

'It is a daily newspaper called *The Inquirer*, which sounds like the English – sorry, *Scottish* – equivalent of *Stuttgarter-Zeitung*.'

Bux whistled in surprise, but Lang hadn't finished.

'Something else, Herr Bux: the pile of papers in Rückeran's flat? They were all editions of Scottish newspapers. There were hundreds of them.'

'Has anyone looked through them?' said Bux. 'Did Rückeran underline anything or cut something out?'

'One of the secretaries is going through them now,' said Lang.

Bux did not really expect a reply but asked anyway,

'Why on earth did Rückeran want with Scottish newspapers? And why telephone that newspaper office in the middle of the night? You said the calls lasted two minutes?'

Lang agreed. Bux drummed his desk with both hands and stared at the map of the world on the wall above his desk.

'Baum, you have excellent English, do you not? I want you to telephone that number in Scotland. Whoever it is will probably give their name when they answer. Then ring off and we will take it from there. Unfortunately, you will have to call at the same time as Rückeran. In other words it will be a late night for you.'

Baum, who was on a second divorce, was used to that and said so.

'While you are in the mood—' said Bux, who always expected a little extra, 'it's unfortunate that the killer has a start, but I want you to check hotel registrations for foreigners and the passports of every passenger on every flight between the United Kingdom and Flughafen

Stuttgart in the last week. Look through all the car hire firms, too. I'll get some help for you with this.'

'What about RAF members, Kommissar?'

'I suppose we must check for those, too,' said Bux without enthusiasm. 'Try all the ones on file – discounting their deceased members, obviously. It shouldn't take long to tick most of them off because many are in East Germany and enjoying new lives, new jobs and new names.'

Bux turned to Hertzog and told him,

'You can make a start with Lang's list of 7th Panzer survivors,' he said. 'We are going to have to interview all of them.'

'In any particular order, Kommissar?'

'Try A to Z,' replied Bux testily. 'If you manage that, take copies of all of Rückeran's photographs to Daimler-Benz. Try our library and see if there are any other images of him. It's a pity about the missing photograph but, assuming everyone else in the photograph is still alive, there must be others. Oh, and get some images of Rückeran sent out to the press.'

'What do I ask them at Daimler-Benz, Kommissar?' to which Bux replied in single-word sentences, 'Do... You... Recognise... This... Man?'

Baum and Hertzog picked up their car keys and left. Lang hung back.

'The thing that baffles me, Herr Bux, is why a killer would want to steal a photograph from a sad old man like Rückeran.'

Bux didn't like that one.

'I would hesitate to describe a holder of the Knight's Cross of the Iron Cross as "sad",' he grumbled. 'Nor are older men sad by definition.'

Lang raised a hand and was about to apologise when a young female secretary with a multicoloured punk hairstyle walked in carrying a large document box and plonked it on Bux's desk.

'This is what we found, Kommissar,' she said. 'We went through every single newspaper, but this was it.'

Bux's big find turned out to be like one of those Russian nesting doll sets with decreasing sizes, and at the end all that was left was the copy of a small black-and-white photograph on a single sheet of paper.

'Is that it?' griped Bux. 'I thought this was the arrival of Magna Carta.'

The girl was already on her way out when she replied, 'It must be important, Kommissar, because someone marked it in red biro.'

The photograph found in Rückeran's apartment was nothing of note, at least at first. It showed an old lady and a smartly-dressed man in his forties shaking hands for the camera. The caption was dated 1969 and said,

Mrs Marie Charlotte Cloutier of Blair Lodge, Braemar, meets the new Conservative candidate for West Aberdeenshire, Mr Colin Mitchell. Mrs Cloutier's daughter, Eugenie, known as Lulu to her family, was murdered by the Gestapo in Paris in February, 1944.

Bux still took his time. He put on his spectacles, and then took them off again. He stared at the photograph for a long time. He turned it over to see if there was anything behind. He squinted from close range and held it up to the light.

'I think I will make a phone call to Scotland Yard,' said Bux eventually.

'Is that Glasgow, Kommissar?' said Lang.

Bux was tempted, but resisted. He lifted his receiver and began to dial.

CHAPTER 9.

Albion Street, Glasgow, Friday, October 1.

Gorman, the assistant news editor (acting), put down his phone and beckoned McKenna over. 'The editor wants to see you after conference,' he said.

High above, a fluorescent light flickered on and off, as it had been doing for a month. Somewhere in the distance a man with a squeaky voice said, 'Get the fuck oota her,' over and over down a phone. A subeditor with a Holmes-type bendy pipe and an eye patch shouted, 'Copy, you wee wanker,' to a teenage messenger.

It was 6.20 p.m. and McKenna, whose shift started at 6.30 p.m., hadn't even had the time to sit down.

He feigned unconcern and asked, 'Did the editor say what he was after?'

'He didn't say anything,' said Gorman, a Pooterish waffler in his fifties, who was still relishing his forthcoming promotion. 'The editorial administrator deals with the masses now, so you'll have to ask her. It sounds to me like a P45.'

Gorman cackled in delight at his wit, but stopped when he realised no one had heard him. McKenna wanted to know more.

'Who's going to do police calls if I'm talking to the

editor?'

'I suppose I'll stand in for you,' said Gorman begrudgingly. 'And you don't talk to the editor. He does things like that. I'll give you some other advice, lad: say as little as possible, don't mention anything to do with sport and don't ask for a rise or a title because it won't wash.'

'But you've got a title?' said McKenna.

'That was with the old boss,' said Gorman. 'Now fuck off.'

The department heads and their deputies – the six members of the student fraternity-like elite known as a back bench – were just filing into conference. It gave him enough time for the long walk down the corridors to the Gents, to wash his hands, adjust his tie and give his Hush Puppies a scrub and a shine. On the way back he stopped by the stationery shelf and lifted four red biros. He wasn't sure about the two notepads, a pack of silver staplers and a copy of yesterday's paper, except that they were free and might impress someone.

Mrs Lucienne Batch operated inside a glassed-in office at the end of the newsroom with a painted sign outside that read *Editorial Administrator.*

Wags said this room was the newspaper equivalent of an airport security scanner because staff hoping to reach the editor had to outflank her first, and that was difficult at the best of times. Others didn't like her acerbic attitude, though it was more likely the fact that she had been in charge of expenses and editorial rotas since her arrival. A few had christened her 'Bitch', though never to her face or within hearing of the new editor, who was very fond of her. Everyone admitted she had her uses and was conscientious, while always managing to make that sound like an accusation.

She accepted McKenna's hand as if it were radioactive and looked him up and down, like a fastidious judge at Crufts. She ordered him to sit by pointing with a finger at the chair and small table in the corner of her office.

'Cawffee?' she said in an odd twang that sounded American.

'Thank you very much,' said McKenna.

'The cups are over there. I'll have one, too: black, no sugar.'

She passed him a coaster with a nice colour image of the Eiffel Tower and cautioned in a clipped, no-nonsense tone, 'Just make sure you don't spill any.'

It hadn't taken *her* long to clock him, thought McKenna.

Women were like cats: they knew within seconds which dog would be dangerous and which would be docile, and she had worked out within seconds which category *he* was in. He sipped away very gingerly at his coffee, and peered at her out of the corner of an eye.

The aggressive black specs and a wonky nose that must have been broken at some stage did her no favours, but she scrubbed up well: sleek black hair cut into a Louise Brooks bob and pale skin. He put her at early forties: a similar age to himself, but in far better trim.

She was organised (or as superstitious) as McKenna, with a separate corner for in/out trays and files that left, leaving her desk clear for an electronic typewriter and a busy bank of telephones. After every call she hung up, American style, without a 'Thanks' or a 'Bye'.

He let his eyes stray to the office next door.

The editor was on his feet, waving a pencil like a baton with one hand and wagging a finger with the other while six members of the senior staff nodded their heads like so many pigeons.

There was a small bar, a large square table neatly stacked with newspapers and magazines ranging from *Private Eye* to the *Wall Street Journal* and one or two foreign papers: *Bild*, which he guessed was German, and *Le Figaro*, possibly French. A sticky label attached to the side of the table warned: *DO NOT TAKE AWAY*.

One wall was devoted to mock-ups of front pages past and a sign that said *Bad Spellers Face Lobotomee*. Behind the largest desk were ten or eleven red and white clocks with varying time zones – New York to Berlin to Moscow to Sydney and some he had never heard of. A wall TV was tuned to Ceefax.

McKenna took another sip of coffee and carefully adjusted his Eiffel Tower coaster so the pointy bit on top was looking away. Then he squared up the coaster with the rectangle of the table.

Mrs Batch didn't look round and carried on rat-a-tatting at her typewriter when she said, 'Obsessive–compulsive disorder.'

'*Beg pardon*?'

'I bet you avoid cracks in the pavement. I bet you have your cocoa at the same time every night, and all your CDs are in alphabetical order. And I *guarantee* you check the door locks twice before you go out. If it's any help, Einstein and Howard Hughes had the same problem.'

McKenna's jaw dropped.

'I thought so,' said Mrs Batch. She stopped typing. 'Out of interest, what's that mark on your face?'

McKenna touched his cheek with a finger, as if making sure it was still there, and worked on his reply. Some thought it was a razor scar – not uncommon in Glasgow – and he never put them right. A razor scar meant *hard man*, but for some reason he didn't think that would work here.

'Smallpox,' he said in a depreciating way. She wrinkled

her nose into a frown and stared at him for some time before going back to the typing.

With nothing else to do, McKenna picked up a copy of the early schedule.

The news desk offering was not exactly cosmopolitan, he thought: the Queen's Park by-election, Braemar in the Highlands breaks record for coldest day of the year (again) and a soldier from Perth tells his Falklands War story.

McKenna looked through the features schedule, searching for the mistakes – and found one immediately, at the top of the weekly film reviews.

'Excuse me,' he said to Mrs Batch, raising a hand like a schoolboy seeking attention from a teacher. 'The review section mentions *Scottish-born fillum star Ian Bannen*.'

'Is that Glasgow vernacular for movie star?' asked Mrs Batch, waspishly.

McKenna gamely laboured on. 'It's not Ian Bannen. The guy who plays the coach in *Chariots of Fire* is Ian Holm. Something else: the Oscar Wilde play at the Theatre Royal? It's not spelt Ernest: E-r-n-e-s-t. It's E-a-r-n-e-s-t.'

Mrs Batch's response was caustic, but droll. 'Well, we're all going to have sleepless nights over *that*,' she said. 'I'll have to bring it up in conference. The editor might even up your salary for that.' McKenna simpered but had just thought of a suitable riposte when the editor's door opened and six men filed out, red-faced and flustered. All six of them frowned at McKenna, as if whatever had been said inside was entirely his fault.

The editor headed straight for Mrs Batch, who was poised with a Parker and notepad.

'We're changing the order of play,' he told her. 'Thatcher is going on the front and the Queen's Park by-election inside. The rest more or less as.' Then, quite gravely and

76

almost threatening, 'I wanna see the news editor, the sports editor and that features guy with the bow tie. What's he called? The one with a double-barrelled moniker.'

'Ashley-Cooper,' said Mrs Batch. 'Daniel Ashley-Cooper.'

'That's him,' said Bloom. 'I want them all in here after first edition.'

Mrs Batch nodded her agreement.

'You can go in now,' she told McKenna as she reclaimed her Eiffel Tower coaster and the coffee mug.

CHAPTER 10.

McKenna's first opinion: Harold Bloom, early forties, medium height but combative and good with the patter. He was totally bald with an alien-sized head and wore Larry King braces, which he got away with when many would not.

McKenna was no expert in accents, but he had seen Kes and heard that fiery former Yorkshire cricketer on TV and this sounded similar. He knew Bloom was *Jewish* – the first word before *Editor* in *Inquirer*speak – so he would need luck. Appointing an English Jew the editor of a Scottish newspaper was like electing a black man mayor of Birmingham, Alabama to McKenna.

Bloom had followed McKenna's eyes to a framed photograph on the side of his desk where a plain woman with Barbra Streisand primps and three girls – the eldest probably ten – were staring back.

'Me missus and kids,' said Bloom, his mouth full of a large sandwich. McKenna thought of Gorman's advice to say nothing, so he just nodded.

The editor was holding a small dossier, and McKenna assumed this was one of the individual get-togethers most of the staff had feared.

'Tell us about yourself,' said Bloom as he dexterously

rolled some Golden Virginia into a Rizla. 'Quick as you can. It says here you were in the shipyards.'

'Accountant in John Brown's.'

'The shipyard, eh? Green or Orange?'

That took McKenna by surprise, as it was probably intended to do, but he kept his eyes fixed on Ceefax. *Transport union blocks Opel sales*, it said.

'Don't worry,' said Bloom. 'I don't give a shite about things like that. You could be a fuckin' Muslim for all I care.'

McKenna kept mum. Bloom moved on.

'What made you choose journalism? You must be the oldest junior reporter in history. How old are you? Forty-odd?'

'Forty-two.'

'Beatles or Stones?'

McKenna was better prepared this time. He pushed his John Lennon specs up and down, Eric Morecambe style.

'Me too,' said Bloom. Then he was off fishing again.

'What do you think of the twilight world of a dog shift?'

'It's OK.'

Bloom leaned back in his chair and blew a smoke ring at the ceiling.

'I started off the same way,' he said.

McKenna sneaked another look at the UK time zone clock: 6.51 p.m. Eight hours to go, if he was lucky.

'Did you really?' he said.

'Nobody likes a dog shift, do they? All those late nights and daytime kips. What does your wife think of it?'

'Single …' said McKenna, then thought it best to add, 'hetero.'

'I see,' said Bloom and changed the subject.

'Did you start on a weekly?'

'*Springfield Herald.*'

That was enough for Bloom.

'Christ, you'll never make it to *This Is Your Life*, will you?' he hissed. 'I'm not a member of the fuckin' Gestapo. I need to know something about you.'

'A reporter,' McKenna said, before adding, 'I did some fillum reviews, too.'

Bloom pointed at a front page mock-up on the wall which read,

EXCLUSIVE: ICE CREAM DRIVERS SOLD DRUGS TO KIDS and said, 'Was that yours?'

McKenna strained to filter out anything that might make him sound arrogant.

'It was mine. I did have a contact, though.'

'Good story,' said Bloom. 'Ice cream drivers selling dope to minors. Most of the Fleet Street papers lifted that, us included. Lucienne was very impressed.'

'*Mrs Batch was impressed?*'

'So she says. Don't get a hard-on, though. She follows all the papers, even the weeklies, in case something is worth lifting.'

'Lifting' usually meant 'stealing', but McKenna still gave himself a proverbial pat on the back. Bloom soon put a stop to that.

'That contact of yours? Was he based at Pitt Street, by any chance?'

'What do you mean, Mister Bloom?'

'*Harold.* I mean there are two members of Strathclyde Police and a guy claiming to be from Scotland Yard waiting to see you upstairs. They gave me ten minutes. So what you been up to?'

'*Cops?* What's cops?'

'Cops who don't wear uniforms. Have you been a

naughty boy?'

'*Not as far as I know.*'

'As far as you know?' said Bloom with a hint of impatience. 'Think about it. If it's to do with the paper I need some schooling. Did the cops get their knickers in a twist over the Ice Cream story?'

'I don't think so,' said McKenna. 'In fact I'm sure. They got four arrests and three sentences out of it. One or two got promoted. What's your opinion?'

'The only opinion I have is that three detectives want to see you, and they're not here to give you a Queen's Police Medal. When did you last speak to a cop?'

'About eighteen months ago. They were on about the Ice Cream story.'

'What about phone calls?'

'I speak to duty officers every night. The conversations never last very long.'

'Tell me.'

'I'd say, "Anything happening?" and they'd say, "Nope. Nothing tonight".'

Bloom managed a wan smile and checked his watch. He looked through his piece of A4 – with neat, very female writing – again.

'According to this there's a DI called Campbell and a bog-standard DC fresh out of school called Hastings, as in Battle of. The main man is Smilie.'

'*Smilie?*'

'Yeah, I thought that, too. But it's S-m-i-l-i-e, not S-m-i-l-e-y. He doesn't look a spy catcher type to me; not one of them that looks like your dad. This one's too young and too well dressed. I don't even believe he's a cop.'

Bloom gave McKenna a few seconds to think about that and then dropped his bombshell.

'I've got some help for you.'

'Help? Help from who?'

'Help from *whom*. Lucienne will go up with you.'

'Mrs Batch? What on earth for?'

'It was her idea, so give her a pat on the back or something. Strictly speaking she should be on her way home by now.'

'Do I really need a burd to help me?'

'Do you have gender problems? A newspaper isn't a bloody male voice choir, you know. How's your shorthand?'

'Sixty words a minute, or thereabouts.'

'Lucienne's on 170 words a minute. That's why she's going up with you. We want detailed notes of what the cops say and what you say back. You've probably got nothing to hide, but there are three of them and we don't want little you outnumbered. My other tip is never try with cops what you tried with me.'

'I don't get that … *Harold*.'

'I mean your impersonation of Robert Mitchum – that Trappist impassivity. Try that with cops and they'll eat you alive. So talk to them. If you are struggling Mrs Batch will help you.'

'How is she going to help?'

'She will let you know if you are saying the wrong thing.'

For Christ's sake, thought McKenna. This is like a le Carré novel.

'What do you mean by "Let me know"?' he tried.

'I don't bloody know. Meet her in the war cabinet before you go up. Suggest she can scratch an ear or dig you in the ribs to shut you up. Play stupid. Think you can play stupid?'

'I can certainly try,' said McKenna.

CHAPTER 11.

The building was a glass and steel monstrosity halfway up Albion Street, and midway between the ties and smart suits of the city centre and the trackie bottoms and shell suits of the East End. George Square, the Royal Infirmary and the Barrows were within walking distance but no walk at all to the Press Bar, which was attached like a remora to its favourite shark.

The offices were on four floors: reception and press room at ground level; compositors, Linotype operators and printers on the first floor; advertising and canteen on the second and editorial, advertising, photographic darkroom and library on the third. The management owned all of the fourth, where there was a penthouse used by the American owners on their rare visits. Mrs Batch must have been highly thought of, too, because she had a key code to take the lift from third to fourth.

Inside it was more posh hotel than newspaper office. The walls were lined with images of hugely moustachioed former owners looking down on burgundy twist carpet and up at eight-arm chandeliers. The boardroom, which had its own bar, was the size of the newsroom, with an oak table surrounded by a dozen leather chairs.

Three men were waiting sitting six feet apart, grim-faced and arms crossed in defensive mode. It was obvious from the start this would not go well.

The Scots, Campbell and Hastings, looked like the cops in Z-Cars, nondescript and with similar little taches. The man they called Mister Smilie was in his early thirties. He was wearing a black three-piece suit, horn-rimmed glasses and he had a butch haircut. His upper-class accent and his condescending tone made it clear he didn't like having to visit a foreign land. Bizarrely, he spoke in a Runyonesque present tense and in the third person.

'We can all smoke,' said Smilie – a fact rather than a request. He made a big deal of unlocking his leather attaché case and pulling out two sheets of foolscap paper. Then, as the other detectives lit up he said, 'Mister McKenna does not smoke?'

'I've given up.'

'Hard work, is it not? Recently?'

'Three days.'

'Aaah. What would Mister McKenna smoke had he not given up?'

'Silk Cut. Or roll-ups if I was desperate.'

'Aaah,' said Smilie disbelievingly. 'DI Campbell?'

They were all armed with personal notebooks and Campbell pulled out his version to say, in cop talk, 'We are endeavouring to find about your assignments here and in particular your telephone calls and whereabouts on the nights of Monday September 20 and 27 this year.'

Campbell waited for a reply but then thought he should add, 'We would appreciate some cooperation in this matter.'

Smilie stared at the ceiling and frowned as if he had just spotted a fly there.

'Mister McKenna is not under caution. Mister McKenna is not a suspect, and can answer "No comment". Or he can simply remain silent, of course.'

'Are you going to tell me what it's about?' said McKenna.

There was no response. Smilie looked across at Mrs Batch.

'Do we need this young lady?'

'I was told she had to stay,' said McKenna. 'Will you take notes?'

'We usually take notes,' said Campbell. 'It's for the good of everyone.'

McKenna remembered Bloom's words: Batch's 170 words a minute shorthand; cops using a crude longhand and having to cut long words and long sentences down to short words and short sentences.

'In that case you have no objection if Mrs Batch takes notes, too?'

Smilie shrugged indifferently. Mrs Batch took off her glasses, blew onto the lenses, cleaned them with an embroidered handkerchief and went back to her notepad.

'So be it,' said Campbell. 'Are you employed by *The Inquirer* UK organisation which resides at 199, Albion Street, Glasgow, Scotland?'

'You know it is. Number 197, though. Number 199 is the Press Bar next door.'

Campbell carried on as if the interruption had not occurred. 'I want you to account for your movements on the nights in question.'

A long silence.

'It would be nice to finish this interview before Christmas,' said Smilie.

'I think he's waiting for a roll of drums,' sniggered Campbell. Hastings guffawed.

'I was just thinking,' McKenna said. 'I was probably in here.'

'Probably?'

'I was in here, both nights. I was on the dog shift.'

Hastings spoke for the first time. 'The dog shift?'

'Night shift. Usually 6.30 p.m. to 4.30 a.m. Dog shift, dog's life, dog shite.'

'Tell us about your ... dog shift,' said Campbell, choosing his words carefully.

'Pretty much the same most nights: check calls to the major police stations, check out TV news, check Ceefax, probably rewrite some of the agency copy, answer the phone, check the foreigners, go home. That's it.'

'*Foreigners?*'

'Rival newspapers.'

'Do calls go direct to you?'

'There's no one on switchboard after midnight – so, yes, calls to editorial are usually routed to me.'

'Are there other members of staff around at that time?'

'It depends what time you mean. Several, if it was before midnight. Things start to die off after 1 a.m. The editor and Mrs Batch often stay late, and there might be a photographer or two still around or someone on sport doing the stats.'

'Stats?' the curious Hastings asked. McKenna thought this was getting like a meeting of the UN when no one had ordered an interpreter, but he tried to help.

'Statistics for readers who want the results of the Super Bowl or the World Series, or stuff like that. Our new owners are Yanks.'

Campbell took over again. 'Who else stays late?'

'There's a guy on the stone – the slab of metal where the pages are set – and he comes up about 1 a.m. He checks the page proofs and then takes off, assuming there's nothing dramatic worth restarting the presses for.'

'Do you ever go out the office?'

'I do the odd death knock. Apparently they think I'm quite good at that.'

'And what makes Mister McKenna so good at death knocks?'

'It helps if you are a local when you knock on a stranger's door and persuade them to talk about their dear departed. It's not rocket science. It's a bit like being an undertaker. I would guess the Pitt Street police see door knocks the same way?'

Hastings nodded knowingly and said, 'No ambulance chasing, then?'

'I don't drive. We have a freelance to do that because there's a dispute about late shifts. Usually he sits in his car all night, following police radio traffic.'

They didn't like that at all. The voices got louder and more aggressive.

'Tell me about a telephone call from a man with a foreign accent on the night of Monday the 20th,' said Campbell. 'Probably just after midnight?'

'If it was after midnight that would make it Tuesday the 21st.'

'Don't be clever,' Campbell retorted. 'We're not in the mood.'

McKenna thought and decided, 'Yes, I seem to remember that, but I'm sure he never rang back on the 27th. If he did, I never took it.'

'We'll come back to that,' said Campbell. 'Tell us about the 20th.'

'Some pissed-up German guy phoned late at night.'

'How do you know he was German? What do you know about Germany?'

'I know it's an anagram for Meg Ryan and I've seen *The Great Escape* and *Where Eagles Dare* a few times.'

Hastings, the junior, tried not to smile. Campbell pursed

his lips and said, 'I advise you to take this very seriously.'

'Look … a guy rang, I took it and he had a German accent,' said McKenna. 'He was pissed. We get plenty of drunks phoning here after closing time, though I can't remember many Germans. He prattled on for a bit. I never understood a word, so I hung up.'

'Did you get his number?' said Hastings, hopefully.

'No. Sorry.'

'You could easily have got a last-call return,' said Campbell petulantly. 'You're supposed to be a journalist, aren't you?'

'I could have done, but two hours of listening to drunks bellyaching about football results is enough. So no, I say again: I didn't get a number.'

'Can you recall what was said?'

'He spoke *German*, Mister Campbell. As I just told you, that's not one of my languages. Are you going to tell me what this is about?'

'Did Mister McKenna take any notes at all?'

'Obviously I didn't take a shorthand note.'

'Did you have a tape recorder?'

A shoe kicked McKenna hard in the right tibia before Campbell repeated, '*Did you have a tape recorder?*'

'Tape recorder?' said Hastings, totally baffled. 'How does it work on a phone?'

McKenna spotted his chance.

'It's just a suction cup device stuck on the phone with the other end plugged into a tape recorder,' he said, deliberately haltingly. 'It works pretty well most of the time. I can actually record both sides of a phone conversation with mine.'

'Don't reporters still use shorthand?' said Hastings.

'Of course we do. You have to. People are always

forgetting to switch on the tape and they're always running out of batteries. That can be a bit—'

'That's enough,' interrupted Campbell. 'DC Hastings, you keep your mouth shut. Now we ask again, Mister McKenna … is that man's voice on tape?'

'I killed it.'

'You *killed* it?' said three men in unison.

'I got rid. I only have a couple, and if they're no use I just tape over the top.'

There was much shifting of chairs, a lot of frowns and some whispering. Smilie dug into his attaché case again, pulled out more bits of paper and made sure everyone could see what he was holding.

It was a copy of a press pass *recognised by the Railway Executive of British Railways, the Association of Chief Police Officers and the Docks and Inland Waterways Executive.* The mugshot was so poor McKenna hardly recognised himself but he certainly recognised the copy of a woman's passport photo Smilie was also holding. Then things got really unpleasant, with Smilie in the van.

'Has Mister McKenna ever been a member of the Communist Party?'

McKenna was taken aback and took some time to think of an answer.

'Not really,' he said.

'What do you mean, "not really"?'

'I was a member of The Young Communist League. There's a difference.'

'You went to meetings, though.'

'Yes, if you call ten- or eleven-year-olds lighting bonfires and listening to a few speeches about the Spanish Civil War a meeting. Are MI5 after me or something?'

'Mister McKenna's father is a card-carrying member of

89

the Communist Party?'

'He was.'

'I assume he still is?'

'Doubtful. He's in a care home.'

Smilie brandished his notes again. 'Mister McKenna was married to a female from Moscow, the woman in this passport photo, was he not?'

'Minsk. Not Moscow. And we weren't married.'

'Same thing, isn't it?' said Campbell and looked round for a laugh. 'What were you, then, if you weren't married? Shacked up, Reds under the bed and all that?'

McKenna had to think about that one, too. Girlfriend? Possibly. Lover? Definitely not: a celibate courtship was closer to the mark, though he wasn't going to admit that to *anyone*.

'I think it's fair if you tell me what you're up to,' he said. 'I'd help any way I could. Everyone knows that. Even Strathclyde Police know that. So far you haven't asked about the night of the 27th. What's that about?'

Campbell and Smilie looked at each other before Smilie decided, 'Would Mister McKenna find it odd if I tell him that a photograph from the pages of your newspaper was found in a German gentleman's apartment two days ago?'

'The same gentleman who phoned you a week ago,' added Campbell.

'Of course it's odd, but how the hell would I know? Why don't you ask him?'

'We would, but unfortunately he is now deceased,' said Campbell. 'Are you sure you've never been to Germany?'

'What the hell do you mean? Course I haven't. I don't even have a passport.'

The three policemen gave each other told-you-so nods.

'I have your passport number here,' said Campbell.

McKenna remembered then: Bloom's brave new world of reporters travelling the globe for his cosmopolitan *Inquirer*. McKenna did have a new passport, but it was still hiding somewhere back home.

'I'd forgotten,' he said truthfully. 'If you have the details you'll know I've never used it. I've never been abroad. I've never even been north of Dundee.'

Smilie's tones were those of an undertaker.

'It may be best if Mister McKenna follows DI Campbell and DC Hastings to Pitt Street, where Mister McKenna will be cautioned and be asked a few more questions. We also need to examine your desk. I assume that's where you keep your tapes?'

The voice was so soft and unexpected everyone looked around and tried to find the speaker.

'Do you have a warrant?' said Mrs Batch. Then, louder, '*Do you have a warrant*? One of those things from a sheriff's court.'

The detectives looked at each other in the hope one might have the answer.

'So I assume you haven't got a warrant?' said Mrs Batch, arms crossed and head on one side. 'In that case I suggest you find a court official and come back here when you have. You should find a court official on St Andrew's Street, though I doubt if they will be open this time of night. If not I'm sure I could find you a number for one of the Glasgow sheriffs.'

Campbell, whose face had gone as red as the carpet, wanted to take it further. Smilie was already stuffing his paper back into the briefcase.

'We won't detain you any longer,' he said. 'Thank you for all your help. Mister McKenna must make sure he has an alibi for the nights in question. DI Campbell will certainly return with a warrant, and may want to talk to some of the other staff.'

He said to McKenna, though pointing at Mrs Batch, 'Please ask your secretary if she would phone me a taxi.'

Batch was just as formal.

'Delighted,' she said. 'Before you go, do you mind if we have a look at this young man's notes?'

'Pardon?' said Campbell. 'His notes? What are you inferring?'

'Implying, I think you mean. *Implying*. If that's the word you were looking for I am implying that detectives taking notes in longhand may make mistakes. I think it's only fair to see those notes. They will go on the record, won't they? I assume you consider Mister McKenna a witness?'

Campbell and Hastings looked to Smilie who just shrugged and said, 'Go on then, Hastings. Read it out for us.'

Hastings found the beginning and cleared his throat.

'Mr McKenna said he took the call on Monday, September 20, and as it was after midnight few other staff would have been working. A gentleman with a foreign accent rang and he was drunk.'

He stopped there and looked around for approval.

Mrs Batch shook her head.

'Mister McKenna has already explained: if it was "after midnight" it was Tuesday the 21st, although he does begin his shifts *before* midnight. You also say a call was from a "gentleman with a foreign accent" but those are your words, not those of Mister McKenna. Mister McKenna described him as "pissed", not "drunk" – a subtle difference, particularly in Glasgow. Need I say more?'

'No, you don't need to say more,' said Smilie.

Lucienne Batch closed her notepad and rose to her feet.

'You can send me a copy of the police statement if you think it necessary,' she said with a tight-lipped smile. 'I'll supply you with a copy of my own notes.'

The detectives tried to look in control as they left, but Mrs Batch wanted a few last words to complete the humiliation.

'Dinnae ever teach yer granny tae suck eggs,' she said, in passable Weegie.

CHAPTER 12.

Harold Bloom poured a large Talisker, lifted his feet high onto his desk and rested his head on his hands.

'Summat to settle your stomach?' he said.

'Pardon?' said McKenna.

'A drink, a bevvy … I've got some wine, if you prefer.'

McKenna tried not to sound prissy when he said, 'Not just now, thanks.'

'Have you given up the sherbet?'

'Pardon?'

'Are … you … on … the … wagon?'

'Third day,' said McKenna, proud but grim. He looked inquiringly next door.

'Missing her already?' said Bloom with a snigger. 'Lucienne's not coming in cos she wants to finish the notes of your interview. So tell us what went on, but don't take too long. I'd like to get home sometime this weekend.'

It took five minutes. Bloom tut-tutted occasionally, and he said what sounded like, 'Nowt like that in Bratfud,' several times. His eyes widened when the German's phone call was mentioned. When he heard of Batch's demolition of Smilie and co. he smiled approvingly and nodded, as if this sort of thing was quite common.

'That Lucienne,' he said. 'Not the sort of lass to scream

on a roller-coaster ride, is she? Or hide from a spider? Who was that bird who beat the shit out of the Alien?'

'Ripley. Ellen Ripley.'

'That's her. They should have had Lucienne in that role.'

'What do you think those cops were up to?' McKenna asked.

'I wasn't there, mate. You tell me why someone got in a state over a phone call from a German.'

'Well, if I were to guess—'

Bloom stopped him, and this time he was not smiling. 'I'm not looking for guesses,' he said. 'I can walk out of this office and find a dozen people to do the guessing. This paper has more guessers than Sheffield has steel.'

'Something to do with that phone call?' McKenna said, hopefully.

'Scare tactics,' said Bloom. 'Classic police ploy to muddy the waters. You were not cautioned, didn't they say? If you're not cautioned they don't need to tell you owt. All that stuff about your ex and the Commie Party was designed to let you know they'd done their homework. What a bunch of bad 'uns. Nowt like that in Bratfud.'

Then, so quietly McKenna hardly heard him, 'Where is it?'

'Where's what?'

'Your tape.'

'In my desk. I have dozens of 'em. Always hoped they'd come in handy.'

It had been a long day and suddenly Bloom was tired, but he wanted to wait until they were off stone, when most of the staff would be on breaks.

'Hang around here until they're all off to the boozer,' he said. 'I don't want them nosy buggers seeing you walking in here with a tape. We'll listen to it when they're out of the way.'

'The guy was speaking German,' said McKenna.

'Lucienne will sort it. Good at stuff like this, is Lucienne. Just imagine it as a foreign language film with her supplying the subtitles.'

He couldn't say better than that, thought McKenna, except to ask, '*Lucienne* … is that French?'

'What do you think?'

'She just looks and acts French.'

'And what do French women look and act like?'

'Skinny, black eyes and they talk with their hands … a bit grumpy, like her.'

'Very good,' Bloom said, and he meant it. 'Anything else?'

'She wears a wedding ring and reads the *Morning Star*.'

Bloom was about to reply when his internal rang.

'We're off stone,' he said after he hung up. 'Go and get your tape now.'

McKenna persisted. 'We were talking about Mrs Batch.'

'Forget it,' said Bloom. 'Keeping a *Morning Star* in her handbag doesn't mean much here. Half the bloody staff are into cornfields and ballet, aren't they?'

McKenna's laughter must have persuaded the editor to add, 'You're half right about the French bit because she worked with the *Agence France-Presse* in Paris. There again, she also lived in the States and Berlin for a time.'

'What was she doing in Germany?'

'She was married to some guy in the British Army of the Rhine.'

'And the wedding ring?'

'A nosy sod, aren't you?' said Bloom. 'You're one of them lonely buggers who say nowt but listen and watch a lot. You should have been a spy. Now get your tape and bring some early editions in while you're at it. Tell Lucienne we're ready.'

'*The wedding ring*?' McKenna persevered.

'Presumably it's to keep the flies away,' said Bloom.

CHAPTER 13.

McKenna thought it a waste of time at first and that Bloom agreed, because he carried on checking his first edition pages while listening to the tape.

It lasted less than three minutes, was hard to hear in parts, and the caller was obviously pissed. It had to be replayed several times, but it did get interesting when Mrs Batch read her translation. Even Bloom threw his paper away then.

She had written, in longhand and in the order of each conversation: Caller, *Lucienne Batch translation*, McKenna's reply. The words she missed were marked 'Inaudible'. They could return to those later, she said.

Caller: '*Sprechen sie Deutsch? Das ist Lukas Rückeran aus Stuttgart.*'

Batch: '*Do you speak German? This is Lukas Rückeran from Stuttgart.*'

McKenna: 'Who's speaking?'

Caller: '*Ich möchte der Familie von Lulu zu sprechen.*'

Batch: '*I want to talk to the family of (sounds like) Lulu.*'

McKenna: 'Are you pissed, whoever you are?'

Caller: '*Ja, ja, Ich bin betrunken. Sehr betrunken. Immer betrunken.*'

Batch: '*Yes, yes, I am drunk. Very drunk. Always drunk.*'

McKenna: 'What do you want? There's someone on my other line.'

Caller: '*Ich muss die Geschichte über Lulu. Sie wurde auf (*inaudible*) Straße in Paris ermordet. Sie müssen die Adler zu finden.*'

Batch: '*I must tell the story about Lulu. She was murdered in (inaudible) street in Paris. You must find the Eagle.*'

McKenna: 'The only thing I caught then was "Paris". Did you say Lulu?'

Caller: '*Lulu: ja, Lulu. Sie war ein mitglied (*inaudible*). Sagen sie ihre familie es tut uns leid. Suchen sie Esso E für Lulu.*'

Batch: '*Lulu: yes, Lulu. She was a member (inaudible). You tell her family we are sorry. Look up (sounds like) Esso E for Lulu.*'

McKenna: I haven't understood a word, mate. I'm going to have to go now.'

Caller: '*Ich sage dir, sie war Schottish. Ich weiss wo sie in Paris ist.*'

Batch: 'I tell you, she was Scottish. I know where she is in Paris—'

The final note from Mrs Batch read: '*McKenna hung up. Tape ends*'.

She wasn't happy. In fact, Mrs Batch was almost apoplectic. She raised both hands in exasperation and spat, rather than spoke, 'A bit stupid, hanging up just when it was getting interesting. He said he had a story to tell … and you missed it. The least you could have done was get his address and what he does for a living.'

McKenna made a meek attempt to explain.

'I understand that now, but you can't expect me to know what was said in a foreign language. The guy was well Brahms and Liszt, anyway. I get loads of calls like that. I did my bit and taped the conversation.'

'Did your bit?' she cried. 'Are you taking credit for this?'

Bloom held up both hands – the referee separating two rival boxers.

'That's enough, you two,' he said. 'This isn't the bloody Press Bar.'

Batch glared at McKenna and he frowned back, but both backed off.

'Now think,' said Bloom. 'This guy had a story to tell, so let's hear it.'

Another long hiatus. Batch tried first. 'The Paris street sounds like Rue de Saussaies. The one I am struggling with is "Esso E". It sounds a bit like Esso Extra, the petrol company.'

'Play that back,' said Bloom. 'Go from "a member" to the end.'

The tape screeched as it rewound, and it was hard to find the right section.

'And again,' said Bloom. 'And again.'

At the end Bloom looked at Batch, who had gone quite pale. Then she whispered, as if afraid others might hear, 'It wasn't Esso E. It was nothing to do with petrol. He was saying S ... O ... E. Special ... Operations ... Executive. Lulu was a British spy.'

They sat in silence and without looking at each other for some time.

Bloom spoke first. 'Does anyone know anything about the SOE?'

McKenna put his hand up at once and suggested, 'There was a woman agent in *Carve Her Name with Pride*.'

'I beg your pardon,' said Batch.

'Come again?' said Bloom.

'*Carve Her Name with Pride*. It was a 1950s movie and starred Virginia McKenna. No relation, of course!'

'Meaning what?' said Mrs Batch, back in glacial mode.

'She specialised in sabotage and ran rings round the Gestapo until she was caught and shot. I think the plot involves Paris, too.'

Bloom was not impressed, either.

'Look, mate, do yourself a favour and think of something that might keep you on this story. I wanted a reporter, not some bloody movie geek.'

He turned back to Mrs Batch. 'What about Adler on the tape?'

'I thought at first it had to be someone called Adler,' she said, 'but then I remembered it translates to "Eagle" in the English. Eagle's Nest was Hitler's mountain retreat. The swastika had an eagle on it.'

McKenna went through the notes again.

'Drunks have a habit of repeating themselves. I wonder if anyone else in the office took a call from him. Shall I ask around?'

'No, we bloody well won't,' said Bloom. Batch agreed. 'We're keeping this to ourselves. The fewer people know the better.'

'Why the hell phone me at the office, though?'

'He may have phoned the first Jock paper he came across,' Bloom suggested. 'He did say this woman was Scottish. Anyway, we'd better find out, and pronto.'

He stroked his chin furiously and looked across at Ceefax. 'Where's our chief investigation reporter this week?' he said.

'On sabbatical,' said Batch emphatically. 'Florida, I gather.'

'Is there anyone else? Someone we can take off rota for a week or so?'

'Possibly, but that means bringing someone else in on the story. Anyway, two of the reporters are down in London for the Falklands victory parade. We could try one of the other specialists: Features? Sport? Obits?'

Bloom looked at her as if she'd used a dirty word and shook his head. He turned to McKenna.

'Just out of interest, what you on next week?'

McKenna tried his hardest to sound enthusiastic.

'Nothing special: I'm down for a death knock on Monday. That's about it.'

'Pull out your notebook then,' said Bloom. 'We're off to war.'

Three of the senior staff were queuing up inside Batch's office, presumably to get to the editor. She shooed them away and closed all the window blinds. Bloom tossed his first editions on the floor so he had more room for notes.

'Here's where we're going,' he said. 'We're looking for a Scottish SOE agent; all SOE agents in France during the war; any murdered ones. Once you find the real name get her place of birth and any living relatives. I think Lucienne might find the time to look after the European angle of things. Stuttgart, Paris and all that? We also need to know more about the German.'

Batch nodded and agreed. 'I'll try some of the German newspapers. I still have contacts out there.' Then to McKenna, 'What about you? Any military contacts?'

McKenna wondered if he was out of his depth here. Mrs Batch was supposed to be an editorial administrator and seemed to have more background and more contacts than Woodward and Bernstein together. He was also beginning to feel like a guard on a runaway train pulling the emergency brake while two drivers pile on more coal. But he wanted this now, probably more than anything ever.

'I guess so,' he said, carefully.

'Well, stop guessing before the rest of the press get on to it,' said Mrs Batch before Bloom also warned, 'We don't want to finish up chasing. It would be nice to break a story instead of following one up.'

McKenna still had a few questions.

'How could other papers follow it up? We're the only ones with the tape. We've got plenty of time, surely?'

Bloom and Batch tut-tutted and shook their heads.

'Was he born stupid, or did he just grow up that way?' she asked dismissively.

Bloom was more forgiving and explained, 'As things stand we have the only story. Isn't that right, Lucienne? But cops are quicker finding names and numbers than a newspaper. It's called an informational advantage. If they are getting nowhere and need help they'll hold press conferences and call in some of *their* paper contacts. Someone might fancy a few quid and take his information around. It won't stay exclusive for long then.'

'BDMs,' said Mrs Batch. 'Another way of losing an exclusive.'

'BDMs?'

She rolled her eyes and gave another exaggerated sigh. 'Births, deaths, marriages,' she said. 'The media is obsessed with anniversaries.'

'Standard silly season fodder to fill pages,' Bloom agreed. 'All that crap like *"On This Day"*, or *"It's 50 Years Ago This Week"*. The only good thing about those is that they don't cost much. Aren't features working on a twentieth anniversary piece on the Cuban Missile Crisis?'

Batch nodded.

'Give it another year and they'll be flogging me a Great Train Robbers anniversary story. All of which brings us back to this Lulu: like where and when she was born, if she was married and where and when she died. Where would you start?'

'The library?' suggested McKenna, who hadn't missed the 'would' rather than the 'will' and still wasn't sure if he was on the story.

'I suppose that's a start,' said Bloom. 'I'd try the local registry offices; maybe the Ministry of Defence. If they clam up, which they will, the Red Cross will have some details about war deaths. When I was a reporter I often pretended I was a relative – but all's fair in love and war, as they say.'

McKenna said, in what he saw as *All the President's Men* mode, 'What's the precise time frame on this?'

'The time frame? Did he say "time frame", Lucienne?'

Mrs Batch just sniggered.

'You mean how long have we got with the tape? Or how long before I hand the story to someone else?'

'The tape,' said McKenna, trying his best to smile.

Bloom leaned so far back in his chair McKenna saw the soles of his shoes.

'The cops have to get the tape before morning,' he said studiedly. 'I don't fancy a charge of perverting the course of justice.'

He twirled the whisky round his glass and half closed his eyes. It took him so long to continue McKenna thought he had fallen asleep.

'Here's what we do. Use one of them Nixon Watergate tape things and make a transcript. Your original can go to them cops, but leave it until way after midnight before you call a taxi. I'd guess Pitt Street will have a night duty sergeant on by then, and he'll be half asleep. Leave a note saying you'd been looking for the tape and it turned up. They won't believe you, but there ain't a lot they can do about it. If you're lucky the night duty officer might think it's a bomb, which will give us a bit more time.'

'We are following it up then,' Mrs Batch said – more a statement than a question. Bloom took his feet off the table and sat up straight to take another swig of Scotch. His eyes were as red as burst blood vessels, but after twelve hours in the building he could be forgiven a tired and worn look. Mrs Batch looked as if she had just come back from having her highlights done at Sassoon's.

'Course we are, Lucienne,' he said. 'We might get some sugar in the cake here. We need a good tale, anyway. Agreed?'

She pointed at McKenna and then, as if he had never been there, 'What do we do about him? Can we trust a rookie reporter, particularly one with red hair?'

'Have we a choice?' said Bloom.

McKenna tried to look nondescript, but asked, 'You don't think I'll cope?'

'We'll soon find out, won't we?' said Bloom. He looked at Batch and she stared back, as if they were still making up their minds.

'Shall we test him?' said Bloom.

'Of course,' said Mrs Batch. 'What shall we try?'

McKenna wondered if this really was a madhouse or if he had strayed on to an edition of *Double Your Money*, with Bloom as the question master and Batch as the hostess. It turned out they had the £1000 winner after Bloom said, 'Here's your starter: what do Natalie Wood and William Holden have in common? And don't say they were famous film stars.'

McKenna tried to keep his face straight and pretended to think about it before he said, 'They died in mysterious circumstances during the same month in 1981, and neither of them made the front pages of *The Inquirer*.'

'And the reason?'

'They weren't Scottish.'

Bloom rolled back in his chair and grinned.

'Not as dumb as he looks, is he?' he said.

He didn't waste time after that. 'Get whatever notes you have on your death knock and leave it for the news desk,' he said. 'Lucienne can sort it out with them. And keep mum about this. In fact, it might be best if you work from home for a day or so. Let's look on this as classified. I don't want anyone else in the newsroom knowing about it. Don't mess up; if you need support let us know.'

'Us?'

'Me or Lucienne. And you go to her first.'

McKenna looked at Batch as she smiled contentedly, like a cat licking the last drop of milk. He wondered if the Bardot-like gap in the front teeth and the crows' feet made her so reluctant to smile.

Bloom stood up and locked his drinks cabinet.

'Now, all you have to do is find a real-life Rosebud for us,' he told McKenna

'No one ever found Rosebud.'

Bloom put on his coat and headed for the office door with Batch close behind.

'That's the problem with films,' he said just before they left. 'Too bloody implausible. Citizen Kane and his dying words? In real life the thickest hack in the world would have found Rosebud with half a day's research. Ready, Lucienne?'

McKenna hurried over to the third-floor window overlooking the executive car park. A jobsworth in a fluorescent yellow jacket was pushing up the barricade and a large, white Mercedes turned left towards Queen Street station and the West End. The car behind, one

106

of those four-wheel drive Jeep things, turned right into George Street and left at the lights towards the A8 and, maybe, the Campsie hills. McKenna saw her as the Aga and green wellies type.

The office gossips had been wrong, then. Batch and Bloom were certainly close, but not that close – more the closeness of Steed and Mrs Peel in *The Avengers*. Two people devoted to a job: colleagues who exchanged friendly banter and occasional innuendo, but nothing else.

On his way back to his desk McKenna stopped outside Mrs Batch's office where she always posted news desk agendas, and there was what he had suspected: the chief investigation reporter was down to interview the Labour candidate in the Queen's Park by-election on the Sunday. Bloom had too much on his plate to know that the chief investigation reporter was back from Florida, but Mrs Batch certainly did, because she was in charge of editorial rotas. As far as this story went, then, the editorial administrator had an agenda. That, at any rate, was the opinion of William H McKenna, and he would stick with it.

CHAPTER 14.

By 2 a.m. there were two tapes. The original was lying on the back seat of a taxi on its way to Pitt Street and its duplicate was in the Grundig reel-to-reel tape machine by the side of the news desk.

McKenna hadn't a clue where to go from there.

Anything after midnight was a bad time for phone calls, particularly at weekends. More out of hope than anything else, he rolled a piece of A4 and five carbon copies into the typewriter carriage and waited, fingers poised, for the arrival of the muse of journalism. Ten minutes later he had typed 'By William H McKenna' in the top left corner. He tried a hypothetical intro because even nonsense was a start – and the background, the names of the people to interview and the justification for starting it in the first place would surely follow.

A Scottish (British?) girl (woman?) who served in clandestine operations (SOE?) during the Second World War (WW2?) may have been murdered, a German (West German?) source has revealed.

Then he was really stuck. Too many question marks, his ancient Adler needed a new ribbon and the S on the hammer kept sticking. He tried it in capitals and italics and then centred it. He wanted a fag and a drink, but he had forgotten Plan B: always keep a supply handy for

108

emergencies – the smoker's version of mouth-to-mouth resuscitation.

There was no Plan C. The Press Bar would be closed and the owners never did a lock-in, even over a weekend. It would be hard to find a working fag machine after midnight in Glasgow. He thought of going through the ashtrays for stubs, but the cleaners were already busy binning whatever was left. His three new biros had been chomped to destruction.

He looked around for help. Saturday was two hours old and the place was empty, apart from a sports desk sub watching TV in one corner and a photographer typing with one finger in the other. It could not have been worse. The sub was one of those born-again joggers desperate to replace one addiction with another. McKenna knew the snapper, Perry, had for months been trying to get the NUJ to ban smoking in the office.

McKenna checked his notes and then cursed and banged away, two-handed, two-fingered, until the typewriter submitted: *British spy, Special Operations Executive, Paris, murdered in Paris, Lukas somebody, a drunk. Stuttgart (West Germany). Lulu and family. Gestapo, Eagle Nest.*

He stopped again. The Gestapo hadn't been mentioned and Mrs Batch said the German had mentioned 'Adler', which also happened to be the people who manufactured his typewriter, and he couldn't see a connection with a murder there. Eagle could be a comic book, the Moon landing module, a large raptor on the American coat of arms or a film starring Michael Caine. If it was Eagles or Eagle's he was in a new ball game: LA rock band, a Clint Eastwood movie, Hitler's mountain home. None of these, of course, After another twenty minutes his wastebasket was full of crumpled false starts and he had to stop himself from throwing his heavy-duty stapler at the flickering fluorescent light a few feet away.

Close to despair, he pushed the typewriter aside and lifted his Halliwells from his desk. He went straight to the front end of C:

Carve Her Name with Pride: *In 1940 the young British widow of a French officer is enlisted as a spy and after various adventures dies before a German firing squad. Halliwell's verdict: slightly muddled, if ultimately moving biopic … blazing war action … and finally tragedy.*

Some additional notes said the film was based on the true story of a young mother, Violette Szabo, born in Paris to an English father and a French mother. Her *nom de guerre* was Louise. She was captured and held by the Gestapo at Rue de Saussaies, Paris and later executed at a concentration camp.

McKenna grabbed his notes and hurried, as quickly as he could without running, out of the newsroom and along the dark corridor outside.

The library was usually overseen by eight middle-aged men wearing knee-length white coats, and all had been coached in the art of total non-cooperation. Any request, polite or not, was treated like someone knocking on a stranger's door and asking to use the bathroom. But the union rules of librarians did not admit work after 6 p.m., so McKenna had the place to himself.

The shelving systems were alphabetised: names of people, subjects – and large grey cabinets for photo files. There was a cuttings section with all key words underscored in red biro and then pasted onto pieces of paper. One corner was given over to reference books and there was a wall to themselves for neatly-bound volumes of past newspaper editions.

McKenna started at S among subjects: nothing on the

110

SOE or the Special Operations Executive. He considered WW2, but that had its own shelf the width and size of a wall of breeze blocks and would take too long. Lulu in the people section was too much of a long shot, but there was a small SOE section in picture files.

There were three photographs. One was an unrealistic publicity shot from *Carve Her Name with Pride* with Virginia pointing a machine gun at someone or something. That should have gone in the people section under McK, but the library staff obviously couldn't tell the difference between fact and fiction.

Another black-and-white snap, already faded and yellow with age, showed a number of smiling people posing on what looked like the lawns of a country house. A brief caption read: **Staff at Special Operations Executive at Briggens, Roydon in 1942.** There were several women, but no names and no credit to the photographer. The final image was more profitable and was of a well-dressed man in his forties shaking hands with a white-haired old lady, probably in her sixties. The photograph had been taken in a street outside an office.

McKenna squinted at the words above the door. **Conservative Party**, it said.

The caption was even more helpful: *Mrs Marie Charlotte Cloutier of Blair Lodge, Braemar, meets the new Conservative candidate for West Aberdeenshire, Mr Colin Mitchell. Mrs Cloutier's daughter, Eugenie, was murdered by the Gestapo in Paris during 1944 and the body has never been found.*

In words the size of the smallest line of an eye test the photo was credited to George Davies, Freelance, *North-East News*, and the date was September 7, 1969 – making it, coincidentally or not, approximately twenty-five years since Eugenie's murder.

He moved to the far end of the room and pulled out

the bound volumes for 1969. There was nothing from September 7 to September 11. Either the library staff had cocked it up or someone had cut it out and made off with it. Staff occasionally did that, usually to add their own stories to a personal CV.

A 12 point headline at the bottom of Page One of September 6 explained: *UK Newspapers Set for Industrial Action.*

'The bloody printers had been on strike,' McKenna said aloud to himself and that *no* printers meant no newspaper.

Energised by this unprecedented surge of motivation, he turned to the reference section of the library's *Collins Road Atlas of Europe* and went to P for Paris. Rue de Saussaies was quite central, and close to the Champs-Elysées and the Eiffel Tower. An *Encyclopaedia Britannica World Atlas* didn't tell him much except that Stuttgart was the capital of Baden-Württemberg in West Germany and was not too distant from the Rhine. Its coat of arms was a black horse on its hind legs.

McKenna was tempted to make copies with the library Xerox, but it would take several minutes to boot and suddenly he felt in a hurry. There was no one in sight so he pocketed two of the photographs and left Virginia McKenna as the only survivor. He switched everything off, headed down the corridor, turned and went back to make sure the lights were off and then returned to the newsroom.

McKenna was on his way past the picture desks when the left leg of a pair of jeans and a dirty Adidas sneaker reached over and blocked his path.

'So you're giving her one, too?' said its owner.

'I don't know what you mean,' McKenna fibbed to Perry.

'The Jew's lemon. That posh English crumpet who

112

thinks she owns the place. I saw all three of you licking each other's arses in his office.'

McKenna pretended to be amused, but said nothing. Perry, who had some title in the chapel, slipped into union senior memberspeak.

'She'd better not be involved in an editorial story,' he said. 'She's a fuckin' secretary.'

McKenna tried to be polite. 'She was working on some notes for us. Anyway, since there's a roadblock here maybe you could help me out on a couple of things.'

Perry pulled his leg out of the way and asked warily, 'What sort of things?'

'Have you ever come across a snapper called George Davies?'

'I remember George,' said Perry. 'He died of cancer about a year ago. Big smoker, more fool him. I went to his funeral.'

McKenna sought the correct amount of disconsolation and said, 'Sorry to hear that. Did he ever get sent on any Westminster-type jobs?'

'Nah. He had a Highland beat and was a freelance anyway. Whatya after?'

'Just an old snap,' McKenna said truthfully this time. 'I found a pic of a Conservative candidate called Colin Mitchell. Ever come across him?'

Perry was quite nonplussed.

'Obviously you've never covered much at all, have you? You're talking about "Mad Mitch", who was a lieutenant colonel in the Argylls – the guy with the bagpipers in Aden. He and his troops saw off a bunch of Arab extremists. He was also the MP for West Aberdeenshire for a time.'

'Did you ever meet him?'

'Sort of, if you think taking pics of someone is meeting them. I was at the count in 1970. He was a Tory, but

113

apparently quite popular. That was the year Wilson was beaten by Heath. You've heard of them?'

McKenna ignored the poor attempt at sarcasm and asked, 'Why would *The Inquirer* send a staff photographer all the way up there?'

'You must be joking, mate. A soldier turned MP, a bit of a nutter, in charge of a Jock brigade and a man who liked the sound of his own voice … Mitchell turned out to be a newspaper man's dream. He quit in '74 and concentrated on daft causes.'

'What sort of causes?'

Perry's time as a helpful colleague seemed to be up.

'What am I, fuckin' Mister Memory?' he said. 'Try *Who's Who*, or Hansard.'

Perry went back to his caption. McKenna returned to the library.

Hansard, the transcripts of, did indeed show that Lieutenant Colonel Colin Mitchell was elected MP in 1970, his 18,396 votes beating the Liberal candidate, Mrs Laura Grimond. The maiden speech was the same year, during a debate on the defence policy. There was a page that consisted of the new MP introducing himself, a few wisecracks and then,

Lieutenant Colonel Mitchell, Aberdeenshire West: I ask the Minister of State for Defence when he will demand details from the West German government relating to murdered female members of the Special Operations Executive from 1941 to 1945. In particular I refer to Mrs Eugenie Rezin, whose mother is a member of my constituency and whose body has never been found. I also ask the Minister of State for Defence when these brave women will be given full military honours. Of the thirty-nine female SOE agents during World War Two, only thirteen have been recognised by this government. It is vital that their work for this country is never forgotten.

There was a cursory reply from a Lord Balniel, who mentioned a thirty-year rule. *Who's Who* didn't take it any further and the *White Pages* for Aberdeenshire did not list a telephone number for C Mitchell, or a Cloutier or a Rezin. They had either left the area, or were ex-directory.

Perry was still slaving away on his caption, typing one-handed and one-fingered, like a six-year-old trying it for the first time.

'Sorry to bother you again,' said McKenna, though he didn't really care by then. 'What's the best way from Glasgow to Braemar?'

Perry was definitely out of patience and very churlish. 'Who do you think I am, fuckin' Bambi Gascoigne? Have you nae got a map or something?' He grumbled on for a minute and then asked, 'Got a job up there?'

'Sort of. Is there a train service?'

'You're no driver, are you? You're no one of them ambulance-chaser wankers?' McKenna's responded only with a diplomatic smile so Perry continued, 'It's about a hundred miles from here. You'll have to change at Aberdeen and get a bus from there. Whichever way you go it's a bit of a slog. Make sure you take your woolly long johns. It's always fuckin' freezing up there.'

Then he lifted a camera the size of his head and pointed it.

'Must you?' said McKenna.

Perry clicked some more and said, 'I always make sure I have up-to-date snaps of people. You might never see them again. You might be knocked down or murdered. Have you got a story up north? Is it something to do with Mitchell?'

115

'I'm just going to see an old family friend.'

'And you don't know where your old family friend lives?'

McKenna turned away, but Perry stuck out his foot again.

'I'd hurry up if I were you,' he said.

'Meaning what?'

'Meaning if you're going up there for a story I'd file it quick. We might be on strike by next weekend.'

'*What for this time?*'

'One of the delivery drivers saw thirty Atex on-screen terminals in the basement.'

McKenna had no idea what they were, but pretended he did. 'That's awful, but what's it got to do with us?'

'Think about it, son. I said *thirty* brand-new terminals. There are sixty staff in editorial. Got it? Chapel meeting on Monday at 11 a.m.'

'I don't think I'll make it,' said McKenna. 'My da's a bit poorly.'

He spent another hour typing up his notes before putting them in a large envelope. Then he pulled them all out again and reread every word.

Does he address her as 'Dear Lucienne' or 'Dear Mrs Batch'? Should he call her 'Dear' at all, though he would like to? In the end he used a new envelope, wrote 'FAO Mrs Lucienne Batch', sealed it with a lick and, feeling like a schoolboy handing in his homework, pushed it under her door.

McKenna had one more job and just before he left he climbed carefully on to his office chair and from there on to his desk, high enough to reach the ceiling light. He had to push up on his toes and it was just as difficult to replace it with the tube he had 'borrowed' from features, but soon it was done. McKenna quite liked the feel of being a deviant.

The Glasgow sky was lightened as he left and one or two early starters were already heading down Duke Street.

'Good night?' asked the taxi driver.

It was 5 a.m., McKenna didn't feel a bit tired and every traffic light between the office and Radnor Street, Clydebank, had been on green.

'A great night,' he said, and for once he meant it.

CHAPTER 15.

McKenna fumbled for the receiver at the first bleep of the bedside phone.

'Hands off cocks; on with socks,' said the female voice. Then, before he asked, 'I'm ringing from the office. Aren't you proud of me?' It was rum, but this affable Mrs Batch seemed more menacing than the usual ball-busting version.

'Just a sec,' said McKenna as he flopped out of bed.

Slowly, his brain began to move into operation. He looked for a cigarette, but then remembered he had given up, so he carried the phone into the kitchen to find some instant. His wall clock said 10 a.m. exactly, but this was Saturday, there was no Sunday paper and she would probably be there on her own.

'I've got your notes,' she said. 'They are quite good, but a bit out of date.'

'What do you mean?'

'I found Thursday's edition of *Der Zeitung*,' she replied. 'That German mate of yours is all over the front page. Campbell said he was deceased, which is true, but he never said he had been murdered, did he? He was shot in the head on Monday this week, not long after his phone call to you: person or persons unknown, as they say. This might explain our visit from Smilie and company.'

'Hang on,' said McKenna. 'He wasn't my *mate* and I don't like the implication he was killed because I didn't like his telephone manner.'

'I'm just giving you the facts. Even a cop wouldn't believe you went out on your break, took a flight to Germany, shot a guy, got a flight back and carried on with your police calls. As we all know by now, you're no Clark Kent.'

McKenna thought that was quite funny, but tried to sound annoyed. 'Thanks a bunch for that,' he said. 'Is there anything else in the story?'

'Not much in the way of words, but quite a few pics. The usual crime scene snaps: cops arriving, body carried out to an ambulance, puzzled locals. If you're interested, the address in Stuttgart is 3b Münchinger Street, Stammheim-Mitte.'

'Wait a sec,' said McKenna and reached for a biro.

'The other pics,' Batch continued, 'were Mum and Dad and the guy wearing an Iron Cross or something similar. There's no mention of his phone call to you, and nothing about Lulu. So that's good news.'

'Who's the suspect?'

'There're no names mentioned, but it could have been the Red Army Faction.'

'Sorry … never heard of that.'

'Well, it's time you did,' she said, in full CSM mode. 'It's a terrorist group, usually abbreviated to RAF. Nothing to do with the Royal Air Force, before you ask. It might be a good idea if you find a library and do some homework on German history.'

That was a bit below the belt, and McKenna tried to ignore it.

'So we've still got it to ourselves. Where do I go from here?'

119

'Where do *we* go from here? We'll start with those notes you left me.'

The rustle of paper and the delay gave him time to pour another coffee.

'I have a few suggestions,' she said. 'An order of play, if you like.'

'Go on,' McKenna said warily.

'In your notes it says *Glasgow University Library.* German newspaper. You don't need that. We've got German newspapers in the office now because I've ordered a supply. I'll get a daily copy sent over to your place.'

'In German? I haven't turned into a Kraut speaker overnight.'

Another long sigh, but she had been waiting for that.

'I'll translate and mark the relevant details in biro. By the way, I've sent a note to your news editor to tell him you're off sick. Better than saying you are on a job somewhere.'

'And what's wrong with me?'

'You fell downstairs at home – the excuse newspapermen will always believe.'

'I don't know if I like that. Couldn't you say I was off diary and working on something important?'

'No one will believe it. All you do are police calls and death knocks and the occasional news in brief, and from what I hear all your NIBs are rewritten by subs.'

McKenna could not argue with that and she continued,

'Now, tell me where you got all the stuff about Lulu and her mother.'

'*The Inquirer* library,' McKenna replied. 'I found a snap of her with an MP. I mention him in my notes. Lieutenant Colonel Colin Mitchell, the former MP for Aberdeen West. He was that guy in Aden who—'

She interrupted. '*Don't* patronise me. I *know* who Colin Mitchell is. I don't need lectures in army history. And it's

Aberdeenshire West. Just try and get things right.'

McKenna waited for her to calm down before he told her, 'Colin Mitchell is not in the phone book, but I should be able to get a number.'

'Have you spoken to this Mrs Cloutier yet?'

'I've only just got up, hen. I haven't even got me trews on.'

But he had given it some thought and said, 'She's not listed, but I'm pretty sure I can find her. If I do, I'd prefer to do this face-to-face. I'm good with old dears.'

Mrs Batch had been thinking too.

'If you are talking about going up to the Highlands I don't think that's a goer. It might be a long way for nothing. Your "old dear" could be dead or she might have moved away.'

McKenna had been emboldened by Batch's rare good nature, or the third cup of coffee, because he said, 'That's a bit negative, hen. I thought this was all about forward motion. I can easily check if she still lives there.' Then, for no reason except that it sounded good, 'I'm quite happy to catch a train and reconnoitre the place.'

'Reconnoitre?' sniffed Mrs Batch. 'What are you, SAS or something? And stop calling me "hen". Hens peck you.'

There was another charged silence, then,

'Train, did you say?'

'Train and bus. I'd have to stay overnight.'

Batch finally made her mind up and agreed. 'Try it, then. If she's still in Braemar and you find your way there use a local B & B – a cheap one. And make sure you get a receipt.'

'What do I do with the words?'

'Bring all your notes and your tapes back here and we can take it from there. If you want a go try and write it as a news story, not a bloody travelogue of northern Scotland.

121

Thinking of which, have you ever used a camera?'

'Couldn't I take a snapper? He could do the driving.'

'No, you can't have a snapper. This is supposed to be a clandestine operation: *clandestine*, as in secret. Three people in the office know about that tape and these are all the moving parts we need. As for snappers – they aren't exactly discreet, are they? It would be all over the newsroom before you arrived back.'

'What if she won't talk?'

'Well, you'll be back on the dog shift, won't you? Anything else?'

McKenna tried sarcasm. 'Nothing. Apart from having to work on a Saturday.'

'This isn't a holiday camp,' she said curtly. 'If I work at weekends so can you. What else would you do on a Saturday, anyway?'

'I fancied Garbo in *Mata Hari* at the Film Theatre.'

There was another of her long, disconcerting silences.

'Just concentrate on finding a *real* spy,' she said eventually. 'One more thing, McKenna: old ladies like men who dress properly, so wear a lounge suit and tie. And make sure you take the lens cap off the camera.'

'I'll do my best,' promised McKenna.

'You'll do *what*? You'd better do better than that.'

'Bitch,' McKenna shouted down the line, long after she had hung up.

CHAPTER 16.

McKenna made sure he was sitting comfortably before he lit his first cigarette in three days, waited for the dizziness to stop and then picked up his phone.

At first McKenna wondered whether he should mention *The Inquirer* or even what he did for a living, because people often hung up right there. Colin Mitchell didn't seem bothered at all. He didn't even ask how McKenna got his home number – an 01 for a London address. He admitted Mrs Cloutier still lived in Braemar, but refused to give her phone number. And, if they were going to discuss her, Mitchell insisted on asking her permission first.

'Never discuss family matters *sans* permission,' he said. 'Call me back in ten minutes.' McKenna agreed, smoked two more cigarettes and then phoned back.

Things went swimmingly from there.

Colin Campbell Mitchell, Lieutenant Colonel Argyll and Sutherland Highlanders, retired, sounded like every man of officer rank in every movie ever made: clipped timbre, a couple of words doing for a whole sentence and a bit Blimpish. It was 'hair lair' for 'hello', 'aawf' for 'off' and 'mi' instead of 'my'.

'Met Mrs Cloutier in late '69,' Campbell began. 'Had an appointment at me constituency office in Aberdeen.

Fine old lady, though not able to travel any distance on her own. Arthritis, I gather. Turned up in an ancient Land Rover with a very dubious driver – a Pole, or maybe a Czech. Never found out, cos he was a mute. Interesting woman, Mrs Cloutier. Lost her husband on the Western Front in '16.'

'The Somme?' said McKenna uncertainly.

'Verdun. Monsieur Cloutier was French. His body was never found, either. Not a lover of the Germans, our Mrs Cloutier.'

She approached the newly appointed MP for Aberdeenshire West in the winter of 1970. It was her attempt to persuade the Federal Republic of Germany to release details of the killings of SOE agents during the war, notably her daughter.

'You gather Lulu was a *nom de guerre*?' said Mitchell. 'Funny, but Mrs Cloutier still calls her that. Don't know what her code name was, so don't ask. Anyway, she was killed in Paris early in '44 and her mother wanted to know exactly where, when and who.'

She was twenty-four when she joined the SOE in 1940, the organisation having been founded in June that year. Although female agents were from different backgrounds they all had two things in common: their fluent French and the excitement, even the addiction, of secret lives.

'It wasn't the Churchill rhetoric that was driving her,' said Mitchell. 'Like many of 'em, she was looking for a bit of drama. Those types are always diving off the high board, climbing mountains, skiing black runs: a risk seeker, in other words. Odd, too, but many had lost families to war: tough cookies with a point to prove.'

'It's hard to imagine a young burd as a spy,' said McKenna. Mitchell guffawed, so loudly McKenna had to move the phone away from his ear.

'Burds, as you call them, are far more dangerous than men,' he said. 'If you know anything about women, my friend, you will know they can be very devious … point that charm at you like a damn pistol.'

'So she was a looker?'

'Not the word I would use but, yes, definitely a looker. Mrs Cloutier showed me some old photos, and I understood then why Lulu had been so good at her job. Beautiful, very beautiful: one of those gals who could quite easily break dozens of hearts … and probably did.'

'I assume SOE women could kill?' McKenna asked. 'I saw Virginia McKenna in a fillum and she was shooting Germans like ducks in a barrel.'

Mitchell chortled and said, 'Saw the same movie. Fairly accurate, I would say.'

After that Mitchell seemed to relish his role as teacher of military matters for the classroom dunce and was hard to stop.

'Killing was part of the job. She'd even have a choice – throttle, knife, pistol, sub-machine gun – but there's more to it than that. How to escape custody and get out of handcuffs, recognise German ranks, know Morse code. I gather Lulu was also rather good at getting Wehrmacht troops in Paris to spill the beans.'

'How would she go about that?'

'Good God, man, you're a bit green aren't you? How do women usually get information from men? It's known as *seduction*: play hard to get, pretend to trip up, lose a shoe, appeal to life's gentlemen – and, bear in mind, many Wehrmacht soldiers weren't Nazis. Mrs Cloutier told me she had another attribute – she could hold her drink. You're a journalist, so you know that people tend to talk a lot in booze.'

'I thought soldiers were forbidden to fraternise with the

enemy?'

'Bit difficult to enforce in Paris, that! Young men away from home are the same anywhere: they want to see the sights, maybe meet an attractive local girl – anything that will make them forget the war. Think of it: if you're a stranger in – say – London, and you're a bit lonely, you'll talk to anyone prepared to listen. Before long you'll be telling them what you had for breakfast. It would be hard to resist a beautiful woman in a city like Paris, and that's for sure.'

'What would she be looking for from a soldier?'

'Isn't it obvious? A uniform would tell her the division. If you know the division you know who the commanding officer is – and after that you look for troop movements, equipment, where they had been, where they were going and if there any dissidents in the division. You might get their cities of residence and their local factories and railheads.'

'Any cities in particular?'

'The obvious ones: Berlin, Dresden, Leipzig, Hamburg.'

'Stuttgart?'

'Of course; you've done some homework, haven't you? The Daimler-Benz factories were there. Still are. So were Porsche. Bosch, who supplied auto parts, was based in Stuttgart.'

'What if the soldiers wouldn't talk?'

'Wait for the next fishing trip and find yourself another juicy cod.'

'How did the Nazis treat SOE women?'

'You mean the Gestapo? Same way they treated male agents. Probably worse. Germans, or anyone else for that matter, didn't think, "Oh, here's a bonny lass. Let's charm her a bit and talk her into submission." Women would be tortured and beaten in the same way; murdered in the same way.'

'You think the Gestapo murdered her?'

Mitchell took some time to think about that before he decided.

'I thought about it down the years and it still baffles me. The Germans always kept detailed notes, but there's no mention of her in any of the Gestapo killing books. We are talking about 1944, when any German with any sense would know they were going to lose the war and it would be a good idea to avoid direct blame for *anything* by then. But it still doesn't explain why the body was never found.'

The young couple in the flat downstairs were arguing and screaming and something broke, possibly glass. Mitchell either didn't hear or just ignored it. McKenna prayed he would hurry.

'I did my best to find out,' he continued. 'I even brought it up at PM's question time. Not that that did any good, either. There were problems, of course: if a body is never found it's even harder to find a perpetrator. By all accounts the Gestapo were involved, but nothing concrete. If you're dealing with a spy you have to deal with guesswork: often it's hard to find the correct age, place of birth – even their family.

'I got some detail. The War Office said she was betrayed by another agent and the Gestapo took her early in 1944. You can make your own mind up about the rest. The War Office claimed she never talked and I believe that, though that is the sort of thing the War Office always say. There was a discreet inquiry in '47 and that was a waste of time, too. There was one story going the rounds that four or five SOE agents were taken to Karlsruhe on the edge of the Black Forest in the spring of 1944: four French girls and an English woman. But that just underlines what I said about the mystery of spies: what do we call Lulu, for example? French or English?'

'Scottish, wasn't she?'

'My point exactly. Born in Braemar: English mother, French father and multilingual. Mrs Cloutier said her German was excellent, too. The other problem is that if she finished up in one of the prisoner of war camps it would be hard to find where, who and what because there were so many. So the review of the Lulu case was dropped in the summer of '47.'

'They just gave up?'

'The War Office probably had their reasons, but I was furious. I know all those SOE operations were clandestine but she had to be worth recognition, even if just some sort of decoration. Those Whitehall buffoons did nothing.'

'If that's the case, why on earth would the War Office hide the details?'

'I don't think it was a question of hiding it. Governments give up in the end. There were thousands of missing persons after the war and the line has to be drawn eventually, hurtful as it may be. Families have to rely on the amateur detectives like me … like you, I suppose. I did manage to find out a few things in '74 but that didn't take her much further.'

'What's the significance of 1974?'

'Dear me. Never heard of the Official Secrets Act – the thirty-year rule?'

McKenna had to admit he had not.

'Right, this will be quick because I have to go: The Public Record Office releases papers every twelve months – the thirty-year rule, it's called. Some documents will stay secret for decades: forty, seventy-five or even a hundred years. We'll never see the full details about the abdication, for example. The files on Himmler's death and Hess's flight to Scotland are still embargoed. All I found out was that she took the married name of Rezin sometime in 1942. Bernard Rezin was a French Resistance fighter cum SOE agent, and that is where the waters get muddy.'

'The man who betrayed her?'

'That was the implication.'

'You don't believe that?'

'There's no proof, and most of it was hearsay. All I know for certain is that they were married, both worked for the SOE and both were arrested in Paris at about the same time. At least the French managed to get his body back.'

'So they knew how he had died?'

'A cyanide pill, according to the autopsy by the French government much later. All of this made it even more frustrating for Mrs Cloutier. The boy, too.'

'*The boy?*'

'Lulu's boy.' Then, when there was no response from McKenna, 'Don't tell me … you didn't know she had a son?'

Downstairs there was complete silence, which was always a bad sign. McKenna though it best to hurry up.

'Is the boy still around?'

'He's certainly no longer in Braemar. Mrs Cloutier offloaded him to a Barnardo's in '46 and hasn't seen him since. As his father was French he may be living over there.'

Mitchell must have sensed McKenna's outrage.

'What was she was supposed to do?' he asked. 'She wouldn't be able to cope on her own and her helper was a mute. I gather the boy was a bit of a handful, so I understand why a lady of her age would look to foster. Anyway, the Cloutier females never struck me as maternal types. The boy was born in '41, and by early '44 Lulu was

129

back in Paris. If it's any help, I gather he was in the army. I never bothered to find out which regiment because it's none of my business. Mrs Cloutier believes he became a handy boxer. I'm sure she will tell you the rest.'

'Do you think she will talk to me? I was hoping to go up there.'

'She's *expecting* you,' said Mitchell emphatically. 'As they say these days, she wants to close this particular book, and even a journalist might help. That's her opinion, anyway.'

'Is she reasonably compos mentis?'

Mitchell laughed very loudly again.

'Don't take this the wrong way, my friend, but she will wipe the floor with you. She is astute and quite mischievous, but I warn you: history has made her vulnerable. I don't want to find out you took advantage. By the way, were you aware she was a member of the Communist Party?'

'I did hear that. Does it matter?'

'Not to me. After the war most people were anti-German, and I don't just mean Nazis. The motherland was preferred to the fatherland back then. I don't think *she* would be regarded as a danger to national security. Is there anything else?'

McKenna had one last question written and ready.

'I wanted to ask about the war and revenge. I wondered if people never stop looking to even the score … maybe family members who lost a mum or dad.'

There was a lengthy silence from Mitchell's end and then, 'What's that screaming? Sounds like a damn murder.'

'Next door's cats,' said McKenna.

'Aaah,' said Mitchell, quizzically. He continued, 'You are talking about Lulu and her family? Someone might not like it if someone gets away with murder, right?'

'Right,' said McKenna.

'Well, first of all, bad blood and vendettas aren't exclusive

130

to people born in Sicily. It's open to anyone if they are given the motivation: "Someone's mother, someone's son", as the saying goes. Have you got kids?'

'No. Why do you ask?'

'Did you ever see the Disney film *Bambi*?'

'A dozen times,' said McKenna.

'I took my three to see it years ago, thinking it was a nice little story of cute little animals living happily ever after in a forest. My children were absolutely horrified. They wanted to know why Bambi's mother was shot and who shot her? Why wasn't the bad man caught and punished? I told a little fib: Bambi's mummy was only wounded, she was hiding and she and Bambi would indeed live happily ever after. I thought I had got away with it, but my eldest wasn't falling for it. Children that age are no fools and he cornered me with, "If someone shot Mommy what would you do, Daddy?" Or words to that effect.'

'And what was the answer, Mister Mitchell?'

'I didn't have an answer; or at least not one for my children.'

Lieutenant Colonel Colin Mitchell wished McKenna good luck and good day and hung up.

CHAPTER 17.

McKenna never used the same pub twice in a week. If he did, others might see him as a regular and he didn't want that. He never drank at home because that meant you were too fond of the stuff. He would have avoided the Glenn Lusset on Dumbarton Road like a plague, but it was the local of what he laughingly called his 'source' so he had no choice.

The Lusset had once been the middle of a row of tenements, but they had gone and the pub now stood by itself, like the only house to survive a bombing raid. There were no street lights, so leaving after closing time in winter was a gamble. Inside, there were vinyl-topped tables, bare light bulbs, glass walls which divided the 'saloon' from the 'lounge' and a permanent smell of piss. The types of clientele depended on hours and day of the week: Buckfast drinkers who had just got their welfare or benefits at early doors, thirsty dockers after work and, on football days, the half-brickers warming up before the march east down Dumbarton Road and one of the Old Firm games.

McKenna had met Myler in '78, at the Sheep Heid Inn on the posh side of Edinburgh at the wedding booze-up of a distant cousin. Myler piped in the guests to the reception: he was a member of a minor industry of tough-looking types to scare people at weddings. Myler wasn't much of a piper, but no one ever complained.

'All the ability of a six-year-old but with my charm,' he said to McKenna after the party broke up. 'Fancy a drink?'

'I do the lot,' Myler had told him. 'Hogmanay, Burns Nights and fêtes. I'll even do a funeral for you if you like. What do you do?'

They were never going to be friends after that, but they were on a wavelength of sorts. Both were raised in Clydebank and both had lost parents in the Luftwaffe's initial incendiary bombings of 1941. Both also needed money, and it didn't take long to discover that they could be useful to each other.

Myler always wore Nike training pants, a T-shirt, no matter the weather, and McKenna had never seen him without his R.P. McMurphy docker's hat. He could have been totally bald for all McKenna knew, and he had never asked him.

He was scary: the battered features of an unsuccessful prizefighter and a smile that could mean anything, but was usually a warning. There was some Irish there, notably a prominent top lip and an appetite for drink and fisticuffs. Myler was the type who was never invited anywhere twice.

When McKenna had done the honours, which were obligatory in this case, Myler sat down and moved close – another part of his intimidation technique.

'Did you get Lieutenant Colonel Mitchell in the end?' asked Myler, who always used full titles of superior officers.

'I did. Thanks for that.'

'I bet Lieutenant Colonel Mitchell wanted something in the paper about the Argylls?'

McKenna admitted that before adding, 'He was a great help: even said I could quote him.'

'What you need me for, then?' Myler demanded as he

helped himself to another of McKenna's cigarettes.

'I need help with some military background.'

'What was wrong with Lieutenant Colonel Mitchell? He'd be more help than a mere grunt. Try the Ministry of Defence or the Red Cross or Army Command.'

'It's the weekend, and I thought it was the sort of thing that might appeal to you.'

'I hate that cheap salesman talk,' said Myler. 'I'm immune to arse-licking.'

McKenna knew how to respond. He used both hands to mimic a GPO counter worker counting out the weekly pension and said, 'I can get you a few quid.'

'How much?'

'About the same as the Ice Cream story?'

'It's gone up since then. You're on a national now, aren't you?'

'Three hundred quid?'

Myler smiled his piranha smile.

'Off you go, then,' he said.

McKenna thought he was beginning to sound like a stuck record, but he explained it all again: the first phone call, the police interview, the tape, Lulu and the SOE and a Braemar mother's fruitless search for a murdered daughter.

Myler did not interrupt, and wrote it all down on the back of a coaster of Queen Victoria on a horse.

'Lulu?' he asked when McKenna had finished. 'I suppose it wasn't a real name?'

'Adele Eugenie, but she preferred Lulu. The family name is Cloutier; married name Rezin.'

'Interesting,' said Myler who was definitely alert. 'A family of Frogs; lots of SOE females were like that. What's the story, though? She's been dead forty years.'

'Like I said, the German was murdered a week after he rang me. I think there is some connection between his killing and this Lulu.'

'Tell me about this screw, then,' said Myler.

McKenna's words were drowned out by the jukebox, where four football supporters, pints in hand and fags in mouths, were piling in the 50ps.

'I won't be a minute,' said Myler. 'Wait here.'

McKenna hated violence, or even the threat of it – but he watched anyway, like a viewer of a wildlife documentary unable to turn away as the lion closes in on the wildebeest. Myler walked – stalked, it could be said – slowly across the room towards the jukebox, bent down and pulled the plug.

'"Mull of fuckin' Kintyre",' he said loud enough for the whole pub to hear. 'I hate "Mull of fuckin' Kintyre".' He eyed the fans up and down and waited for a reaction. They hesitated and the biggest of the four considered it, but one of his mates said something and within another minute they had drunk up and left.

Myler sat down again.

'Now, where was I?' he said.

'The screw: he was killed by a single shot to the head. That was the 27th, the Monday, and four days later – yesterday, that is – three cops are in The Inquirer office and clambering all over me.'

'Did they tell you anything?'

'Like what?'

'A suspect. Did they name names? No? So the cops haven't got far. You said three of them turned up. Plods?'

'Detectives. Two from Pitt Street and an Englishman with a posh accent, though we're not sure if he was a real-life cop. They tried to play the heavies, which struck us as a bit odd. We had a copy of my chat with the German on tape, though.'

135

'Who do you mean by "we"?'

'The editor and a lass who did the translation for us.'

'And the German?'

'A prison officer in Stuttgart. The guy was pissed and rambled on about this and that, but then he mentioned Lulu and Paris and the stuff about the SOE. He said she was Scottish a couple of times so he must have known her.'

Myler took another swig of his Guinness, thought for a few seconds and then,

'Did you say this Lulu had a son?'

'No, I never said that. Not to you, anyway. You know him?'

Myler didn't reply to that and said instead, 'I'll see what I can do. It might take time, so meet me in the Copthorne – Wednesday lunchtime next week.'

'The Copthorne? You're coming up in the world.'

Myler had his newspaper out and was waving at the barman for a refill. McKenna was on his feet and about to leave when he thought of something else.

'Ever hear of a guy called Batch? He was in the Rhine Army but he's probably in Northern Ireland now.'

It took several seconds before Myler replied.

'Never heard of him,' he said. 'Copthorne, 1 p.m., and make sure you bring cash. I've always fancied a session in there.'

Then, without looking away from his *Sporting Life*, 'If I were you, I'd go and see the old burd in Braemar.'

CHAPTER 18.

At 8 p.m. on the Saturday Bux finally picked up coat and hat and car keys and got ready for home.

'That's it,' he said to his three colleagues. 'Silke will be thinking I have got a girlfriend!' Lang, Hertzog and Baum smiled, because this was the Kommissar's standard joke. It usually meant they could go home, too.

Then his internal line beeped.

'Is it still snowing in Stuttgart?' the caller said after introducing himself. Bux took off his coat and hat, dropped his car keys on the desk and sat down again. He switched to hands-free speaking so the others could hear. Lang had recognised the signs, too, and he activated the Grundig to record.

Bux tried to be patient, knowing the British always discussed the weather before anything else. 'It must have been a bit of a shock, all the white stuff in September,' said the caller. 'It's still raining up here in Scotland, not as bad as—'

Bux interrupted. 'Have you any news for us, Herr Smilie?'

Smilie sounded quite hurt when he replied,

'Oh, very well,' he said. 'I'm just trying to be polite. Anyway, I do have odds and sods for you. Are you sitting comfortably?'

'Just get on with it, Herr Smilie. This is a murder case, remember.' Then, under his breath, '*Dummkopf.*' His three colleagues smiled.

Smilie began, 'I have the tape of the conversation between your deceased prison guard and a Scottish journalist. I have also interviewed the journalist in question, not that that came to much. I must also warn you that the prison guard was drunk, and I don't think a drunk will take you very far in a murder case.'

'Let's hear it,' said Bux.

'The Kommissar wants it over the phone? I was going to mail it.'

Bux didn't think *anyone* could be so stupid. Baum, sitting opposite, must have agreed, for he covered his mouth like the wise monkey who speaks no evil. In other words, Smilie was being obstructive on purpose.

'I don't think it wise to send sensitive material through the post, do you, Herr Smilie? Now if you would be so kind, I am in a hurry.'

'Give me a minute, *mein freund*,' said Smilie.

The tape was coming third-hand: from tape to phone to another phone, and it was difficult to hear in parts. Smilie was told to rewind and replay it two or three times to make sure the copy had gone through correctly. The crucial sections were in German and Bux had enough English to follow the rest, from Rückeran's drunken rambling to the journalist's obnoxious response.

'This SOE woman in that tape,' said Bux. 'Is there a real name? Are there any family members still alive?'

'I interviewed her mother today,' said Smilie, quite proud of himself. 'A hell of a trek, and the weather was absolute awful. Always is up in the frozen north, apparently.'

'Weather apart, what else did you find?'

'She was elderly and infirm, so I didn't get much from her. We had some stuff from the Ministry of Defence: an SOE agent obviously, signed up in '41 and shot early in '44. She called herself Lulu in France. Code name Eagle Face: real name Adele Eugenie Cloutier. She had a hubby, Bernard Rezin, who was a French Resistance fighter. He was killed by the Gestapo a few days before she vanished.'

'Vanished? What do you mean by "vanished"?'

'She was shot trying to escape, but for some reason the body was never found. That's it for now, old boy.'

'*That's it*? That's her life story?'

'I have to tell the Kommissar that a lot of it is still classified,' said Smilie after another of his long pauses. 'I did gather she was highly regarded in SOE circles – a bit of a Mata Hari type, apparently. There was an inquiry in '47. It came out then that her husband broke during interrogation, and the Gestapo had tracked her down from there. One of the golden rules of espionage: never marry a fellow agent. Doesn't the Kommissar agree?'

'What of the inquiry?'

'They found very little. In '47 the country had other things on its mind – Russia and the Iron Curtain, for starters. No point wasting time and money trying to find out what became of one SOE agent. It was just a mother keeping an obsession alive. Agreed? The inquiry was quietly dropped in the end.

'Did her mother discuss a family? A family is mentioned in that tape.'

'There was a son – James – born in 1941, but obviously soon an orphan. Granny then got rid, and after that it was the usual routine for kids who have lost parents: foster homes, running away, a couple of police arrests … one for GBH – that's grievous bodily harm. He was also done for poaching.'

'Poaching?'

'Illegal hunting: the favourite sport of Highland Scots, apparently. His redemption, or so they call it, came when he joined the armed forces at eighteen.'

Smilie was unwilling to elaborate and Bux had to ask, 'Are you going to tell me which of the armed forces? Where is the boy now?'

'He was in the army.'

'*And?*'

'I think the Kommissar will have to take that up with the Ministry of Defence; or perhaps someone at Defence Staff headquarters.'

Bux sighed and subsided into his chair.

'So this James Rezin is still operational?'

'I think it may be fair for the Kommissar to surmise that.'

'Have you any recent photographs?'

'I can try, but you know what the Ministry of Defence will say…'

'I can guess,' said Bux. 'Out of interest, how long were you with the old lady?'

'There was a bit of a panic; something about IRA terrorists landing at Stranraer so I had to get down there lickety-split. The Met is pretty uptight about things like that – the Hyde Park bombings, and all that. So the interview was truncated.'

Bus looked round at his colleagues. There were blinks and raised eyebrows from all three. They thought Smilie was lying, too.

'I'd like your opinion on the journalist you interviewed,' Bux said.

'I have a rough transcript of the conversation, if that is

any help. Basically, he was a Jock halfwit. I didn't get much cooperation from the other staff, either.'

Bux almost dropped his coffee on the floor.

'*Other staff*? Do you mean others know about this tape? Who are they?'

'There was an editor with a Yorkshire accent. We obviously spoke to him first but he didn't go into the interview. There was also a bolshy female secretary.'

'Bolshy?'

'Feisty; aggressive. It must have been PMT or something.'

Bux didn't bother trying to find out what that meant and raised his tone.

'What happened in the end?'

'He first denied he had a tape, but then handed it over. Claimed he had just found it. Not a lot we could do about that.'

It did not take Bux long to work that one out.

'Don't tell me … you went in without a warrant?'

There was no response.

'Any more bad news for me?' asked Bux, and he knew there was.

'There *may* be a duplicate of the tape,' said Smilie quietly. Bux squeezed his biro so hard it broke.

'So there is more than one tape. The journalist made a copy.'

Then, in his best sardonic tone, 'Did anyone manage to get his full name?'

'McKenna. His name is William Holden McKenna.'

'*William Holden*?'

'It takes all sorts, doesn't it? His parents must have been film buffs.'

Bux took down the home address and phone number.

'And the woman?'

'Her name is Lucienne Batch.'

'Address; telephone number?'

'Erm … Strathclyde police are still working on that,' said Smilie defensively. 'They made a real balls-up with that interrogation, don't you think?'

Bux was out of patience.

'*Interrogation*?' he shouted. 'I expected an *interview*, not a session with the KGB. Did this journalist have an alibi for the night in question?'

'Yes.'

'And he is definitely the man on the tape?'

'Yes.'

'Did you talk to any of the other staff?'

'Haven't had the time, *mein freund*.'

Bux took a few seconds to regain his composure before he said, 'Herr Smilie, do you know anything about the newspaper business?'

'Only what I read in *Shooting Times*.'

'Well, write this down somewhere: an editor and his staff will spend most days looking for a story that would sell their newspaper. That would include the staff of your *Shooting Times*. In the case of this Scottish newspaper I am sure they would read *something* into detectives charging into their office and *interrogating* a member of staff. Any half-decent journalist would see something suspicious in that. As far as that tape goes it sounds as if you were stung. Has anything appeared in the paper?'

'Nothing yet,' said Smilie. 'If Bonn is concerned I could always get in touch with the Attorney General's office and organise a D-notice.'

That was enough for Bux.

'Thank you, Herr Smilie. We will be in touch.'

'Roger that,' said Smilie as he hung up.

When Bux had rewound and replayed the tape for the fifth time he found a fresh piece of chalk and cleared the board above his desk.

'I assume you all know what an SOE agent was during the war?' he began.

It was odd because Hertzog and Lang keyed notes into their computer while Baum used old-fashioned shorthand, but all three nodded in agreement.

'Rue de Saussaies, Paris?'

Baum, the historian, was first there.

'Headquarters of the Gestapo, in the 8th arrondissement,' he said.

'Perhaps the body is still there,' said Lang.

'I don't think so, Lang,' said Baum. 'The Allies searched the whole place. They even dug up the floors. The body must be elsewhere. It should be easy to find in the Federal Archive.'

Bux chalked 'Eagle' with a question mark on his board.

'Eagle Face was the code name for that Lulu girl,' said Hertzog.

'Rückeran said "Eagle", not "Eagle Face",' said Lang.

'Eagle Face could be the name of a local landmark,' said Baum.

'I disagree,' said Lang.

'Me too,' said Hertzog.

Bux raised a hand.

'That's enough. Let's forget the Eagle for now and go back to the phone call. Rückeran was obviously drunk but this is beginning to sound like a confession to me: *You must tell her family the truth. Her name was Lulu. Lulu was murdered in Paris*. We must also remember that Lulu and

Paris were mentioned by Rückeran's landlady when they spoke of the photograph that went missing. Can I remind you she also mentioned *three* Wehrmacht soldiers with Lulu, snow on the ground and the Eiffel Tower in the background.'

'I was interested in Smilie's choice of the name Mata Hari,' said Baum. 'In other words it sounds as if Lulu was a bit of a honeytrap expert.'

'Honeytrap?' said Hertzog.

'A professional seductress,' said Bux. 'A woman – although it could just as easily have been a man – whose job is to seek information from an enemy.'

'What of the family?' said Baum. 'The tape says, *Tell the family the truth.*'

Bux picked up his notes and read it out.

'James Rezin, born April 8, 1941, Blair Lodge, close to Braemar, spelt B-r-a-e-m-a-r. On that basis, Lulu must have fallen pregnant in July 1940 or thereabouts. So far, Scotland Yard has been unable to find the whereabouts of the boy. I think it is fair to surmise, however, that he is *not* a member of the RAF.'

'Do you think this is the Rückeran killer?' asked Baum.

'I think it fair to describe him a suspect.'

'Forgive me, Kommissar,' Hertzog said, cautiously. 'But why would Rückeran be the target after all these years? This woman died in 1944.'

Bux's response was to point a stubby finger at Paris on the map of Europe on the wall. 'It's true that a body has never been found, but that does not stop a family – let's call him a son for now – from doing his own detective work and suddenly being offered a clue. As things stand, Rückeran's tape and his missing photograph are the nearest we have to a clue. Agreed?'

All three nodded.

'This woman Lulu and the tape and at least one member of the 7th Panzer Division appear to be interconnected. Agreed?'

They nodded approvals of that, too.

'So if we find out what happened to that woman in Paris and the names of the men on that photograph the better chance we have of finding the killer. For a start, we can drop all these notions about the RAF. Agreed?'

They nodded, but only out of courtesy this time.

CHAPTER 19.

The *Yellow Pages* for Aberdeen in Clydebank Public Library had a dozen Braemar guest houses. The Fife Arms on Glenshee Road looked ideal – close to the village centre and with a licensed bar. McKenna used the library's public phone.

The woman who answered sounded Australian, because every sentence seemed to be a question and she called him 'mate'. She put him on hold to go through a room list. The 'medication time' music from *One Flew Over the Cuckoo's Nest* piped in the background as he waited until she reappeared to suggest an executive suite with views of the Cairngorms.

'You're lucky, mate?' she asked. She took his address, asked how he would pay and what time to expect him.

'Before you go,' said McKenna. 'Have you lived there long?'

'Braemar? Five years, mate. I got spliced with the bloody owner?'

'Ever come across a family called Cloutier?'

'Missus Nikita?'

'Missus *who*?'

'Nikita, as in Khrushchev. My little joke, that. It's well known she was a Red and maybe still is. Are you family,

146

by the way?'

'Sort of. I couldn't get her on the phone, though.'

'She's ex-dee. She'll be there, though. She never goes out. She's in a wheelchair most of the time and some Polish geezer does all the shopping? Did you say you were related?'

'No I didn't say that. I was just hoping to get a chat with her.'

'A chat? Are you from the fuzz, too?'

'You mean the police have been to see her?'

'Yeah. One turned up in an unmarked vehicle this morning.'

'How do you know he was police, then?'

'This is Braemar, mate. Nothing here stays secret for long, especially geezers whose car radios can be heard a mile away. By the time he punctured on the way back to the village and had to call in the local garage everyone here knew the size of his dick – pardon the French. It was the biggest drama round here for years. It will be in the local rag before you can say Germaine Greer. What did you say you did?'

'I didn't, but I work for a local rag.'

There was a long pause before she went into efficient receptionist mode. 'Dinner is from 6 p.m. to 8.30 p.m. If you want grog after that the main bar will be open till eleven. Look forward to seeing you soon. Have a good one!'

The train was only half full, and no passengers in sight, so McKenna reached over to lift a copy of *The Inquirer* discarded on the seat opposite.

It was Saturday's edition, two days old, but it still seemed quite exciting to see the outcome of something that had started life as a discussion inside a Glasgow newspaper

147

office. McKenna had little interest in the mechanics of the operation. To him anything post the typewriter stage was like Chinese acrobats, the first man on the Moon or a surgeon doing a successful heart transplant: he wondered how it was all done, but it was so far out of his sphere he never bothered trying to find out. But there it was – his marks on an edition of a newspaper: Ian Holm had replaced Ian Bannen as the sprinting coach in *Chariots of Fire* and a word in the title of the play at the Theatre Royal had been changed from *Ernest* to *Earnest*.

Also, as had been anticipated, the front page lead was Thatcher and her unemployment statistics and the latest on the upcoming Queen's Park by-election had been moved to Page 3. Opposite that, on Page 2, the list of senior staff members had also been amended. The features editor, sports editor and the news editor were still there, but there the deputy editor just below 'Harold Bloom, Editor' had been replaced by 'Editorial Administrator, Lucienne Batch'. McKenna chortled to himself and thought, My … how they had all misread *that* little girl.

The rain was getting heavier, barrelling past the window on its way south, and swishy waves were battering the coast to the east. He wondered if he would make it past Aberdeen, let alone a bus to Braemar.

The unease had begun, as expected, when the 11.41 from Queen Street tiptoed past platform 9 and into the great unknown. Anything twenty miles in any direction from Clydebank was a foreign land, and ahead were people and places he knew only from newspapers, television and books: Gleneagles, famous for golf, Perth the city of the Picts, Dundee the home of Desperate Dan, Forfar and its Maw Broon's bridies.

An invisible British Rail voice announced in a monotone, 'Change here for Montrose, cultural capital of the county of Angus. Your food and drink operator for today is Hamish. Please have the right amount.'

McKenna coughed up for a can of Coke and an egg sandwich and wondered what the editorial administrator was up to.

Her first day at Albion Street was memorable. A tiny force in black with the ten to two walk of a dancer marched across the editorial floor like Boudicca heading to war as forty men pretended to be working. Within a week she had seen off the usual office sharks and 'Batch' was 'Bitch'. McKenna didn't think *that* would give her sleepless nights. She might even enjoy it.

On her second day he overheard a girl from accounts telling her friends in the canteen that 'the new woman in editorial' was probably a foreigner because she wrote the number seven with a line in the middle and crooked at the top. And calling someone *Lucienne* was too la-di-da by half and she wasn't particularly attractive anyway, with those horrible glasses and broken nose. Another girl with a lip piercing raised a laugh when she said that to christen someone Lucienne was like those Glasgae folk who called restaurants *brasseries* and clothes shops *boutiques* and went to trendy cinemas with foreign films without subtitles.

There was a jolting and a scraping and the same BR voice announcing, 'Aberdeen this stop. All change here.'

From Guild Street a single-decker plodded north through places he had never heard of: Westhill, Torphins, Banchory and Ballater, with the bus stopping at every one. At Aboyne there was a half-hour wait to change the driver for someone even older and slower, and this one had to stop when a large deer decided it wanted to cross the road ahead. Finally, after two hours, the driver told his only

149

surviving passenger, 'Auchendryne Square. All change.'

It was snowing – not heavily, but enough to cover some of the hills circling the village. A lone snowplough clobbered its way down the middle of the street and back again. A dirty, battered Land Rover was parked in the middle of the square with a handwritten sign which said *Taxi Driver* clinging to its window.

'Can I get a taxi here?' said McKenna.

A man in his seventies, rosacea cheeked and puffy faced, wound down his window and said belligerently, even for a taxi driver, 'That's what I'm here for.'

'I'm looking for a local estate called Blair Lodge.'

'Another one?' said Taxi. '*She's* popular all of a sudden.'

'You mean the guy who got stuck?'

Taxi didn't like someone spoiling his story so he didn't answer.

'Bet this place swings at night?' McKenna said, pointing out at the teahouses and sporran shops in an effort to get a smile.

'*Bet this place swings at night?*'

'I heard you the first time. I'm no deef.'

It was funeral-parlour cold inside the car, so cold it made McKenna dizzy. He rubbed both hands together and shivered, meaningfully.

'Any chance of putting the heating on?' he asked politely.

Taxi said nothing and drove on.

First they went north in the direction of the big hills, then east past a small castle alongside a river whose banks had overflown into the neighbouring fields. There was a short stretch of single road and then a right turn on to a unmetalled dirt track with potholes so deep Taxi had to jag from side to side. He watched through his mirror when McKenna banged his head on the roof and refused to slow down. Then, just as McKenna was about to complain, they turned a final corner and through the gates of Blair Lodge.

It was what some would call a small estate and was shielded by trees in the middle of a small valley of undulating meadows. Two small hills – one round and pointed, like a woman's breast, and the other flat, like an iron – looked down on the house. Its large gardens were unkempt, with grass so high a small child could hide there. Some hundred yards from the front door was what looked like a graveyard surrounded by wooden fencing, but there were no visible headstones. The windows were boarded, except the downstairs front which had two French windows. To add to the dark mystery of the place, a mist suddenly rolled down from the hills as far as the main house.

A man in his sixties, with the attitude and looks of Norma Desmond's creepy butler in *Sunset Boulevard* was waiting at the entrance. A large black dog that was with him barked unenthusiastically and a female voice called 'Shut up, Bruce,' from somewhere inside. The man pointed McKenna in and stepped aside. An old lady, who resembled every nodding, smiling old lady who do weekends at Oxfam charity shops, was waiting.

'I am Marie Cloutier,' she said. 'How lovely to see you again.'

CHAPTER 20.

McKenna was beginning to regret this even before he got past the front door

Mrs Cloutier was in a wheelchair and in her nineties but the country air must have treated her well, for she looked much younger. She pushed and pulled the wheelchair around unaided and the voice was strong. But this was mid afternoon and she had on a heavy dressing gown and a pair of old slippers. The snow-white hair was a mop of tangles.

She guided McKenna into a dark room the size of a tennis court. Everything was in disarray: clocks telling different times, curtains attacked by moths and intricate cobwebs clinging to all four corners. The paintings on the walls – roly-poly nudes and several *Monarchs of the Glen* – were dusty, and there was a large desk falling down with letters and books, with several others left on the floor. Two busts of Lenin were staring at each other, one on either side of the fireplace, and above that was a large mirror which, to McKenna's horror, was cracked. Blair Lodge was Miss Havisham's Satis House from *Great Expectations* transplanted to the Highlands.

She had mistaken him for someone else, too.

'Things must have changed since your day,' she said. 'How long is it now?'

Colin Mitchell had warned that she was a tad eccentric, but McKenna thought this might be worse: senility or the early stages of dementia, perhaps. He mumbled something non-committal, hoping that, if she was anything like his father, she would forget everything within seconds.

There was still time to catch the last bus to Aberdeen so he turned down the offer of alcohol for coffee and little biscuits.

Mrs Cloutier and the bouncer seemed to communicate with a mixture of Tarzan-English from her and an odd sign language from him. When he brought over port in a glass the size of a vase without being asked McKenna remembered Mitchell and his mention of the family's mute helper.

'This is Janek the Pole,' she told McKenna as if by way of introduction and then to Janek, 'You Warsaw War Horse?' Janek nodded and gave a lopsided smile, like someone hearing the same joke for the hundredth time.

She pointed at her own lips, then at the Pole.

'You show,' she said.

Janek opened his mouth. There was no tongue.

'Nazis,' said Mrs Cloutier, almost as if announcing the menu for lunch. 'It happened in Dubrovitz Ghetto. The Germans were into experimenting with children. Our Warsaw War Horse hates Germans. Don't you, Janek?'

Janek nodded his agreement.

'They cut off his tongue?' said McKenna.

'*They cut off his tongue*,' Mrs Cloutier mimicked, like a clever parakeet.

'What happened?'

'Ask him.'

'I assume he managed to escape. Sounds like a good story.'

'My God, you are really on the ball, aren't you?' she said. 'And it's *Klutje*, not *Clue-tee-ay*, and stop checking the time. There's nothing ruder than that.'

McKenna began to realise then that here was another bossy cat dealing with a docile dog and this might take some time.

'I think I'll take that drink now,' he said.

Mrs Cloutier moved carefully off her wheelchair onto the sofa and signalled McKenna to sit down next to her. Janek vanished and reappeared with several bottles, whose labels all started in Z and ended in K, that he had never seen before.

'I gather the police came to see you?' he asked by way of openers.

'A man arrived on Saturday morning,' agreed Mrs Cloutier, who was halfway down her port already. 'He didn't stay long and the idiot punctured on the way back to the village. Odd, don't you think, people wanting to talk about Lulu after all these years? It must be a bit like a convoy of buses.'

'What was he after?'

'Well he started off by pretending he was here to talk about Lulu and that he might have a "new angle". He left right after the phone call.'

'Someone phoned him here?'

'That's what telephones are usually for,' with something close to a sneer. 'It was a man with a foreign accent, and he wanted to speak to my guest. He didn't give his name, either.'

'Can you remember what was said?'

'There was a "No"; a "Yes" or two from this end. The last thing he said was, "Roger, copy that". The caller must have

154

been someone called Roger.'

McKenna thought she was taking the mickey, but he slogged on, determinedly.

'Did he mention the transcript of a tape at all?'

'A tape?' she asked suspiciously. 'What sort of tape?'

McKenna reached into his knapsack and pulled out the documentary wallet, inside which was Mrs Batch's transcript.

'This one,' he said.

It took some time to find her reading spectacles and even longer to get through two pages. There was little reaction, though she did ask, 'Are the police chasing this up, as you call it?'

'I'm not sure.'

'Have they spoken to your prison guard friend?'

'Not a friend, Mrs Cloutier, just a man who happened to phone me at the office. And no one will be talking to him – because he is deceased.'

'What happened?'

'He was murdered. That was probably the reason that cop came to see you on Saturday.'

'I don't think it was a cop,' said Mrs Cloutier. 'He was too well dressed, and they usually come in twos, don't they?'

McKenna took some time to think of the best way of framing his next words.

'I think certain people are keen to talk to your grandson,' he said.

'Why?' she demanded almost before he had finished.

'Look, Mrs Cloutier, the police always have to tick off a list of suspects.'

Mrs Cloutier was outraged, or pretending to be outraged.

'Suspects?' she said waving her hands. 'I don't like *your* implication. In any case, I haven't seen James since '46. Not even a telephone call.'

'You haven't spoken to your grandson in all that time?'

'I just said that. Are you deaf?'

She lightened her tone then.

'Look, I decided long ago I would never try to contact him. It wouldn't be fair on the fosterers if I appeared out of the blue and told him, "Hello, this is your grandmother". It's like a pet dog: you leave it to the new owners and make sure it never sees you again. James and his fosterers must have decided that, too, because he never came back here. I can't help you with this.'

'Do you know the foster parents?'

'No.'

'Mitchell told me he joined the army, but didn't tell me which group.'

'*Group* … hear that, Janek?' she snorted. 'I think he means which *regiment*. Groups are something to do with pop music.'

There was another long silence, broken only by the crackling of wood in the huge fire.

'I thought you were here to talk about my daughter, not the boy,' she said. 'You haven't asked *anything* about her. How are you going to write a story without the main character?'

McKenna knew by then it would be a night in the Fife Arms. He waved his empty glass at Janek and settled down on the settee.

'I'm curious to know why you called her Lulu,' McKenna began.

'I didn't call her that,' she said, for the first time beginning to sound like a grieving mother. 'It was her field name in

156

France, but in the end it became part of the furniture here. Everyone calls her that.'

'Why *Lulu*, though?'

'She thought it sounded naughty and seductive, but dangerous. Something she had seen in an old silent film, I think: a beautiful girl who brings down all who fall for her. I think it was a German film. Somewhat ironic, don't you think?'

'Sounds like *Pandora's Box*,' said McKenna. 'It was made in Berlin and an American woman called Louise Brooks played Lulu.'

Mrs Cloutier wasn't listening or wasn't interested so McKenna moved on.

'Colonel Mitchell told me SOE operators had a short lifespan. What made her choose a job like that?'

'*Lieutenant Colonel Mitchell.* Try and get things right.'

Then she softened again.

'A job is a job and people tend to pick what they are best at. I suppose someone thought that journalism might be the best role in life for you?'

McKenna wasn't inclined to move there but pretended to agree.

'Someone once told me,' she continued, 'that my daughter had a special gift for SOE work, but I knew that. She was the sort of child who was always hiding in cupboards or in the woods. SOE work to her was like another game … but with real guns.'

'Did she tell you anything about her operations?'

She tut-tutted, 'Good God, mister, you're not very good at this, are you? Operations like that are clandestine. She sent me occasional letters with London postmarks so I was supposed to believe she was still in Britain. She claimed she worked for the Ministry of Agriculture which, if you knew anything about Lulu, was one of the funniest things ever.'

'Can you remember the last time you saw her?'

Mrs Cloutier stared out into the mist blanketing the French windows before she spoke. 'February 20, 1944,' she said. 'Most of the roads were impassable. It gets cold up here but nothing like that. There had been a heavy snow, so heavy it covered most of the Pap and Eagle Face.'

'*The Pap and Eagle Face?*'

'Our local landmarks,' she said. 'The tallest one is the Pap of Braemar and the other looks like an eagle, at least from the other side of the valley. You will have seen them both before.'

'Missus Cloutier, I've never been here,' he insisted. 'I've never even been north of Glasgow.'

She looked at him from out of the top of her spectacles and said, 'You must have forgotten.' A pause and then, 'Your father will tell you all about it.'

McKenna thought it unfair to quarrel with an old person so he just frowned and pretended to be angry. 'I think this joke is running a bit thin, Mrs Cloutier. You are mistaken.' Then he spelt it out. 'My father isn't talking to anyone. He is in an advanced stage of Huntington's disease. He has trouble remembering his own name.'

Mrs Cloutier was totally unabashed.

'Huntington's…' she said. 'Isn't that genetic? Then, before McKenna could respond, 'I understand your concern. At that age it's hard to know what was real and what was imagined. Children have to rely on what other people tell them. You were only here for six months, but I still remember that birthmark.'

'It's not a birthmark, Mrs Cloutier,' he said. 'It was smallpox.'

'As you wish,' she said. 'Don't worry, I won't mention it again.'

McKenna was running out of tape so he asked Mrs Cloutier to move back to the story of her daughter and the last time they met. They had twenty-four hours together before the flight to France, she recalled.

'That was nice because she never had much time at home. On the last day here she climbed Eagle Face with Janek and the dog. That was it.'

'The lad didn't go with them?'

'He was still a baby and it was a very cold day. When she left we kissed by the front gate and smiled one of those pretend bye-for-now smiles. There was something fateful about that day. Bruce must have known it, too because he refused to come back in the house. Dogs are quite astute about things like that.'

'Is that Bruce?' McKenna said, pointing at the dog asleep by the fire.

She laughed, raucously. Even Janek came close to a smile.

'*It's not the same dog, mister.* The one we are talking about was ten in 1944 so that would make him forty-eight today! It's the same breed and we have always kept the same name. This one must be our fourth or fifth Bruce.'

McKenna felt foolish but, doggedly, moved on.

'I gather the War Office weren't much help?'

'By the time I heard anything *new*, the War Office had changed its name to the Ministry of Defence. They told me she flew out on February 23 and parachuted somewhere near…' She looked to Janek and he signalled back. 'Caen. It was Caen. Two days later it was obvious they had taken her. No coded messages, you see? I got a telegram from the War Office and then the standard letter with a name typed to show they'd done some homework. The telegram arrived in March, 1944, and the letter a year later, closely followed by a letter of condolence from the King. From then on, I was virtually on my own.'

'Didn't the church help?'

'We were not churchgoers,' said Mrs Cloutier contemptuously. 'Lulu even refused to have the boy baptised.'

'Can you remember what was said in the letters?'

'I can do better than that,' said the old lady. 'I will show you them.'

Janek found them in the drawer of the desk close to the window. She started with the telegram:

We regret to inform you that your daughter, Adele Eugenie Cloutier, was posted missing on (exact date unknown but believed to be late February, 1944). The report that she is missing does not mean she has been killed as she may be a prisoner of war and if she is a prisoner of war news of that may take some time to reach this country. In this case we ask you to send any letters or postcards at once to this office. Any news like this should not be forwarded to the general public and the media. Any such notification will be returned to you as soon as possible.

The 1945 letter was signed by General Sir Henry Colville Barclay, Military Secretary's Department:

I am commanded by the War Office to state that in view of the lapse of time since our last communication and the absence of any further news regarding your daughter since the date she was reported missing we must regretfully conclude she has lost her life, and death is presumed.

'Is that it?' said McKenna. 'The longest words are that general's name.'

Mrs Cloutier cackled and agreed, 'It doesn't tell you much, does it?' Then, more seriously, 'It's better now than it was then. I used to wake up every morning believing she would suddenly appear from somewhere. Denial is said to be the first stage of grief, isn't it?'

'I heard someone grassed on her?'

'I assume someone grassed on her, too,' she said drily. 'Lots of grasses during the war.'

'But nothing about how she died.'

'I had to guess. My view, and that of everyone else I talked to, was that the Gestapo couldn't get her to talk and shot her "trying to escape," as they liked to call it. There were execution chambers all over Paris and it probably happened in one of those. Why they thought it necessary to conceal her body is another mystery; lots of mysteries in this story.'

'I heard some SOE women seduced Germans. Is that true?'

'Possibly,' she replied carefully. 'She was good at making fools of men.'

'Did she hate men?'

'Hate men? Definitely not. She was married, after all. She just hated anyone in a Wehrmacht uniform.'

Something odd had struck McKenna.

'How do you know all this, Mrs Cloutier? You told me SOE operations were clandestine. Colin Mitchell even told me agents never even told their families.'

Another Wicked Witch of the West cackle and then, 'Most girls of that age usually keep a personal diary, don't they?'

'And you read it?'

'Come, come, mister. Don't try and look outraged! Every mother has the right to look through a daughter's diary.'

McKenna took a risk. 'Do you still have it, by any

chance?'

'So you can have a read yourself? Typical journalist! Sorry, but I burned it a long time ago. If the War Office weren't going to give her a medal or even acknowledge her existence I certainly wasn't going to let them wade through her personal stuff.'

McKenna checked his watch, this time without hiding it.

'It's 3.36,' said Mrs Cloutier. 'You've missed the late bus. I don't have the diary, but I do have some old photographs … if you have the time.'

Janek wandered off into the house and reappeared a few minutes later carrying three large photo albums, which he placed on the small table next to Mrs Cloutier. She squeezed his arm with her bony fingers and pulled him closer so he could see better.

The collection was coded: red, yellow and black, and the photos were the sort of amateur efforts that families are too embarrassed to hang on a wall and of little interest to anyone apart from the people who took the pictures in the first place. McKenna thought it intrusive; like peeping into a stranger's bedroom.

The red album was the early years: bonny baby in a pram, sitting on the knees of a very young Mrs Cloutier and playing in the garden. Then, aged ten or eleven, dressed in black and performing what looked like a seductive dance.

'The school play,' Mrs Cloutier explained. 'She was picked for the Salome role. Rather daring in those days, don't you think? I don't know which boy had the misfortune of playing John the Baptist.' McKenna politely joined in when she laughed at that.

In the second album, also in black and white, Lulu was wrestling with a Bruce dog, riding a horse and skiing in a place with a background of high mountains.

'Mont Blanc,' Mrs Cloutier explained. 'Look at that sky … like a field of cornflower. And there she is, swimming in the ocean in Corsica.'

Three pages were devoted to ghosts of boyfriends past. Lulu must have been a busy girl because there were dozens of them, lined up like big game that had just been shot. Some were holding her hand and others were smiling hopefully into the lens.

'She was popular with men,' Mrs Cloutier said. 'At least the ones I saw.'

The last image on the final page was of Lulu posing on a rock face, grinning and playing the fool for the camera. Both her arms were hidden behind her back and one leg was raised, like one of those wading birds.

'That's her impersonation of a flamingo,' said Mrs Cloutier. 'I think that was taken in the mid thirties.'

'Unusual,' said McKenna. 'That rock face looks like a large bird, too.'

'Eagle Face. The hill across the valley. One of her favourite walks.'

As McKenna had expected, the black album was only half full. There were a couple of Mrs Cloutier pushing a pram and Lulu pulling a large horse through a field.

'Land Army in 1939,' said Mrs Cloutier rather contemptuously. 'A year later she was in the SOE.'

The final few shots were in colour. There was another version of Lulu on Eagle Face, then a camping holiday perhaps: a small tent, a shoeless and brown-footed Lulu happily cleaning her teeth, and cooking by an open fire.

'And that's it,' said Mrs Cloutier. 'The life and times of my little girl.'

She closed the last album and handed all three to Janek. McKenna was puzzled.

'If you don't mind me asking, Mrs Cloutier,' he said, 'but where are all the photographs of the boy? And where's her husband?'

Mrs Cloutier did mind and told him so.

'These are family photographs,' she said huffily. 'They were not supposed to be the works of Robert Capa. She didn't have time and she was married to another SOE operator, so they would not go around taking photographs of each other. I never even met my son-in-law, let alone saw a photograph of him.'

'Not even a wedding pic?'

'Their choice. And before you go all weepy-eyed about families and children being close, that doesn't apply here. I told you: Lulu made up her own rules.'

Mrs Cloutier gave a fake yawn, the sort people use to escape from something or someone. She signalled Janek to help her back into the wheelchair.

'I'm tired,' she said. McKenna got the message, pocketed his notepad and got to his feet. 'Janek will give you a lift in the Land Rover back into Braemar,' she said. 'I hope you keep me up to date with your story.'

Janek was about to make off with the photo albums when McKenna said, 'Do you have a printer here? A few family snaps are always a help.'

'Hear that, Janek?' she said. 'He thinks this is a branch of Boots! Braemar post office has one of those copy machines. Make sure I get them back. If not, I'll have to get Janek to have words with you.'

The Pole nodded and McKenna promised.

Car heating systems seemed to be illegal in Braemar, and by the time he checked in at the hotel he was pink-nosed and half conscious with the cold. He climbed the stairs to his room, hanging on to Mrs Cloutier's photographs as if carrying three Ming vases.

CHAPTER 21.

The Fife Arms minded him of one of those old Hammer Horror movies: a small village pub, a sign outside creaking in the wind – even when there was no wind – and locals who fell silent as soon as a stranger walked in.

A gang of Young Farmer types standing on one side of the bar stared and then went back to their dirty jokes. Four middle-aged men arguing over a game of cribbage stopped for a few seconds before carrying on and three silent pensioners stared at nothing in the other corner. A juke box was playing 'Wooden Heart' by Elvis.

By the time Ken Dodd was into 'Tears for Souvenirs' McKenna was close to the end of his third pint, and ready to call it a day. Then there was a shove in his back so hard he spilled most of the beer.

'How's it goin'?' said the assailant. 'Get your job done?'

It was the Braemar taxi driver and he was the worse for wear, his nose as red and lumpy as that of W.C. Fields. McKenna began to work out the best way of escape.

'You're frae Glasgow?' said Taxi.

'So I am,' said McKenna downing the remains as quickly as he could.

'Did you see the old dear, then?'

'Mrs Cloutier? I did.' McKenna got to his feet and pocketed his cigarettes.

'Bet you didn't get much from her, did ya?'

McKenna shrugged.

'Was the boy there?'

McKenna pulled his cigarettes out of his pocket and sat down again.

'You knew the son?'

Taxi knew how to tease out a story. 'Nah. Wouldn't say I knew him, but—'

'What did you say your name was?'

'I didn't, but it's Angus.'

Well, it would be, wouldn't it, thought McKenna, but he stayed polite and asked, 'Fancy a drink … Angus?'

He wanted a Talisker 'and a pint of heavy'.

McKenna got him a double, asked the barman for a tab for Room 3a and found the furthest, quietest corner. He waited until Angus was looking elsewhere, pulled out his recorder and balanced it on his knee under the table.

Someone, possible McKenna's editor at the *Springfield Herald*, had told him that interviews should always be formulated like an edition of *This Is Your Life*. It was best in chronological order: the boring childhood stuff first, work, marriage and children in the middle and the dramas last. He left the tape off for the humdrum bits: Angus, Gaelic for rock, born and bred in Braemar, too old to enlist but did his bit 'for King and Country'. He drove to Loch Ewe in the far west and shared a crofter's cottage there so he could stay there and help load and unload for the Atlantic Convoys. McKenna switched on at 'coming home at weekends'.

'Did locals see much of the Cloutier family?' he asked.

'The granny was well known round here. You know she

166

was a Commie? She had her own little newsletter, and dropped it through doors once a week. Then she started to hold meetings in the village hall, but no one ever turned up. Everyone just saw her as a dotty old hen but then it turned out she had been grooming kids; telling them stories about the motherland and the Revolution.'

'Kids? What kids?'

'The ones evacuated from places like Glasgow. There were nine or ten of them living in the house early on in the war, but she was warned off. She was either too daft or too Commie, so the kids had to be moved on. Didn't you hear that story?'

McKenna took a big swig of his Guinness and then said, 'No, I didn't hear that story. Did you see much of the daughter?'

'Lulu, wasn't she called, the one who got murdered by the Gestapo? She was never at home and when she was she never came into the village. I did see the lad with his granny and the Pole a couple of times.'

'What do you know about the lad?'

'Apparently he was a bit of an imp and even the Pole had problems with him, though it can't help if you're a mute and can't tell kids off. The boy was taken on by a Barnardo's near Dumfries round about '46 or '47. I heard later he'd joined the army.'

'Did the granny explain why she got rid? Some locals must have known.'

Angus waggled his empty glass meaningfully.

'I'll have to think about that,' he said.

McKenna brought him another Talisker and two more pints. The Beach Boys were picking up 'Good Vibrations' and one of the Young Farmers was lying on the floor below the bar rail. The others ignored him; it was just like Clydebank, except there he'd have lost his smart jacket

167

and shirt by now.

'I told you he was hard to handle,' Angus continued. 'My guess is he was just shuffled around after that.'

'Why do you say that?'

'Families who adopt expect a kid who is reasonably well-behaved, ya ken? And he wasn't. I did know he joined the army.'

'You told me that already,' said McKenna, with a note of irritation. Angus was becoming repetitive. 'Mrs Cloutier mentioned that, too.'

Angus gave one of those disbelieving looks old people often use to show how wise they are and said, 'Bet she never said the boy was here a week ago?'

Angus was well gone, and McKenna didn't believe him.

'Are you certain?' he said. 'She told me she hadn't seen him since '46.'

'She's telling porkies,' said Angus. 'I should know because I drove him over to the Lodge from the village.'

'You're telling me an army man didn't have his own transport?'

'The weather was shite,' answered Angus, and this time McKenna did believe him. 'He'd have needed a Land Rover or something and obviously didn't have one. He arrived late on. There was no moon and I had to keep defogging the windows.'

McKenna was about to ask the obvious but Angus got there first.

'He said bugger all, if that's what you're thinking. He told me where he was going and that was it. Not even "thanks", or a "goodnight". I ken him opening the back door an inch or so, so he could use the courtesy light. It was definitely him.'

'How did you *know* it was him?'

'He had a birthmark on his cheek. A bit like yours.'

'*Mine* was smallpox.'

'Whatever it was, people remember bairns for things like that.'

'How long did he stay?'

'No idea, pal. He never took a return trip. For all I know he might still be there.'

CHAPTER 22.

Bux became quite agitated when he read the death notice for the first time.

Friends and colleagues of Lukas Rückeran, it said on the back page of the local newspaper, *of Münchingerstraße, Stammheim-Stuttgart, are invited to his funeral service at 2 p.m. on Tuesday, October 5. Dornhalden Cemetery, Landeshauptstadt, 70161.*

Bux repeated 'Dornhalden Cemetery,' and waited for a reaction.

Baum the historian answered first. 'The RAF suicide trio are buried there.'

'Quite correct,' said Bux. 'A murdered prison guard will soon be feeding worms in the same cemetery as the terrorist group alleged to have done the killing. The press will have a field day. I can imagine the headlines now: *MURDERED STAMMHEIM GUARD BURIED WITH RAF SUICIDE TRIO.*

'Do you think the killer will appear at the funeral?' asked Hertzog.

Bux guffawed. Much as he disliked the 'us and them, young versus old', policy among some senior colleagues, but he could not help himself.

'Our *junge* has been watching too many films,' said Bux

directly to Baum, who chortled in return. 'Murderers do *not* turn up at the funerals of their victims, Hertzog. That was something invented by Hollywood.'

Hertzog's face reddened and Bux softened his tone.

'Look, Hertzog, you can soon discover that for yourself because I want you and Baum to cover the funeral. Lang will accompany me to the coroner's inquest.'

As the detective in charge of the case Bux had no choice but to attend the inquest at the regional courthouse, close by the parliament building. He would have preferred an hour or so at Dornhalden Cemetery because while a killer would never be stupid enough to turn up at funerals mourners often offered a clue. Whoever paid for the newspaper death notice, for example, would surely attend.

The courthouse was packed with journalists and photographers with half a dozen TV crews waiting outside to catch the comers and goers.

Bux had an hour before the start, so he bought a coffee at the small cafe in the annex close to the main entrance. He plonked himself on one of the wooden seats in the long corridor running the length of the building, from where he could keep an eye on everything.

There were several familiar faces: his forensic and ballistic team, Dietrich the doctor and Drescher, the public prosecutor, who was also there to give evidence. Then, another face Bux recognised: a man in his fifties walking past less than a metre away and pretending he hadn't noticed him.

Bux called out, 'Hello, Homann!' which forced him to stop and look round. The former chief commissioner of the Federal Criminal Police Office (BKA) hardly blinked.

'Bux, how are you?' he said pleasantly. 'I must have been miles away. Are you here for the inquest? Terrible thing, wasn't it? How is the lovely Silke?'

Bux said nothing until Homann had no choice.

'A drink, Kommissar?' he said. 'There are seats in the cafe.'

Homann answered the first question with the first lie as soon as the coffees arrived.

'I had some work to do in the area,' he said. 'I also wanted to hear the verdict on the murder of that poor prison officer.'

Bux thought that unlikely: Homann lived at Wiesbaden, 200 kilometres to the north, and was long retired from the BKA. Homann would also know all about the Rückeran verdict because Bux had just seen him coming out of the coroner's office, and the coroner would have made up his mind by then.

Bux had met Hans Homann in the mid seventies, when many *Kripo* officers had been seconded to Operation Watersplash, which was Homann's plan to bring the RAF to its knees. He was clever: the BKA soon became the country's first coordinated police agency – not unlike the American FBI – and the first agency to use computers, soon to become the bêtes noires of every detective over a certain age.

This resourcefulness, an excellent speaking voice and the look of a benign bank manager meant that Homann enjoyed a high profile with the media and the public. He retired in 1980 with more honours than the British monarchy. Bux had never trusted him: a man who wore silk bow ties and smoked a pipe had to have a devious streak somewhere.

Homann had an agenda here, too, for he soon started to fish, sipping carefully at his coffee and never looking Bux in the eye.

'Terrible, that Rückeran business, wasn't it?' he said. 'I gather he was an exemplary prison officer? Wasn't he found two days after the murder? I thought that would be difficult for a detective, Bux, even a detective with your abilities.'

'Progress has been very slow,' said Bux, determined to ignore the flattery. 'We should have more to go on after today's funeral.'

'I assume you are chasing the RAF lead?'

'What RAF lead is that, Homann? This was nothing to do with the RAF.'

Homann didn't quite roll his eyes, but he certainly disagreed.

'I read some of your quotes to the press, but with respect, Bux, I never saw it as a lone killer. There is too much of the RAF about it: a prison guard, the rumours about an escalation in terrorist attacks. That cigarette brand in the dead man's apartment? Such cigarettes are obtainable anywhere in Germany.'

Bux thought for a moment before he said, 'I never mentioned the cigarette to the press, and certainly not in public.'

Homann shrugged non-committedly, which made Bux even angrier.

'Do tell me, Homann,' he said, 'when you spoke to the coroner a few minutes ago was he going to decide that it was a RAF killing, too?'

'The coroner is an old friend, and I was not there to discuss the RAF or the Rückeran murder,' said Homann.

'The RAF *could not* have been involved,' said Bux. 'The press and the public might swallow that, but not me. Now what was said to the coroner?'

'What I said to the coroner is my business,' said Homann. His tone hardened.

'I do not normally interfere in *Kripo* cases,' he said. 'I do have opinions about this case, however.' Then, with what he made sound like a warning, 'I am certain Bonn will see it that way, too. I have a meeting soon with the new Minister of the Interior, who also happens to be a friend of mine.'

Bux knew where this was going even before Homann pulled out the knife.

'I am sure he will be happy to hear your views on the progress of the case,' he said with a sneer. 'My personal view is that one of the special response units should have been used in this case some time ago. I will also remind the Minister of the Interior that we are no closer to finding the killer.'

'Oh, *we* are no closer?' said Bux.

Homann got to his feet and threw a few Deutschmarks on the table as if giving money to a street beggar. 'I do hope your noble career ends happily,' were his last words as he left.

The inquest went almost exactly as Bux had expected. Almost.

Homann's coroner friend, who was in his seventies and deaf in one ear, was fond of his loud, theatrical rhetoric, which always went down well with journalists and media hoping for quotes. He was shocked, he said, that a state prison officer had been 'silly enough to supply a killer with what amounted to a loaded pistol'.

'My ninety-year-old granny could have murdered this man,' he almost bellowed. 'This amounted to a form of suicide by Herr Rückeran.'

In the words favoured by many coroners, the 'likelihood' was that Rückeran had been murdered by one or more members of a RAF gang of urban guerrillas. The coroner would also be writing a 'prevention of further death report' to the incoming Federal Minister of the Interior and other government agencies.

'The RAF,' he said, 'are plainly still fully operational,' and that, 'prominent citizens of the country should consider their day-to-day operations.' A bodyguard or two seemed an excellent idea.

Finally, the results of the autopsy completed that morning: the bullet that had killed Rückeran and the time of the murder were not new, but the report of the pathologist was and there was a buzz in the courtroom when the coroner read it out. Herr Rückeran had been suffering from an alcohol-related disease and his liver had been close to total failure. In the opinion of the pathologist, Herr Rückeran had six months to live, and that was generous. The likelihood was, then, that alcohol would have killed Rückeran even if a RAF gunman had never appeared at his door.

'Anything to add, Kommissar?' the coroner asked Bux.

'Nothing to add,' said Bux. 'Nothing at all.'

The Kommissar's mood lightened at mid afternoon when Baum and Hertzog arrived back from Dornhalden Cemetery.

'It was a bit like the funeral of that American who shot Kennedy,' said Baum as soon as he sat down.

'No mourners, then,' said Bux who had expected that. 'But several members of the press, I would think.'

'That's right, Kommissar,' said Hertzog excitedly. 'I counted three funeral attendants, the priest and his choristers … and *seventeen* members of the press.'

'Ah,' said Bux with a little smile. 'The pigs had been watching the same American movie as you, Hertzog. They thought the killer would turn up with his personal floral

175

tributes. Did anyone leave flowers?'

'Quite a few,' said Hertzog. 'One of the floral tributes said, "All your colleagues at Stammheim". There were other flowers but few had left a name. The prison deputy had left one which simply said, "Mario Koch".'

'Brave of him,' said Bux sardonically.

'Not much of a send-off, was it?' said Baum. 'I would have been ashamed of that had he been a friend of mine.'

'It's understandable in many ways,' said Bux. 'The press, the public and virtually everyone else had decided this was a RAF killing. If poor Rückeran did have friends or colleagues still alive they would think it too risky.'

'I thought his landlady would have attended,' said Lang.

'If you recall, Lang, they're away seeing their grandchildren,' Bux pointed out impatiently. Then to Baum, 'Who were the pall-bearers?'

Hertzog jumped in before Baum could even begin.

'There was a boy in his twenties, an older man in his sixties and a young woman,' he said. 'She thought I was a mourner and asked if I wanted to drop a few pieces of dirt on the coffin. "A last farewell to your friend," she said. So I showed her my card and she showed me hers, which read: *Dagmar Reich, Director. Abel Reich of Stuttgart, the best burial service in the city.* The man in charge was her father, Frank Reich, and the other was her brother; a family business.'

'I think I worked that out for myself,' said Bux scornfully. 'But who paid for the funeral service and the coffin? And priests don't come cheap, either.'

'This Dagmar woman did not want to discuss it,' said Hertzog. 'So I had to wave my warrant card at her again. It was a gentleman called Adler. No first name.'

'Was it *lavish* coffin?' asked Bux.

'The most expensive, according to Abel Reich of

Stuttgart,' said Baum.

'Does that mean something, Herr Bux?' said Lang and Hertzog together and waited for a response. Bux wanted to make sure so they had to sweat while he went through his notes.

'If I am correct,' he said eventually, 'and I think I am, the person in question is Leopold Adler, the deputy managing director of Daimler-Benz at Untertürkheim. If you recall, that was the office Rückeran was so keen to telephone before his death.'

CHAPTER 23.

'Too much grog, mate?' asked the Aussie, pushing the plate with its egg, bacon and sausage at him. 'You look like you're going to chuck a sickie any second?'

'Stomach ache,' McKenna lied.

'Yeah, right,' she said. He tried to remember. There had been lager, lots of whisky and some whiskey, that much he knew, and some concern about how he was going to charge *this* on expenses.

'Good night?' he asked the Aussie, thinking she could elaborate.

'Oh, a great night, mate,' she grinned. 'We all liked the impersonations. My favourite was John Wayne; the Burt Lancaster not so good.'

McKenna cringed, left his breakfast and scuttled back to his room.

He had three hours to kill before the midday bus to Aberdeen so he used his last free packets of Nescafé and lay on the bed to think.

There was something odd about that battered little mansion, its dotty lady owner, the family tragedies, the burial ground with no graves and a Pole who never spoke but could read minds. And the grandson – the army boy who may have turned up in Braemar after thirty-five years

… an event ignored by his grandmother.

He knew old folk forgot, and often made mistakes, but not Mrs Cloutier. She was definitely *not* trapped in reverse like his father, who most of the time couldn't even remember his own name. He thought of going back to have it out with her, but he didn't really fancy another drive with Angus, and the more he thought about it the less important it seemed. In any case, he had other things to do.

'How do I get to the post office?' he asked Aussie as he paid his bill.

'A short walk down Mar Road, near where the stagecoach stops,' she said with a smirk.

'Very funny,' he said. 'What time does it open?'

'Oh, it's not open on Tuesdays, mate. Have a good one, Pilgrim.'

McKenna phoned the office from the village public phone at 10 a.m., as he had been ordered.

'Did you see the old lady?' demanded Mrs Batch without any sort of preamble. 'What did she say about Lulu? How long did you stay? Hurry up: there's a fire drill in a few minutes.'

He told her everything he could remember but left out the drinks and the bill. When he mentioned Angus and his last words she became quite animated.

'Say that again. What about the son?'

McKenna went through it for the second time. Dead silence.

'Are you still there?'

'I wouldn't believe a Highland taxi driver if I were you,' she said eventually. 'This one obviously saw you as an easy touch.'

'I'm not that stupid,' said McKenna.

179

'Aren't you?' asked Mrs Batch scornfully. 'And what if the son *had* turned up? It's not a crime, is it? Old ladies forget, and if the boy was in Braemar he certainly wasn't killing someone in Stuttgart.'

She let him think about that for a few seconds before adding, 'I've something more plausible for you.'

'Go on,' said McKenna carefully.

'I got the latest copies of *Der Zeitung*, and spoke to one of their reporters. She gave me some background on our pal Rückeran.'

'She? You mean a *female* reporter?'

'Yes. Some do exist.'

'I thought we were supposed to keep this to ourselves.'

'I told her we were working on a piece about the Red Army Faction. I never mentioned Lulu and the tape. She believed me.'

There was a pause and a ruffle of paper.

'She had good local contacts, which is more than most people here can say. The coroner is going to decide it was unlawful killing, probably by a member of the RAF. So, like I just said, you can forget Lulu's son.'

'Is Rückeran still big news over there?'

'It's still the lead on the front page. The usual stuff about "this quiet neighbourhood" and "a killer in our midst", and quotes from local politicians. The police over there either aren't giving much away, or are getting nowhere. The reporter said the best they got was one sentence of quotes from "Kommissar Markus Bux, Stuttgart *Kripo*", the detective in charge. Do I read it?'

'Please.'

The case of the murder of Lukas Rückeran is ongoing and we welcome any help from the public in this matter. We do not rule out the possibility there may be a connection with members of the Red Army Faction.

'Doesn't say much, does it? A bit like one of Strathclyde Police's press conferences. What do you think?'

'All I can think of is that the police are desperate if they have to appeal for help from the public. The forensic and ballistic teams have probably failed.'

McKenna took the plunge.

'Don't fly off the handle,' he said, knowing that she would. 'We haven't got very far either, have we?'

'Meaning what?' she said icily.

'I was thinking at breakfast, "If all these government departments haven't found Lulu after all these years what hope have we got?"'

He took another deep breath before adding, 'Where do we draw the line?'

'We draw the line where the editor decides,' she hissed. 'I told you before: we *need* a story. A newspaper is not like a school, where everything is based on overall grades. It's based on success. As things stand *The Inquirer* is about as successful as one of those student rag week papers. Something else: if we can't push stories along there'll be what Yanks call "a net headcount". You know what that means?'

'I can guess,' said McKenna. The tone hardened even more then.

'Are you going to come along with me on these things? If you feel you can't cope, go and get a job as a street cleaner or something. Make up your mind.'

McKenna was making up his mind when the office fire alarm went off and Mrs Batch hung up.

He was still considering it two and a half hours later on the Aberdeen to Glasgow train, too tired to do anything but stare out of the window at nothing. He had a headache from hell and all the rattling and swaying was making it worse.

He searched for a bottle of mineral water and the aspirin in his rucksack, but all he found was something that hadn't been there on the journey out.

He still had the Lulu family albums.

CHAPTER 24.

B ux got the call he had waited for on the Wednesday, when a secretary said the deputy managing director of Daimler-Benz would be happy to meet him. She gave him a time and the directions, then added, 'Herr Adler tells me he is looking forward to talking with such a distinguished police officer.'

Bux was still thinking of that when Lang pulled into the car park outside the main assembly plant at Untertürkheim, nine kilometres east of the city centre. The Kommissar disliked such statements because they meant someone was either being sarcastic or was hiding something, and Bux was immune to flattery. Nor did he like people who drove fast, expensive cars, and the brand-new S-Class stationed in front of a *deputy managing director* sign was as fast and expensive as one could find.

'That's his wreck,' Bux told Lang sarcastically. 'And those are the thugs looking after him,' he added, this time pointing at two hefty bodyguard types sitting in a small room on the side of the all-glass reception area.

An attractive woman in her thirties introduced herself as 'Herr Adler's assistant' and led the way out of the offices across the factory floors to the body shop assembly line, where dozens of workers, male and female, were welding and bonding bits of vehicles like so many robots.

Leopold Adler, a handsome figure of booming authority with hair cropped short like a Prussian aristocrat, was talking to three members of staff, but sent them away when he saw the detectives arriving.

'Let's talk in the office,' he said. 'It's quieter and more private there. Then I will tell you all I can about my friend Lukas Rückeran.'

It did not start well.

'There is no smoking in here, Kommissar,' said Adler as soon as the three men were seated. 'It is just a house rule here.'

Adler smiled politely and almost sorrowfully. Bux obeyed, dimped his cigarette and smiled back because he could be as impolite as he wished now.

'We were talking about your friend Rückeran's funeral service on the way here,' he began. 'Weren't we, Lang? I think we both found it odd that there were no mourners. I discount all the journalists, of course. You were too busy to attend?'

Adler hackled and said, 'I was not too busy, Kommissar.'

'All his former colleagues at Stammheim gave it a miss, too,' continue Bux as if he hadn't been interrupted. 'It appears the man your call your friend was buried by strangers.'

'It was not a question of having other things to do, Kommissar. It was a case of protecting oneself. Every police press conference I have heard implied that this was a RAF killing. Nazis apart, the RAF target what they like to call the country's "imperialists". I was not a Nazi, but I am certainly a well-known industrialist.'

That was clever, thought Bux, and Adler had a point.

He went back to the beginning. 'Tell me about Rückeran. I gather you two went back a long way.'

184

'I would describe Lukas as a normal youth,' said Adler. 'He was an only child and something of a loner, but his parents were good people – the types who go to church every weekend and are always engaged with the local community. Rückeran and I went to the same school and I spent a lot of time with him.'

'Do you remember anything notable about his youth?' said Bux.

Adler sighed and said, 'He loved animals.'

'I said *notable*, Herr Adler.'

'Oh, I think it is important if looking back on the history of Lukas Rückeran,' Adler insisted. 'It will seem like nothing to you, but perhaps this incident best sums him up. If you have the time, of course, Kommissar?'

Bux thought he was playing for time but said, unenthusiastically, 'If you have the time I have the time.'

'I will certainly never forget it,' Adler continued. 'We were in the Schwaben Hills and came across a roe deer lying on the edge of the forest. It had been hit by a car and the driver had left it for dead. The deer was like a Bambi type; very young and very small. I wanted to carry it to the nearest village. Rückeran insisted its back was broken and he did not hesitate. He sat on the grass next to it, patted it like a damn pet, held it with one hand and broke its neck with the other. He had never struck me as capable of something like that, but people are always surprising you. Don't you agree, Kommissar?'

This man was either playing for time, or trying to annoy him, thought Bux, so he moved him on and asked, 'After college?'

Adler pointed at a large framed photograph on the wall and said proudly, 'You know our Lord Mayor, Manfred Rommel? Rückeran and I joined his father's 7th Panzer in October, 1939. We were barely out of our teens.'

'Odd you should mention *Feldmarschall* Erwin Rommel,' said Bux. 'He also won the Knight's Cross of the Iron Cross.'

'I do not understand, Herr Bux. A Knight's Cross?'

'Of the Iron Cross,' corrected Bux. 'Did you never see the Rückeran photograph?'

'The one in his apartment?'

'Was there more than one, Herr Adler?'

'He didn't talk about it,' Adler decided after a short pause. 'He kept many things to himself.'

'You were friends in the same division and you never heard about it?'

'I was a driver in a Tiger I,' said Adler haughtily. 'Rückeran was infantry. We did not go around holding hands. In any case, were not many records lost towards the end of the war?'

'Possibly,' said Bux rather derisively. 'What else can you tell me? So far all I know about him is that he avoided work and never cleaned his apartment. Did you know he was close to drinking himself to death?'

'I read of the coroner's report,' said Adler quietly.

'Were you surprised?'

'Not really. I knew he had been heavily into drink for some time.'

Bux sighed and said, 'Tell me, then: how does a boozer turn into a war hero?'

'He wasn't always like that,' said Adler cautiously. 'In any case, it might have been the other way round.'

Adler checked his watch; always a bad sign. Bux picked up the pace.

'*Tell me*. Believe me, we are all ears.'

'It was after his parents died in the bombings. I know he felt guilty about that.'

'He felt guilty about the death of his parents?' said Bux incredulously.

'He was miles away from home. He could not attend the funeral.'

'But they died in the bombings of 1940,' said Bux. 'According to his superior at Stammheim he began drinking heavily *after* the war. Did he drink a lot in Paris?'

'I am not a damn psychiatrist,' Adler replied testily.

'You *were* in Paris during the war?'

Adler didn't hesitate. 'Late June of 1940, not long after the end of our French campaign. A marvellous week … but then it was off to the Russian Front.'

'You never went back to Paris?'

Adler didn't falter there, either.

'Obviously I went back on business, but just that one time during the war.'

'What about Rückeran?'

'Summer 1940; the only time Rückeran was there, too.'

Bux kicked Lang's shins to stop him interrupting, but Adler had not noticed.

Bux pretended to follow his notes and didn't look up.

'Tell me about that French girl you met in Paris,' he said.

Adler tried to turn it into a little joke when he said, 'How unusual, a French girl in Paris!'

'Let me jog your memory,' Bux replied doggedly. 'There was a photograph in Rückeran's apartment: a French girl and three members of the same 7th Panzer division as you, Herr Adler. It was taken close to the Eiffel Tower and the girl was wearing a beret. One of the men was Rückeran; were you one of the others?'

'Come, come, Kommissar,' retorted Adler. 'There were hundreds of photographs of German soldiers in Paris,

187

many with local girls. Rückeran did not follow me around Paris like a tame dog. He must have had other friends in the 7th and other divisions and I certainly *do not* remember a French girl called Lulu. I never saw such a photograph in his apartment, either.'

Bux left it a few seconds before he spoke again.

'I didn't mention a girl called Lulu,' he said.

Adler did not move and did not speak for several seconds. The only sounds were the buzzing and whirling from the factory floor.

'Herr Adler?'

Then the office telephone rang.

Adler leapt to his feet and hurried to pick it up, which was exactly what Bux would have done. Nor was he surprised when Adler immediately went on the offensive, like every clever senior management figure.

'You must forgive me, Kommissar,' Adler said, while holding a hand over the mouthpiece so the caller could not hear. 'In retrospect, I think Rückeran may have mentioned a woman called Lulu. My friend was a great romantic.'

Then he pointed to the door and said, 'My assistant will show you the way out to the car park. I will help you with this case, obviously, but I do not see how a missing photograph of some woman Rückeran may have met in France is going to help. Now, gentlemen, if you do need to talk to me again you have my number.'

CHAPTER 25.

McKenna was bang on time, but there was no sign of Myler. He tried the main foyer, the bar and coffee shop and the loo, but nothing.

He was quartering the hotel for the third time when he heard a voice.

'Over here, dickhead,' said Myler.

McKenna thought he must have been watching from the same dark cranny in the bar for some time as McKenna wandered round like an idiot trying to find him. He wasn't sure, but that was the sort of thing Myler would do.

But he might have been difficult to find in daylight because this was a different-looking Myler: black suit, black tie and white shirt. The McMurphy hat had gone, and for the first time the world could see he was as bald as a billiard ball.

McKenna asked, as facetiously as he dared, 'Why the daft glad rags?'

'I've got a meeting,' said Myler as if that explained everything.

'Am I allowed to ask who?'

'*Whom*. With your boss; though he doesn't know it yet.'

McKenna tried to look indifferent to this calumny.

'You want to meet the editor? What the hell for?'

'I told you I'd find some bells and whistles for you but quid pro quo, as they say. You have to do some backscratching for me.'

McKenna didn't like the sound of this, even less when Myler explained.

'I'm going to write my life story,' he said proudly, and as if expecting a round of applause. Then it got worse.

'If I write a wee book about my time in the service will your editor use it? One of those … what are they called?'

'Serialisations,' said McKenna. He tried to think of a survivor's way out and how he could let Myler down gracefully. Bloom wasn't keen on serialisations and would certainly *not* want to meet someone like Myler.

He played for time.

'Fiction or non-fiction?' he asked.

'I just fuckin' told you it's about *my* time in the service.'

'The service being?'

'*Special* service; that's all I'm saying.'

'Look,' said McKenna politely. 'I don't think that is going to get us far. If we talk to the editor he will want some detail. He will want to know more about you. If you were hoping to sell a few copies you'd have to mention a few things like where and when and if you jumped off planes and shot people. At least give us a few clues.'

Myler hadn't been listening or was just ignoring him.

'Can you get me in to talk to him this afternoon?'

'Today? He's a busy man and we can't just march in. I can try and get an appointment, but it won't be this week. I have to finish this story first.'

Something else occurred to McKenna then. 'If you were in the army didn't you sign the Official Secrets Act?'

'There's a way round it.'

'Go on,' said McKenna warily.

'There's a rumour that someone high up at Hereford is doing a book about *his* time in the regiment. I know who it is but all I'm telling you now is that he won't need the money. I definitely *do* need the money and you can't have one rule for the officers and one for other ranks, can you?'

'Can you write?'

'No. That's your job. You can ghost it for me. There's no bread, though.'

McKenna was outraged.

'I'm supposed to write it for eff all?'

'It's not for eff all,' Myler said. 'You are going to get the benefit of my experience and knowledge, just as you did for the Ice Cream Doping story. That did all right, didn't it? Bet you never told your editor where that came from.'

McKenna couldn't argue with that.

'Let's hear what you've got,' he told him. 'A few things I could sell to him.'

'Have you got one of them recorder things?' asked Myler, holding his gaze.

'I have,' admitted McKenna.

'Make sure it's switched off, then. All this is off the record. No shorthand and no scribbling on the back of your fag packet. If I find out you have been recording I'll cut your balls off with a rusty saw.'

McKenna nodded to agree, but switched on the tape inside a pocket anyway.

'Do you remember the Iran Embassy siege in 1980?' Myler began.

'I saw it on TV. I remember ITV wouldn't drop *Coronation Street* for it.'

'I don't think people will make that mistake now,' said Myler, dangerously close to a smile. 'The service is big news so I always thought it would make a good book for

191

someone. There are stories nobody has ever read about – Malaysia and Borneo, Aden, Oman. I have some stories about the Iran Embassy siege, too.'

'Northern Ireland?'

'I've never been there,' said Myler without trying to pretend that was true.

'It sounds interesting,' said McKenna. 'I can put it to the editor and I'll do my best. But I tell you now: we're going nowhere until I crack the Lulu story. So what about her?'

Myler pulled out his paperwork.

McKenna was surprised at the small and neat writing from a man who was basically a Clydebank hooligan. It was as immaculate as any work from Mrs Batch. Perhaps this was typical of people with military backgrounds. He didn't ask how Myler had got the information, though he guessed much of it was from the registrar at Braemar because there was a bill of a pound per person per copy at the bottom of his notes.

Mrs Cloutier, Lulu's mother, was on the electoral roll as Marie Charlotte Cloutier (née York), born Blair Lodge, Braemar, February 1891. Husband: Charles Cloutier, born Paris, 1890, died at Verdun, December 1, 1916.

'They sure died young in them days,' said Myler before he continued, 'Adele Eugenie Rezin (née Cloutier), born Blair Lodge, Braemar, on March 8, 1916, deceased, Paris, France, February, 1944. No exact date on the death certificate but occupation given as "secretary", the standard moniker of female SOE agents. Now the boy: James Rezin, born Blair Lodge, April 8, 1941. I also got the copy of a wedding certificate from London, September 20, 1940, of Adele Eugenie Cloutier to Bernard Rezin, a Paris viticulturist – or a winemaker to you.'

'Hang on,' said McKenna. 'Married in September 1940; child born April '41?'

'I saw that, too,' said Myler.

'And what's your opinion?'

'The registrar at the time may have made a mistake, which is possible if there's a war going on, or it must have been a shotgun wedding,'

'Mrs Cloutier never mentioned that.'

'Of course she never mentioned it,' said Myler. 'Illegitimacy was like a crime in those days, so people kept quiet. At least this mum and dad did the decent thing, not that the French have ever bothered about things like illegitimacy. Talking of which, that guy Smilie who interviewed you?'

'What about him?'

'He tried to sweet-talk the Braemar registrar, too.'

'I guessed he would do that.'

'Bet you never guessed Smilie wasn't the only one,' said Myler. 'That registrar must have thought this was like paid overtime.'

'Shit! You mean another journalist?'

'A guy with a foreign accent,' said Myler. 'He phoned the registry office a couple of months back. He claimed to be working for the West German government.'

'What was he after?'

'The same everybody else was after: a copy of the birth certificate.'

'Did the registrar agree?'

'She told him she would check with the grandmother first. She agreed, as long as the German gave his contact number.'

Myler loved to string out a story and went back to work on his Guinness so that McKenna had to ask in the end.

'Did Mrs Cloutier get the number?'

'Oh, she got it all right.'

'*And?*'

'It's the main switchboard at Stammheim prison in Stuttgart.'

'You are a bastard,' said McKenna.

'So I am,' said Myler. 'Now you'd better tell me what happened in Braemar.'

By 2.30 the lounge was down to two men at opposite ends of bar stools, drinking with weary determination and pretending not to notice each other.

McKenna gave him a short history of the family snaps, Blair Lodge and Janek the Pole. He even mentioned the taxi driver and Bruce the dog, but left out the bit about Mrs Cloutier's and her war children from Glasgow.

Myler listened to the end and then carefully took his time over another roll-up.

'Braemar,' he said. 'Funny place. A sort of sheep-shagger's paradise, isn't it? That old burd and the mute sound interesting. Did you say the dog is called Bruce?'

'I did. But why do you ask?'

'It just put me in mind of a guy in the regiment.'

'That's a bit of a long shot, isn't it?'

Myler carried on as if he hadn't heard.

'He came from somewhere near Braemar and there can't be many of *them* around. Interesting guy. His operational name was Bruce: Robert Bruce, as in Robert *the* Bruce, the guy who hid in a cave with an itsy-bitsy spider.'

McKenna took a deep breath before he asked, 'You think that was Lulu's lad?'

'I suppose it could be. Bruce was one of us, no doubt about that. He was in the Hereford Mafia – 22 SAS to you – but got bombed out around '73.'

'What happened?'

'He beat the shit out of a couple of locals in one of the Hereford boozers, probably over a burd. Not exactly punishable by firing squad, so he got a talking-to and a warning from the CO. He had to go and apologise to the locals. Fair dos, but then I heard he failed his medical.'

'Hadn't he passed a medical when he joined?'

'Of course he passed his medical, but you have to be tested every six months. The second time round they found he was epileptic.'

'What kind of epilepsy?'

'How would I know?' Myler growled. 'I'm nae fuckin' doctor. If it took a medical to find out it couldn't have been that serious. No one ever mentioned him throwing a wobbler on duty. He had to leave the service, though.'

Myler let McKenna think about that before he added, 'It might not have stopped his full-time job, anyway.'

'What full-time job?'

'You have to find work and most are only good at one thing. Some get jobs as bodyguards for foreign dictators and others go into covert operations, doing the dirty stuff for governments. They are like freelances everywhere, including newspapers, I would think. They're not staff, so all their missions are deniable. If they get caught, or killed, a government can always disclaim them. It saves a few quid on tax and company pensions, too.'

'You seem to know a lot about this guy. I thought the SAS were supposed to be secretive.'

'Well, you don't go on holiday together, and you might not recognise someone in the street, but you hear things. Some are better known than others, particularly the one we are talking about.'

'Meaning his illness?'

'Sort of.'

'You must have an opinion.'

'My opinion is he is still involved in covert operations.'

The bar staff were busy emptying the ashtrays and stocking up for early doors. Myler waited until they had finished on their table before he continued.

'Did you ever read about that plane hijack that ended up in a shoot-out in Mogadishu?' he asked.

'About five years ago, wasn't it?'

'The baddies were Palestinians and, like most terrorists, they wanted money and comrades released from prisons. It was a Lufthansa flight and most of the passengers were German so Bonn sent in a special service unit: GSG 9. They are all former cops, which doesn't necessarily make them bad people, and they are quite efficient. To cut a long story short, by the time they landed at Mogadishu the terrorists ran out of patience, shot the pilot and threw him out onto the runway. There was a bit of a stand-off while people worked out what to do next. It turned out then that GSG 9 had the use of two boys from 22 SAS to help.'

'I assume Bruce was one of them.'

'He was *not* one of them,' Myler said testily. 'I told you, he failed his medical. If you stop interrupting I'll tell you the best bit. The regiment had got new stun grenades for confined quarters, a 737 being about as confined as you could get. So in went the grenades and in went GSG 9 and out went the terrorists. All the passengers were rescued unharmed. Good operation.'

'Where does Bruce come into it?'

'The two SAS guys weren't German speakers so Bonn found a Brit who was fluent. The idea was for him to do the translations between the SAS boys and the GSG 9 team: English to German and back again. Our two guys were never there officially and just vanished as soon as the job was done. The third guy didn't travel with them. So for a long time there was a rumour there'd been a third man in the Mogadishu operation and he had been working for Bonn.'

'God, that's a hell of a story.'

'It gets better. I told you how terrorists operate: the Palestinians wanted leaders of the Red Army Faction released from jail. Within a day of the Mogadishu gang getting smoked the RAF leaders topped themselves. Or, as they say, it was "alleged" that they topped themselves.'

'By any chance was it that prison in Stuttgart who has just lost one of their officers and who phoned a newspaper in Glasgow just before he died?'

'You're catching on now, McKenna. I'll have another pint.'

McKenna was approaching binge territory, so he stuck to a half. Myler seemed to be there for the night so he excused himself to the loo, found an empty cubicle and put a new tape in the recorder.

'Is there any way I can get in touch with those SAS guys?' he asked when he came back, feeling like Michael Corleone plotting to shoot that bent cop in a New York restaurant. Myler still hadn't noticed the tape, or had stopped caring by then.

'No,' he replied. 'They are both still operational, and there's no guarantee they even met Bruce. I don't know anyone in GSG 9, either.'

'What became of Bruce after Mogadishu?'

Myler considered this for a time.

'I think that's as far as I go,' he said.

'Come on, Myler!'

'I'm being serious. If you want to follow it up I'd go and talk to your boss about my book idea. After that, persuade him to put you on a flight to Stuttgart. Then you can do some investigations of your own.'

'I can't see him going for that.'

'Well, you're not going to get far sitting on your arse in Albion Street. The Germans will have records somewhere about captured SOE agents and what the Gestapo got up to in Paris. Believe it or not, they are better at keeping details like that than us. You might even get that exclusive you've been looking for. I'll even give you a headline: *EYE FOR AN EYE*, you could call it.'

'You're *certain* about that?'

'It's pretty obvious, isn't it? Someone has been evening the score about something that happened during the war. Good luck to him is what I say.'

'So you believe in revenge, too?'

'Course I do. If it was someone in my family I'd want to know what had happened and who did it, and then I'd sort it out.'

'What about the German bombers who killed your ma – mine, too?'

Myler's response was quite logical when McKenna thought properly about it.

'We're not going to find the guy who dropped the bomb, are we? I'm not going to take out every Luftwaffe pilot from the last war. It's a bit easier if a German drunk phones you and admits he knows all about a murder.'

McKenna paid for the drinks and crisps and tipped the barman a quid for some spare receipts. Myler looked set for the night.

'Don't forget my bread,' he shouted as McKenna left. 'And don't ever mention the war to a German.'

McKenna took a bus home and arrived back at 4.30 p.m. He was in a happy, half pissed mode and as he climbed the steep stairs he even hummed to himself in competition with the heavy rain outside. Then he stopped.

He smelled something nice just as he saw the black leather pants and slingbacks on the steps. The sun from the fourth-floor skylight high above lit half her features but left the other half in shadow and, for the first time, he noticed how small her feet were. McKenna hadn't drunk enough to ask her what she was doing there and, for now, she wasn't going to tell him.

CHAPTER 26.

The lights inside the Daimler-Benz offices were on and it was still only mid afternoon. Bux bent his head so he could see the huge clock on the Daimler-Benz Untertürkheim sign high above: 3.43 p.m., Wednesday, October 6, 1982 – or, as Bux preferred, six days, 144 hours, 8,640 minutes left to retirement.

Bux had never been the sort to indulge in navel-gazing, but Silke had been right: he should have retired in 1977 when he had the chance. She had been quite brutal about it. He was slowing down and should leave it to younger men. He was too heavy, even for the hard stuff. He was beginning to resemble that old Communist leader Khrushchev on television, or England's Henry VIII in those Holbein paintings. She tried everything, quoting from an old poem about the 'days of wine and roses' and how short they were. If he retired then he would see more of the grandchildren, make that tour of Europe he had promised her for so long and spend the rest of his time as an affable, if rather large, lotus-eater.

Bux had never been noted for his affability.

He blamed his bouts of bad temper on overwork, which was probably true, although some *Kripo* colleagues insisted he had always been like that. The surgeon who had removed the bullet from his right leg after a gun battle outside a Hamburg branch of Deutsche Bank in '57 may have been right.

'You'll have a lot of arthritis in those ankles,' he warned. 'I think you will be quite short-tempered in your old age.' How right he was.

Bux came out of his soul-searching as soon as rain began to batter the roof of the Mercedes like bullets from a gunship. He turned to Lang and told him, politely, to switch off the radio and to pull out his notes.

'Read out the section about Paris in the Hubers' interview,' he said.

Police officers seldom had shorthand and relied on abbreviated notes, but Lang's attempt was close enough.

'Frau Huber said, "I remember it well now. A French girl with beret; taken in Paris; snowing. Quite a large photograph, though blurred. Three Wehrmacht soldiers with her by the Eiffel Tower, and none looking at the camera".'

'And the missing photograph?' said Bux.

'The landlady remarked about the front cover of a photograph which said "Lulu and Friends". Frau Huber then insisted that the girl was called Lulu.'

Bux nodded and said, 'Rather odd, is it not, that a man of his import could not tell the difference between Paris in summer and Paris in winter? Herr Adler is hiding something.'

'But Kommissar, I had details from the Federal Archive,' Lang insisted, not for the first time. 'The 7th Panzer Division never returned to Paris after 1940. Why would Herr Adler fib about something like that? The Hubers must have made a mistake.'

'Landladies never make mistakes, Lang. Landladies are nosy. They know *exactly* what is in a tenant's apartment, and that includes his private photographs.'

'Perhaps the men in that photograph were from different divisions.'

Bux had already thought that through.

'Soldiers in a foreign land stick together,' he said. 'They are territorial in many ways. You would not find members of the Heer wandering round Paris with the *Luftwaffe* or the *Kriegsmarine*. They would stay with their division, even the same platoon members. Men from Stuttgart would stick with other men from Stuttgart – and don't forget that Rückeran volunteered, so he had the choice. Didn't Adler say that he and Rückeran joined the 7th together?'

Lang opened his glove compartment to find some of his mother's chocolate cake and offered some to Bux.

'I'm on a diet,' Bux said huffily.

'Why didn't you mention the snow to Herr Adler?' Lang wanted to know.

Bux regarded that as criticism and he responded icily,

'I think I told you before, Lang, it is best to keep a few things to oneself when talking to a suspect. If you tell them too much they will head for the hills and you'll never see them again. I wanted to keep Adler guessing.'

Bux was deciding between Frau Lang's chocolate cake or another cigarette when, suddenly, the lights on the cars of Adler's bodyguards flashed on and off.

'*Hello* … see that, Lang?' said Bux, pointing at Adler, who was hurrying towards the car park. 'Herr Adler's phone call must have been urgent.'

Lang looked at Bux and Bux looked back as Adler and his bodyguards drove off at speed.

'Do we pursue?' asked Lang, and Bux was still considering that when the car radio crackled into life.

'Another one, Kommissar,' said Hertzog who was in something of a panic.

'*Another what, goddam it?*' Bux shouted back.

'A man fell off the castle walls at Ittersbach.'

'And? People are always falling off castle walls.'

'His name was Fiedler.'

'Hertzog, I swear to God...'

'Manfred Fiedler, born in Sigmaringer Straße, Stuttgart 4, private first class in the 7th Panzer division from 1939 to 1945.'

Then, much quieter, 'He was on our list of interviews, Kommissar.'

Bux was already putting on his seat belt.

'I can be in Ittersbach in forty-five minutes,' he told Hertzog. 'Baum and you will follow as soon as possible. Is there a local police station in Ittersbach?'

'A state volunteer officer, name of Klein. He owns a small factory there.'

'Good. Phone him and tell him we are on our way.'

'Something else, Kommissar,' said Hertzog before Bux hung up.

'Hurry, then,' said Bux.

'There was a telephone call from the deputy governor at Stammheim.'

'*Saying what?*'

'He said Birgita Springer is well enough to see you.'

CHAPTER 27.

B ux remembered Ittersbach from his courting days, late in the summer of '49.

Germany had just been divided into East and West and everyone was waiting for the new 'economic miracle'. The two lovers cycled all the way from Stuttgart to Baden-Baden, deep into the Black Forest. They slept in a tent with room for one and cooked on open fires. Every day was summer then. They laughed when they struggled to cope with the new Deutschmark. Money wasn't important then, either.

As for Ittersbach, both had hated the place from the start.

It was one of those Nordic, chocolate-box retreats where the locals still refused to admit a war had ever occurred. Silke despised *Oktoberfest*, where men got drunk in that foolishness unique to Germans: red-faced, loud and obnoxious. Bux could put up with the drink, but not all those prancing men in leather pants.

The village's little castle, *Die Teufelstreppe*, or the Devil's Ladder, was not up to much, either. This thirteenth-century fortification had been uninhabited since 1875 and had fallen into total disrepair after the war. The only things that remained were the gargoyles, some ancient cannons and the tour buses with visitors, who could climb to the top battlements for the spectacular view of the Black Forest.

The death of Manfred Fiedler had not stopped the *Oktoberfest* revellers at Ittersbach on this occasion. Several men, and two or three women, were already drunk when Bux and Lang arrived. An oompah band, trailed by dozens of girls in straw hats – some red and some black – marched, radios boomed and several campers, surrounded by dozens of tents, were washing in an outdoor sink on the edge of the village.

Klein, the volunteer officer, was overweight and far too old for police work, but he had had the sense to use a blanket to cover the body. A dozen *Landespolizei* stood around, smoking and talking among themselves and waiting for someone to tell them what to do. Bux ordered Lang to organise some of them into groups to knock on each door for potential witnesses while the rest were to concentrate on the campers and their tents.

Bux lifted the blanket and pulled it back.

Fiedler had landed like an accomplished high diver. The face was crushed and unrecognisable, but most of the rest was intact, with legs and arms all pointing in the right direction. He had been wearing lederhosen and a shirt which had been white, but was now deep red.

Bux stepped back a stride and strained his neck up at the battlements high above. The rock's face from base to top was sheer.

'One hundred metres,' said Klein, who must have read Bux's mind. 'No one could ever survive that.'

'Has he been moved?' Bux asked.

'He has not been touched,' insisted Klein and then, perplexed, asked, 'Why do you say that, Herr Kommissar?'

'I am just wondering,' said Bux as Lang put up some tarpaulin fencing to keep away the inquisitive, 'how

205

Fiedler managed to land six feet away from the bottom of the rock face. Or do you think he took a flying leap?'

'You think it was suicide, then, Kommissar?' Klein asked.

'No, I do not think it was suicide,' said Bux.

He left it to the forensic teams, the photographer and Doctor Dietrich – 'and how are you today, Kommissar?' – and followed Klein up the Devil's Ladder.

The spiral stone steps were steep and narrow, with the awkward stride length of all ancient castles. It would be difficult for most people to squeeze past, but particularly for Bux. For Klein, too, and after ten metres he had to stop and sit down.

'These … stairs … will be the death … of me,' he wheezed. He watched as Bux lit up and added, 'I … have never … had to face … a situation like this here.'

'A situation like what?' asked Bux.

'An accidental death in Ittersbach,' explained Klein. 'People do drink too much during *Oktoberfest*, but this is appalling.' Then as if this might explain everything, 'Herr Fiedler, of course, was not a local.'

Bux sat down on the stair and said, 'You had better tell me about him, then.'

Fiedler and his wife had lived in the village for some fifteen years and owned the *Gasthaus* Fiedler, a small guest house in Drasco Straße. They were popular with the locals, said Klein, though still thought of as 'city people'. The guest house would never have made the Fiedlers rich, according to Klein, but they had a regular clientele.

'Many returned on a yearly basis,' said Klein. 'Frau Fiedler was famous for her *Lebkuchen* – gingerbread – and there were nice views of the Black Forest hills from the bedroom windows. Or so I am told.'

Bux, flicking his cigarette stub out of the turret's window

206

and said, 'Do you know anything about him, apart from Frau Fiedler's gingerbread?'

'Like what, Kommissar?'

'His background, his family … did he have any friends?'

Klein was aghast.

'Oh, we never ask things like that in Ittersbach,' he said. 'We are proud of our privacy here. Speak no evil, hear no evil is our view.'

'Tell me what Fielder was doing at the top of the castle' said Bux.

'It's a tradition on the first Monday of *Oktoberfest*. At sunset those fit enough always climb the Devil's Ladder. There is a firework display which is quite spectacular.'

'But not as spectacular as a man falling a hundred metres?' said Bux.

'Herr Kommissar?'

'I am just being facetious. Please continue, Herr Klein.'

'Fiedler acted as a sort of unofficial guide, though he had never been asked. He was a non-drinker, see? He showed people to the top and then made sure they got down in one piece.'

'Would any of those people be under the weather?

'Herr Bux?'

'Inebriated. This Devil's Ladder looks dangerous to me, particularly if someone has had too much.'

'Some people go at it to excess, but it's fairly safe,' insisted Klein.

'Tell me about the accident. What did you hear?'

'The firework display had just started when he fell, though others insist the display was over by then. All *were* convinced that Fiedler had tripped. He must have lost his sight in the gloom, or maybe he had had too much drink.'

'You just told me he was not a drinker.'

'There's always a first time, Kommissar. Shall we continue to the top?'

Bux spent over an hour on the battlements. He walked from one end to the other, occasionally stopping to look down at the village. There were several discarded cigarettes, which he told Lang to bag, and several used fireworks, which must have landed from the village when the show began. He tried to imagine the death because that was all he had: the victim leading his party to the top in slow, single file, the searchlights from the village square and the fireworks, the killer waiting for the party to look away, or perhaps trusting them to be useless with drink.

It was no accident, and no suicide. That much was plain. The battlements, where bows and bricks were once flung at enemies, were three metres high and two metres apart and guarded by metal railings. Fiedler – a big, heavy man, according to Klein, must have been lifted and flung over the edge by someone even stronger.

Bux was still considering that when he realised the pager inside his jacket pocket was beeping. He hurried down the Devil's Ladder stairs as fast as he dared.

One of the *Landespolizei*, a boy about Lang's age, claimed to have found 'a witness', a railway worker at Ettingen station, three kilometres down the valley and a stop on the train journey from Stuttgart to Karlsruhe.

Bux's 'witness' turned out to be Rainer Hasek, the stationmaster for over twenty years. Herr Hasek was not exactly senile, but he was certainly no speedster when it came to discussion. He also had that infuriating habit of all country folk of never getting straight to the point.

Herr Hasek had not been involved in *Oktoberfest* because he had been on duty. That was why he was still wearing his railway uniform, he said. He heard about the Fiedler incident over the radio and hastened over to help. He claimed he had seen 'a suspicious character', who bought a ticket at Ettingen station about three hours before Fiedler fell to his death.

'Excuse me,' said Bux, who was recovering from the Devil's Ladder climb and was not in the mood for prevarication, 'but *what* was suspicious about that?'

'It was a man with a dirty, unshaven appearance,' said Herr Hasek.

'Is that a crime in the villages of the Black Forest?' cried Bux.

'No, Kommissar, it is not a crime here,' said Herr Hasek calmly. 'But I thought it unusual to see a man wearing green trousers, German dragon boots and a winter parka around here. He was also carrying a huge rucksack.'

Bux had underestimated Herr Hasek, so asked politely, 'Where was he going?'

'He paid for a one-way ticket.'

'*Where was he going*? West, I presume?'

'He was going east, Kommissar. He bought a ticket to Stuttgart.'

'And did he get the train to Stuttgart?'

'Not while I was there. As I said, I hurried to Ittersbach when I heard about the fall. In any case, the station office is closed after six.'

'When he bought his ticket did you see his face?'

'He had a hood, and it was quite dark.'

'Did he speak?'

'Three words: "Single to Stuttgart". He did not even say "please".'

'Right,' said Bux decisively, 'tell me this: if a stranger intended to travel from your station to Ittersbach what would be his best way?'

'Five minutes by car,' said Herr Hasek. Then there was a little pause before he added, 'Though of course he would not be driving.'

'Why so?'

'In their wisdom the Ittersbach elders have decided that vehicles would be banned from the village during *Oktoberfest*.'

'What about walking?'

'Thirty minutes. There's a track through the forest used by local loggers. It's popular with hikers on the Stuttgart/ Baden-Baden trail.'

Bux thought furiously.

If a killer wanted to distance himself from pursuers a car was ideal, but not as unpredictable as walking because police would never expect that. A strong hiker should get from Stuttgart to Ittersbach inside two days and Rückeran had been murdered eight days ago: ample time for anyone. Fiedler's killer must have bought his ticket in advance, walked from Ettingen to Ittersbach and then back before taking the Stuttgart train at a time when there would be no stationmaster.

He tried to think of the forests, the tracks and his walks with Silke all those years ago. It was similar to the Ardennes in many ways: steeply wooded and difficult to find an army, let alone a man on his own. There were herdsman's barns which would be unused in late spring or early winter, so ideal for a man on the run. He could use the gravel roads on the Stuttgart/Baden-Baden trail during the night and sleep during the day. Damn it, he thought. Someone has done his planning.

Bux knew he was struggling. As things stood his best hope was Birgita Springer, although it might be unwise to put faith in a member of a terrorist group who had just tried to commit suicide. He had solved cases swiftly in the past, in less than a day on one occasion, but he knew now he might have to wait for his wristwatch, pension and trip to Europe with Silke. He could pass the case on, of course, as some had suggested, but to do that was as abhorrent as an unsolved murder to him. Setbacks and challenges had always brought out the stubborn old mule in Markus Bux, too.

When Baum and Hertzog arrived all four of Bux's team watched as the second member of the 7th Panzer Division to be killed in eight days was bagged into a cadaver pouch and carted into an ambulance for the trip to Stuttgart's city morgue.

Bux sensed a combative mood among them, too, for they didn't need to wait to be told what was needed next: house-to-house searches, interviews with locals – if any had seen a foreigner – and who had climbed the Devil's Ladder on the fateful night.

'I want to hear from everyone,' said Bux, 'and that includes the drunks.'

CHAPTER 28.

There was something different about her, thought McKenna, as she wandered round his flat, opening doors here and picking things up there; a bit like a potential homebuyer.

When she sneered at the flying ducks above the fireplace and looked closely at his *Green Lady* painting on the wall he realised what had changed.

'Your specs?' he said. 'Do you have them contacts now?'

'I've got twenty-twenty vision,' Lucienne Batch replied. 'I don't need specs. I always use clear lenses for work.'

'What for?'

'Men don't make passes at girls who wear glasses,' she said, 'and the scarier you look the more people do as they're told.'

She moved to the opposite wall, where McKenna hung his film posters.

'What have we here?' she said, though she obviously knew. 'Ingrid Bergman always having Paris, Audrey Hepburn on a scooter in Rome, Rita Hayworth putting the blame on Mame … and who's this?'

'Louise Brooks as Lulu in *Pandora's Box*,' said McKenna. 'Weird, isn't it?'

'What's weird about it?'

'*Lulu*: Paris, and all that. Mrs Cloutier said Lulu nicked the name from the movie. Incidentally, has anyone ever said you look like Louise Brooks with that hairstyle? The film was made in Berlin, too. Weren't you over there for a time?'

'No resemblance *whatsoever*,' she said emphatically and moved on to the single framed photograph on top of the television.

'Your little babushka?' she asked. 'What was she called?'

'Anastasia.'

'That's original, isn't it?' she smirked. 'What happened?'

'Do you really want to know?'

'Moderately interested,' she agreed. McKenna told her,

'She came over with a trade delegation from Minsk in 1979. They were about to start on a new metro and thought Glasgow underground fitted the bill. Her English was good so she did some translating. I quite liked her, for all her foibles.'

'And what were her foibles?'

'Phone calls home that went on for hours, the childish tantrums and her ability to spend money like Imelda Marcos.'

'Your only picture?' she asked curiously. 'Where are all your family snaps?'

'There aren't any. They went up in the Clydebank fires.'

'Your parents?'

'Dad was away in the RAF. Mum was killed in the first Luftwaffe raid in '41.'

Batch looked only moderately sorry and immediately moved on.

'I assume you were evacuated?'

'How did you know?'

'I just guessed.'

213

'What about you?' asked McKenna.

'What about me?'

He tried a little quip and said, 'What did you do in the war, Mummy? You can tell me if you want.'

Mrs Batch stared at him until he was forced to look away.

'I don't want,' she said.

She was back in full boss mode after that.

'Time to get on with business,' she said. 'I haven't much time. You smell like a brewery, so I guess you saw your army mate?'

'I've just come from him,' McKenna admitted.

'And…?'

McKenna gave her the abridged version and when it was done she dropped the Myler tape into her posh leather satchel.

'What's next for the great Sherlock Holmes?' she asked then.

There was no smile and McKenna didn't like the sarcasm, but he wasn't in the mood so he just told her. 'I was going to try the Ministry of Defence,' he said. 'I want to see if there are any details about this James Rezin. I'm tempted to tackle Mrs Cloutier, too. I'm *definitely* going to contact the Braemar registry office.'

The temperature plunged a little then.

'What the hell for?'

'It was Myler's suggestion. He thought the birth and marriage details were a bit odd and we should find out more.'

'*It was Myler's suggestion*?' she demanded. 'Is he editing the paper now? Believe me, he's pointing you in the wrong direction. As for Mrs Cloutier, I don't think it's a good

214

idea to hassle an old lady.'

'I've no intention of *hassling* her.'

Mrs Batch crinkled her nose and thought for a second.

'I've got a better idea,' she said.

It might have been the way she said that, or the black diary she pulled out of her satchel, but there was a horrible feeling of foreboding then.

'Do you still have your passport?' she said.

'I think so,' he replied cautiously.

'You either have, or you haven't.'

'I have, somewhere. Why do you ask?'

The black diary was held up towards him like a court witness reading the oath.

'You are booked on the 1.05 p.m. LH2473, Glasgow to Stuttgart, changing at Heathrow. It should take about three hours.'

She held her head on one side and waited for his reaction.

'I'm supposed to fly to Germany?' was all he could think of. Then he began to look for a way out, smiling at her with what he thought she might see as affability.

'I'm flattered,' he said, 'but I am not an investigative reporter. There're several in the office who would do a better job. I can't see me coping in Germany: I don't have the lingo and I don't drive. I don't even know where Stuttgart is.'

'I'll look after that,' said Mrs Batch. 'I think we'll get on fine.'

McKenna was sobering up and he felt a headache coming on in competition with the gut rumbles.

'I'm not sure about this at all,' he said.

She pointed a finger, Kitchener-style, and said stiffly, 'Do you have any ambition? Are you one of those members of staff who see dignity in failures?'

Then a little bit of flattery and something else. She stretched out on the settee, told him to sit alongside and said, 'You've done well so far.'

'I've been lucky,' McKenna said, correctly.

'Well, *use* that luck,' she said, digging him in the ribs. 'Most people would die to be involved in a story like this, particularly if it meant a trip to Berlin.'

'Berlin?'

'I meant Stuttgart.' She thought for a while and then poured him another drop of gravy. 'If we crack the story and file it in time I could show you round West Berlin; do the tourist bit.'

McKenna thought he had spotted the exit.

'I hate to say this,' he said, 'but the NUJ won't like the idea of a non-union member working on a news story. Have you thought of that?'

'How are they going to know, unless you tell them? I'm owed time off, anyway. I could be on holiday for all they know. If it damages your ego we can say I'm your secretary, that you needed a translator or someone who knows the area.'

'What about Bloom?'

Mrs Batch shrugged non-committedly and said, 'I've cleared it with him and he knows what to say if the union objects. He also knows a good thing when he sees it.'

Then it sunk in.

'A good thing when he sees it?' said McKenna. 'That's why you chose me. That's why I became so bloody indispensable all of a sudden?'

Mrs Batch did not respond and McKenna ploughed on,

'You wanted a reporter who could do some donkey work, but wouldn't pinch too much of the glory. You needed an

216

NUJ member to go with you, am I right? That's why you picked the office thicko.'

Mrs Batch's smile could have been one of triumph.

'Oh, I wouldn't put it quite like that,' she said.

She gave him another minute, but by then both knew what he would say.

'I assume you'll do all the driving?' he said limply.

'Correct. The translations, too.'

'We'll need some photographs?'

'You're the David Bailey for this one.'

'I'm not a snapper. The NUJ chapel won't like that, either.'

'*They won't know.*'

The diary joined the tape in her satchel and she stood up, her job done.

'Make sure you're there before 11.30 a.m.,' she said. 'There's a forty-minute wait at Heathrow, which should be enough time for a drink. I've fixed up the travel vouchers and tickets. We're staying in a hotel near the centre: cheap, but good enough for us. If it makes you any happier, it also has a bar.'

McKenna tried to sound caustic. 'Anything else while you're here?'

She didn't answer and was on the way out when, totally out of the blue, she stopped and pecked him three times on the cheek, French style: left, right, left again. He blushed. She smiled and told him, 'Don't forget your passport.'

She had reached the ground floor before he thought of something to say and shouted down, 'See you tomorrow. Looking forward to it.'

She didn't stop and didn't look round.

'I like your outfit,' he called, feeling even more stupid

than before.

Then she did stop.

'Dressed to kill,' she said, before disappearing into the streets of Clydebank.

CHAPTER 29.

Birgita Springer, two armed guards, one doctor and a nurse – both in uniforms, too – had a complete floor of the US Army Hospital at Bad Cannstadt to themselves.

A putty-faced female guard with a bossy American twang showed Bux and Lang the way and told them, 'You have half an hour.'

Bux peered through the window. The girl was dressed in a hospital gown but had been allowed to sit on a chair on the side of her bed. She was reading *Threepenny Novel* by Bertolt Brecht, a favourite of left-wingers, and looked pale and sorry for herself.

Birgita Springer was attractive, even without make-up, but hard-faced, like many female prisoners. The needle marks on both arms told a story, too, and Bux reminded himself that addicts were invariably highly strung and manipulative.

Bux stepped back so Lang could have a look.

'I want you to handle this one,' he said.

'Are you sure, Kommissar?' said Lang anxiously.

Bux explained. 'She is more likely to talk to someone her own age.'

'Where should I start, Herr Kommissar?'

Bux's sigh was like a gust of wind.

'Where everyone starts,' he said. 'Age, place of birth, childhood, parents, lost innocence, the RAF and her time in jail. *Then* we can discuss Rückeran.'

'What if she clams up?'

Bux squeezed Lang's arm and slapped him, quite firmly, on both cheeks.

'She won't clam up, Lang,' he said. 'You'll soon have her jumping all over you like a little puppy. Show her some sympathy, show off your muscles – but don't try and intimidate her. Don't pepper her with questions. Let her do the talking.'

In the end she did do most of the talking, chattering away like a little bird, and far too astute for Lang. He introduced both detectives and used her first name, which was a good start, but then he began to blush, and of course she spotted that immediately.

Birgita Springer was born to comfortably middle-class parents in Frankfurt, where her mother and father owned a health food shop. After their divorce she dropped out of college and moved from student protester to something more radical. She was still a teenager when she joined the Red Army Faction.

Springer was not a terrorist, or so she claimed. She had never carried a gun and would not know how to use one, but that did not stop her being sentenced to ten years for firearm offences in '77. A month later she joined a dozen other RAF detainees on the seventh floor of Stammheim Supermax.

They were single-cell, she said, but she was allowed out two hours a day. She disliked most of the RAF group, Andreas Baader in particular, and soon found herself isolated from the rest of the people in the prison.

'But not from Herr Rückeran,' said Lang.

'In prison you need an attachment,' she replied, widening

her eyes and fluttering her lashes. 'It does not have to be a relationship – just someone you can talk to, who may have the same interests. It keeps one sane. You could describe Herr Rückeran as a father figure. He gave me advice and we had similar tastes in books and music.'

'It all began to fall apart in 1981,' she said.

'He told me he had found an apartment outside the complex and it was best if we didn't speak from then on. He had been disciplined because we were "too close". That is what he said, anyway.'

'You didn't believe that?'

'Of course I didn't believe it,' she sighed. 'There seemed to be no reason for it. It's a fact of life that guards all have their favourite prisoners and vice versa, but I was certainly no Gudrun Ensslin or any of the other RAF leaders. I was not a troublemaker and never once considered an escape. Incidentally, have you worked out who killed him yet?'

'Rückeran? No. But we have our opinions.'

Springer's response was almost a reprimand.

'Your opinion has not taken you very far, has it? You should have asked me.'

'And what could you tell us, Birgita?'

'It was a RAF insider … but not a RAF insider,' she said insistently.

'That is rather enigmatic, Birgita. Can you elaborate?'

'I need a cigarette first.'

Bux gave her the remains of his pack, and she must have been on jail rations because she lit up a second while the first one was still going. She leaned back in her chair, as close to contentment as a prisoner could be. Then she told them,

'The man who killed Herr Rückeran is a foreigner.'

The female guard peered into the cell and pointed

meaningfully at her watch, but gave up when Bux responded with a fearsome frown.

'Your insider?' said Lang. 'A member of the RAF was a foreigner?'

'There have always been foreigners,' she said. 'There was a Swedish girl who called herself Greta and an Irishman called Patsy O'Hara who turned out to be French as soon as he opened his mouth. Then there was the man you should be looking for: Robert Bruce, the Scot.'

Lang did well, thought Bux. He showed interest, but avoided excitement. He kept his eyes on his notes when he replied.

'Robert Bruce, Birgita? A Scot, did you say?'

'I studied medieval history at school and I know Robert the Bruce was the king of Scotland during a war of independence. The famous story was that the Scots had taken a beating and he was hiding in a cave, wondering what the hell to do next. He was inspired by a spider spinning its web time after time, until it succeeded. When I mentioned the story to Robert he smiled, which was rare for him.'

'Tell us about this Robert.'

'He appeared in the spring of 1976 and he hit it off with most of the girls, me included. He was in his thirties. His German was excellent, though you can always tell a foreigner if you listen long enough. Robert Bruce wasn't his real name, obviously. I don't know what it was, so it's no good asking—'

Bux interrupted. 'Did he ever mention a family?'

'No. He never spoke of friends and family. He managed what none of us ever could: he kept a veil around himself; he was a mystery.'

'You were obviously quite close to him,' said Lang.

The girl smiled and licked her lips, like a little cat.

'Close?' she asked.

Lang was blushing again so Bux decided to intervene.

'I think my colleague means, "Were you friendly with him?"'

'Yes, I suppose you could call it that. We were *all* friends. Boys and girls shared baths, sat on each other's knees and slept together. It didn't make us engaged or anything.'

Lang was oddly prudish for a young man and tried to move on.

'If we send you one of our sketch artists do you think you can remember some of the salient features?'

'*The salient features?*'

That was enough for Bux.

'His looks, Fraulein,' he growled.

'Black hair and black eyes, but a pale face: a pretty boy. Charismatic, you would say: one of those people you notice in a crowd. He was below average height but muscular. As I said, good-looking, but there was always a sense of danger about him. I don't think people would want to upset him. There was always this feeling that when he walked out of the door you might never see him again. I also remember a scar on his face. I think it was a birthmark.'

'Left or right?'

'On his right, I think. Yes, I am sure: it was on his right-hand side. Oh, and his army issue watch: a huge black thing with different time zones. He said he could use it to forecast the weather and know the height of hills.'

'I assume he carried weapons?'

'Of course, though I don't remember him actually using one.'

'What was his function, then?'

'With the girls?' she said, but stopped smiling when she realised Bux was not amused. 'There's not much a lot more I can tell you. He took part in some of the bank robberies, usually to keep an eye on the street. He did some of the training, choosing firearms and discussing forthcoming operations. He knew a lot about guns.'

She started to fidget, and the army doctor appeared at the window again. Bux thought they may have to wind it up. Then, totally out of the blue,

'Why ask me this? You know all about him, anyway.'

Bux looked at Lang and Lang stared back.

'How would we know all this, Fraulein?'

'I thought police officials shared *everything*. You didn't know he was working for Bonn? That there was a fifth columnist inside the RAF? That's what I meant by "a RAF insider, but not an insider". Understand now? Another cigarette, please.'

Bux had run out so he sent Lang out to scrounge some from somewhere.

'What was he doing for Bonn?' said Bux.

'You *really* don't know?' The girl was enjoying it now. Bux shouted so loudly she almost jumped off her chair.

'No more games, Fraulein,' he warned. 'Just remember this is a murder investigation, and it would be best if you tell us what you know. Things can go in your favour, or I can make sure they do *not*. I gather you are expecting parole soon?'

She was more cooperative after that.

'I told you he arrived in '76?' she said. 'All of a sudden the RAF were struggling. The police seemed to know all the plans in advance. You knew that much, Herr Bux? There were several arrests and a succession of failures: that American warmonger Haig escaped a landmine at Mons in Belgium; an attack on an American Security Police office at Kaiserslautern was a disaster. It didn't take long to work it all out.'

'You never mentioned it to anyone in the RAF?'

'I had my reasons,' she said. Bux didn't push.

'Wasn't there a weeding process in the RAF? He was a foreigner, after all.'

'A lawyer called Haag looked after things like that – checking people's backgrounds and warning off the ones they didn't fancy. He's doing ten years in Landsberg, as you are no doubt aware, so obviously he didn't know, either. Robert never had *any* such problems.'

'Why a foreigner, though?'

'Less likely to be caught,' she said. 'If you were looking for a RAF killing would you start with foreign passports? Of course not: you head for Berlin or Hamburg, even Stuttgart, and round up all the German-born RAF members you can find. Right, Herr Bux?'

'Right,' said Bux ruefully. 'When did you start suspecting him?'

'Almost immediately. We were in one of the Berlin hole-ups, late at night. We were sharing a bath when he started to ask about the RAF in the sixties and seventies and the targets: police officers, judges, former Nazi party members, Gestapo ... everything. It was the sort of thing people ask. Like a school history lesson.'

Lang reappeared with a pack of Marlboro. She took another long swig of water and started on the cigarettes.

'Do you remember the Hans-Martin Schleyer affair?' she said.

'The Daimler-Benz board member?' said Bux.

'I prefer to describe him as a capitalist pig, but to each his own. Most of the leaders were in Stammheim and this was an attempt to free them. Schleyer was kidnapped on his way to work and his bodyguards were shot dead when they got in the way. It was regarded as a major coup for the RAF – kidnapping a prominent industrialist who happened to be a former Nazi SS officer.

'Bruce was fascinated by the way it had been organised: a girl pushing a pram into the road to stop the vehicles and distract the bodyguards. It was so clever. No one would suspect a mother with a child – which was really a doll – would be hiding a Uzi inside the pram. Bruce kept asking for the details: the RAF girls involved, the number of bodyguards, the pram – even the whereabouts of Daimler-Benz.'

'But I am sure there have been no copycat murders,' said Lang.

She snorted and addressed the young detective like an idiot.

'I know that. He wasn't thinking of the best way of murdering people – he was looking for RAF details he could pass on to Bonn.'

'Did he get anything from you?' asked Bux.

'Not then. I mistrusted him. Things started to go wrong after he arrived.'

'*Not then, Fraulein Springer*? Later, perhaps?'

She didn't reply and drew furiously on her cigarette.

'This is all off the record, Birgita,' said Bux.

Then she did speak, but so quietly he had to ask her to repeat it,

'I saw Bruce the night before Rückeran was murdered.'

Lang was nonplussed.

'How did you manage that?' he demanded. 'You were in jail at the time.'

Bux, who had seen it all then, answered for her. 'He came to see you inside Stammheim.' Springer nodded in agreement.

'Tell us what happened,' Bux said.

'About nine at night a guard told me there was "a

gentleman" to see me, and I was to go to one of the interview rooms. I don't get many visitors and I nearly fell off my chair when he walked in. He only stayed half an hour, and pretended to be my lawyer or something. At first he just carried on like Berlin: a little peck on the cheek to start. How was I? How's the food? How long before I was released? He had friends at Bonn who could help. Shall we meet up when I got out? I was terrified.'

'Terrified?' asked Lang. 'But why?'

The girl looked towards Bux and shook her head in disbelief.

'Where did you find this one, Herr Kommissar?'

Then she hissed at Lang, 'Look, boy, have you never heard of Death Night? There were more suicides that night than a handball team. I thought I was going to finish up the same way.'

'But Bonn reduced your sentence.'

'But I am still here, am I not?' she said. 'It all adds up now.'

'What adds up, Fraulein?'

Her lips trembled and tears began to fall on her anti-suicide blanket.

'Poor Rückeran. I should have seen it coming.'

'*Fraulein Springer*?'

'It was quite clever – the sort of tittle-tattle you take for granted. I think he said something about Bonn wanting to interview prison guards who had been around in the Baader–Meinhof days. He showed me a photograph of Herr Rückeran taking me to court for the parole hearing.'

'Rückeran was his target, then,' said Lang.

'Correct!' she shouted. 'You got something right.'

'Why kill this particular prison guard, though?'

'I don't know. You are the detective. Perhaps Herr Rückeran knew too much, or Bruce just didn't like screws.

227

Either way, I blame myself. It was a mistake to mention where he lived and his work schedule, but it didn't seem to matter at the time. They were both supposed to be working for the state, were they not?'

'Is that why you attempted suicide?' said Lang. 'You felt guilty?'

'*It wasn't a suicide attempt*,' she said derisively. 'It was to save my skin. I was making sure the government would never find me in my cell hanging from a towel. I got my retaliation in first, if you like.'

'I still don't understand, Birgita.'

'I'll give you a clue,' she said. 'Bonn does not like the idea of prisoners topping themselves now. Stammheim has something of a history of things like that, has it not? It used to be a good way of getting rid of undesirables, but you can only fool the people some of the time. Suicides in prison don't win votes for a government, either. Now, when you go back to school tomorrow, ask for the name of our new Chancellor. His name is Helmut Kohl.'

Lang was tempted, but just shrugged and didn't interrupt.

'I don't know what Kohl and his party have in mind, but one thing is for sure: they don't want to read about another suicide in Stammheim at election time. That's why I am in a military hospital, well away from the press and the public. Right, Kommissar? Something else: I thought if I made a fuss *certain* people would remember I had been promised an early release.'

'Certain people?' said Bux.

She didn't answer and looked down at the floor. Bux edged closer.

'Tell me who offered you an early release,' he said. 'You were a RAF member, and in the current climate it would be difficult to secure a release. It would need someone

228

with authority – maybe someone in charge of the anti-RAF operations. Didn't Bruce mention "friends at Bonn"? He would definitely answer to someone like that. Just tell me: *unter vier Augen* (under four eyes).'

She thought for so long Bux was about to give up, but suddenly she moved closer, held his arm with a tiny hand and whispered in his ear.

Then Bux did understand the whole ghastly operation.

CHAPTER 30.

Lucienne Batch's bonhomie had vanished somewhere between the pecks on the cheek and the Caledonia Bar at Glasgow Airport.

'It's a bit early to be drinking,' she began before the first sip of his McEwan's heavy. She didn't like his gear. 'You look like Val Doonican,' she said. 'We're supposed to be nondescript. And someone saw you coming: fancy paying nineteen quid for a Pringle sweater.'

McKenna was taken aback.

'How do you know the price?' he asked. 'I never told you.'

'You don't need to tell me,' she said without the merest hint of a smile. 'You've still got the maker's name and price on.'

She tut-tutted when he struggled to find his passport at departures and then asked, 'What's that smell?'

'Brut aftershave,' said McKenna.

'Well, it would be called *that*, wouldn't it?'

She sniggered when an air hostess on the flight to Heathrow told him that 'passengers do not pay for food and drink in flight' and took offence at anyone in a BA uniform. One was too pushy, the others too snobby and the male attendant had to be queer. McKenna thought the

Lufthansa attendants' folk costumes charming, but they weren't to Mrs Batch's taste, either.

'*Oktoberfest*,' she explained. 'Any excuse for Germans to dress like idiots and drink too much.' Two blonde Germans arrived to serve drinks and she decided, cattily, 'Here comes the hairy armpit brigade. And see the cabin skin? That's what pressurised berths do for you.' After that she shuttled as far away as she could, lest anyone thought they were together.

'We now cross France,' said a male steward with a fake suntan and dyed blond hair. 'Lille and Roubaix on right side and Bruges to left. Our friendly staff now goes round with perfume, cosmetics and spirit. Unfortunately, we have not change.'

McKenna pushed himself half up his seat to look out, but all he could see was a bit of sky and a reflection of Mrs Batch, staring back through the Perspex window.

His father may have flown this way during the war, McKenna thought, though he wasn't sure. He knew he had been a rear gunner, usually in a Wellington, and he may have mentioned France and possibly German cities, but never in any detail. McKenna would have liked to have known more, but after the usual childish questions – 'What did you do in the war, Daddy?' and 'What happens when someone dies?' – and the scornful responses, he never tried again.

McKenna had always been able to distance himself from things he didn't like or didn't want to remember, which was exactly like his father. He was certainly no Mrs Cloutier, able to spend a lifetime digging under her personal rubble, but there were questions he should have asked: the medals you kept hidden in the cupboard, Dad? What was my ma like? Above all, perhaps, where did Glasgow children go when they were evacuated during the war? Now he would never know.

The tannoy crackled, a female voice said something lengthy in German and almost at once the aircraft slowed and began its long descent.

'*Vielen Danke*,' said the younger of the blondes, who had been collecting the food trays and drink bottles when she saw McKenna had managed to rearrange the condiments and cutlery into the correct square or circle. Mrs Batch looked on, with what was either contempt or pity.

Mrs Batch was an excellent driver and handled the vehicle, a hired Beetle, like a female James Hunt, with lots of overtaking and several aggressive beeps.

'You must have been here before,' McKenna decided, because she had not once checked a map or asked directions.

No reply.

'Weird motor this, isn't it?' he said affably. 'The engine's at the back.'

Another pip of the horn followed by a left turn onto a dual carriageway.

Still no response.

'Nice-looking city, isn't it? A bit like Glasgow in parts.'

'Shut up,' said Mrs Batch.

The Mercure in Stuttgart-Nord must have been half empty because there were only a couple of cars in the underground park and no buzz of guests in the main reception area. A girl with good English took their passports details, asked for signatures and handed over the room keys.

'This is your number,' said Batch. 'The lift's over there. I'll see you in the bar in twenty minutes. Then we can decide on a plan.'

'What sort of plan?' said McKenna uneasily.

'Who does what and who goes where.'

'I thought this was a joint operation.'

'It is a joint operation, but we need to divide the tasks,' she said. 'There's no point both of us going to the same press conferences, is there? We'd look a bit stupid interviewing the same detective. Anyway, we can discuss this later.'

Then, the Batch sneer. 'Can you find your way to the lift?'

'The lift?' he asked and then realised the number on his room key said 401. 'What number are you?'

'I'm in 106,' she said.

CHAPTER 31.

B ux was told a dozen times that 'Herr Homann is unavailable,' until he found the right secretary in the right place at the right time and she agreed to pass on his message.

'Can you repeat that, Kommissar?' she asked down the crackly line. 'Did you say "Robert Bruce"? Two words: is that all?'

'That is all I need,' said Bux.

'I will pass it on to Herr Homann, but he is very busy.'

'Just do it now, please,' said Bux.

She was back within five minutes. Homann would certainly meet him – in the transit bar at Flughafen at 10 a.m.

'You are fortunate, Kommissar,' the woman added. 'You caught Herr Homann just in time. He is due to fly to the United States this morning.'

Homann was in the coffee shop close to a flight information display. The departure time for the next flight to the United States was 11.30 a.m., which gave Bux an hour, if he was lucky.

What Homann was up to in Washington DC was none of his business and Bux wasn't going to ask, though he did know the headquarters of the Federal Bureau of Investigation was on Pennsylvania Avenue and Homann had collaborated with them in the past. It was thought Homann's Operation Watersplash had been copied from the FBI dirty tricks campaigns against groups like the Black Panther Party and some Hollywood film stars. Some blamed the alleged suicide of the American actress Jean Seberg in Paris in 1979 on FBI harassment, and there had been several suicides among members of the RAF.

Homann didn't look up from his newspaper and asked, rather facetiously, 'And how was the lovely Fraulein Springer?'

'Fraulein Springer sends her regards,' said Bux, just as facetiously. He pulled out the police sketch and wafted it at Homann, who took a cursory glance and went back to his newspaper.

'I think you may recognise this man,' said Bux. 'I believe Bonn knows him quite well, too. He called himself Robert Bruce. His real name is James Rezin.'

'I believe that is the case,' said Homann.

'*You believe so*?'

Homann turned to look at Bux for the first time.

'I have never met him, but I think it is a good likeness,' he said. 'But obviously not good enough for you, Bux. Has it been circulated yet? I thought not. You would not be here talking to me otherwise.'

'But you know who he is,' said Bux. 'You might even know *where* he is. I would *love* to interview this man – but unfortunately, while one agency is trying to find James Rezin, others are doing the opposite.'

'Really, Bux,' said Homann disdainfully. 'You say I know where he is? One should be careful with such statements.'

'So you deny that James Rezin was employed by Bonn? That is not the opinion of Fraulein Springer, who knew

235

him well.'

Homann put down his newspaper.

'You are prepared to believe the word of a prison hophead who is also a member of a terrorist group?' he scoffed. 'Remember your training days at police academy, Bux? One of the first things I was taught is that one must never trust a drug addict. If she is not very careful, Fraulein Springer is going to finish up back in one of the quiet sections at Stammheim. She should remember her next parole meeting and *you*, Kommissar, should think about your pension.'

'I believe her,' insisted Bux. 'She knew Rezin and she knew Rückeran. She was also aware of your marvellous wheeze of planting a double agent inside the RAF. It must be quite annoying for you to see it all fall apart.'

'Fall apart, Bux?'

'Your operator has turned rogue.'

Homann shrugged and checked his watch and then the flight display.

'Let me help,' Bux continued. 'While James Rezin was embroiled in your operation he discovered that Rückeran and two 7th Panzer Division colleagues had been involved in the killing of a female SOE agent. There was a photograph in Rückeran's apartment of all four of them in Paris in the winter of 1944. Unfortunately for you and Bonn, the female agent was the mother of James Rezin. Two of those Wehrmacht soldiers in that Paris photograph are now dead. Perhaps you can tell me how I save the life of the third, Herr Homann?'

'We have been through all this before,' Homann replied testily. 'The coroner decided Rückeran was killed by the RAF. Fiedler sounded like an unfortunate accident to me. Hadn't he tripped after drinking too much?'

'Fiedler was *not* a drinker,' Bux said and tried to keep

his temper. 'It would have been difficult to trip over a three-metre high balustrade, too. As for the notion that Rückeran was murdered by the RAF, you well know that was not the case.'

Homann wouldn't answer, and some of his fellow passengers were already checking in. Bux thought he had another twenty minutes of battling Homann and his prevarications when his demeanour suddenly changed.

'Sit down and listen, Bux,' he said and pulled back a chair. 'I will tell you all I can, but if this goes any further I will deny everything and it will be your word against mine. And *please*, none of your famous tantrums.'

Bux sat down to listen.

Homann took Bux back a decade, to the Munich Olympics of 1972.

'I will not bore you with detail because it is a well-known story,' he said. 'Palestinian extremists rushed the quarters of the Israeli team, the Munich police blundered and eleven of the Israelis were killed. It is *not* known that some competitors, notably a British team, were staying in the same apartment block.'

'James Rezin,' said Bux.

'We will call him that for now,' said Homann, 'though there have been several aliases. He was an officer in the Royal Scots Fusiliers and I think he boxed at light heavyweight. I do not know if he was a good boxer because in the end he didn't compete. What I *do* know is that he was quite good at other things. Professional soldiers recognise sounds, even at 4.40 in the morning: screams, shouts of anger, the language and, crucially, the number of shots fired and the types of weapon.'

Things moved on from there, according to Homann. The Briton was interviewed by a liaison officer with the

Federal Border Protection.

'You will know Ulrich Wegener, of course,' said Homann.

'Yes, I know Colonel Wenger,' said Bux.

'Wegener was quite impressed with this Briton: lucid and blessed with a very good memory. By all accounts it was like the meeting of long-lost brothers: boxers, avid sports followers – and both possessed the rogue element of members of the Special Forces. After the botched rescue attempt Wegener was determined that this must never happen again – hence the birth of his elite counterterrorist unit, now known as GSG 9. It was modelled on Sayeret Matkal, the Israeli General Staff Reconnaissance Unit and the Special Air Service in Britain. Wegener had trained with both.'

Homann checked his timing again but, to Bux's relief, called a waiter over to order two more coffees.

'That should have been that,' he continued. 'Bruce would go home to his regiment and Wegener would continue the war against terrorists. Then their lives converged again.'

'So Rezin joined Wegener and GSG 9?' Bux asked.

'It didn't *quite* work out like that. Rezin joined the British SAS after Munich but was thrown out – something to do with assaulting a civilian in a bar. What does a soldier, who is qualified for only one thing, do in such circumstances?'

'Mercenary,' said Bux. 'Either that or prop up a bar stool for the rest of his life.'

'He chose the former. The seventies were the golden era for men paid to fight. Most of the work was in the Third World: Congo, Sierra Leone, some of the Asian countries – but Europe, too.'

'West Germany?' asked Bux.

'Quite so,' said Homann, sipping daintily at his drink. 'Wegener's first GSG 9 operation was in 1977 and you know that story, too. A Luftwaffe flight, with eighty passengers on board, most of them German, hijacked by four Palestine terrorists: all four shot, three of them fatally, at Mogadishu Airport. Wegener would not give me the full details but it was well known that two members of the SAS were involved. There was a third man, another Briton, but *not* a member of the SAS.'

'James Rezin,' said Bux.

'By the time Wegener was called in the 737 had made what amounted to a tour of Europe and the Middle East: Rome, Cyprus, Bahrain, Dubai, Oman and then Mogadishu. The rescue operation had become multinational, so Wegener thought it a good idea to take a fluent language speaker with him. Rezin had excellent German and was in Berlin, working as a close protection officer for a senior manager at one of the big banks. He seemed an obvious choice.'

'I am sure Wegener's English is excellent,' said Bux.

'It is, but Wegener never leaves *anything* to chance. The SAS men, for example, were no linguists. It turned out to be a flawless operation.'

'So that was how James Rezin became Bonn's male Mata Hari?' said Bux.

'Quite so, Kommissar, though I would not frame it that way.'

'I'll frame it this way, then,' said Bux. 'Bonn started to follow the notion of Dirty Wars from the FBI, or was it the Stasi?'

'Very good, Kommissar,' said Homann. 'East Germany's Ministry for State Security had done it for years. There was a shortage of West German men after the war and many single women were chosen for high office. The Stasi decided that all that was needed then were good-looking men to talk to gullible women.'

An announcer from somewhere said passengers for

Washington could now wait by the departure gate, and Bux tried to speed things up.

'So that was how the RAF was tackled from the inside?' he said. 'I know half of their members were female.'

'I brought it up at a meeting with the Federal Minister of Defence in Bonn,' said Homann smugly. 'From then on things moved apace. All I had to do was find the correct Romeo spy and point him in the right direction.'

'The art of seduction certainly ran in that family,' said Bux quietly.

'Meaning what, Kommissar?'

'It's not important, Homann. Please continue.'

'Wegener mentioned a man who knew Germany, its culture and of course the language. Rezin, or Robert Bruce as he called himself, was also handsome and quite charismatic. It worked wonderfully well, though I say so myself.'

Each week Rezin left his findings in a clear plastic case in the same pine tree. It was like a gold mine for Bonn. All his information was accurate and key RAF figures were arrested. Weapons, explosives, and documents were snatched. James Rezin saved many lives, according to Homann.

'Well, all of that begs the obvious question,' said Bux. 'Why would a Briton risk his life on a cause that was nothing to do with him? He must be a strange character.'

'For obvious reasons I never met him, but I have my own opinions,' said Homann. 'If you were looking for such a type he would be dysfunctional in many ways – probably a man addicted to danger, a loner who may have lost parents or family and a marriage that had failed. If a person like this hadn't been in the services he would probably be in prison.'

Then something else occurred to Bux.

'This one is not going to finish up in prison, is he? Or, assuming he survives and is caught, he will not face a trial.'

'Please elaborate,' said Homann, well aware of what was meant.

'To put it crudely, Bonn will have to disappear this one,' said Bux. 'Do you agree? He will know too much for his own good.'

Homann got to his feet and pulled a passport from an inside pocket.

'Don't worry, Bux,' he said bitingly. 'There are other ways of making people disappear. Bonn will have to find a new name and a new country for that Springer woman, for example – if she behaves herself.'

'If she behaves herself?'

'I think you know what I mean, Kommissar.'

'And James Rezin?'

'He is more of a problem, admittedly, but I am sure something will be found. He is a hero, after all.'

'A live hero or a dead hero?' said Bux.

Homann frowned and pushed past towards his gate.

'If I were you, Bux,' he said with what sounded an explicit warning, 'I would leave state security operations to others. Remember, in cases like this there is a point when a case is no longer the responsibility of a detective.'

'I haven't reached that point yet,' Bux called as Homann showed his passport and plane ticket to the air hostess. 'This case is *still* my responsibility.'

Bux knew Homann had heard him, but he did not reply and did not look back.

CHAPTER 32.

'Two walk-ins for you, Kommissar,' said the desk sergeant at reception. 'Foreign journalists, they say.'

'What do they want?' Bux demanded irritably.

The sergeant looked at the couple seated a few metres away and said, 'I didn't ask, but it seemed quite urgent.'

'*What do they want?*'

'They mentioned a woman. Lulu, it sounded like: L-u-l-u. They said you would know what it was about, Kommissar. I can send them away if you like.'

Bux told the desk sergeant he did not want them sent away.

'Show them to the sweat box,' he said. 'Tell them I'll be along in a minute.'

Bux made them wait twenty minutes, which is why he liked to call the interview room the sweat box. He watched from behind the two-way mirror to check the body language and listen out for any conversations. He was out of luck.

It was obvious which of this pair was running this little game. The woman, attractive but quite hard-faced, had spotted the red light high on the wall at once and poked her companion hard in the ribs to warn they were being monitored. The man with the scar on his cheek but with a tame demeanour could not stop his right foot from shaking and chewed at his pencil as if it were a piece of gum. All the while the woman stared, unblinking, straight ahead at Bux on the other side of the mirror.

When he realised they were not going to talk Bux turned to Lang.

'We'd best go and have words with them,' he said, then paused a second before adding, 'I'll do the talking this time, Lang.'

McKenna thought it was like a war movie about occupied France: two well-dressed cops (Gestapo) in a windowless cubicle (prison cell) with a large sink (water torture) and a mirror the length of a wall (so others could enjoy the view).

The big cop minded McKenna of Cannon, the fat private eye in the TV series – overweight and slow, but the type you wouldn't want to tackle at arm's length. He did all the talking and insisted on English even after Mrs Batch introduced them in German. The young cop, Lang, had excellent English too, but looked as though he was fresh out of school.

There was something else new to McKenna: Mrs Batch was now 'deputy editor of *The Inquirer*' and he the 'chief investigative reporter'. She had also come armed with a push-up bra and a V-neck top and began with the *Babes in the Wood* routine: childish voice, flickering eyelashes and lots of smiling.

'Mind if I take this off?' she asked politely. 'It's hot in here, don't you think?' McKenna guessed, correctly, that the fat cop would be immune to this: the boy was not. He blushed as he helped her off with her jacket and carefully placed it on the back of her chair. Then she pulled out the little black diary.

She began with the Rückeran phone call and the transcript.

'I'm sure you heard that tape,' she said. 'So you will be well aware that it is on record that the SOE spy used the name Lulu.'

No response, not even a nod.

'Then I will assume then you have listened to it,' she smiled. 'So let's say straight away we have no interest in finding the murderer of a citizen of West Germany – just what was said in the tape. It is our attempt to help a mother find the body of the daughter she lost during the war.' She stared meaningfully at Bux and added, 'Incidentally, the mother has been waiting for three decades so there is no time restraint for us.' Slight pause and then, 'Though there may be for you, Kommissar Bux.'

You clever little pretty girl, thought Bux. I will have to be careful with you. She returned to her notes.

'Some of the background on Rückeran between 1939 and 1945 would certainly help us: his division, colleagues … if he spent time in Paris. We will obviously try war records, but it will take time'

'You just said you had no time restraint,' said Bux.

Lucienne Batch continued as if she hadn't heard him.

'If we could check the Federal Archives and where—'

'We have all those details on my word processor,' Lang interrupted.

Mrs Batch beamed and leaned back in her chair.

The Cheshire Cat smile and the flirting was *not* going to work with Bux.

'I apologise for my companion,' he said. 'But we cannot help you with this. You have come a long way for nothing.'

'Some of our details could help with your case.'

'I do not see how,' said Bux dismissively.

'I don't think you would be sitting here with us,' said

Mrs Batch imperiously, 'if you *didn't* believe the murder of the prison guard involves a British spy called Lulu somewhere. Am I correct?'

Bux still wasn't biting, so she softened her tone.

'Kommissar Bux, my colleague recorded a number of other interviews that might be pertinent to your case. For example, Mister McKenna spoke to the mother of Lulu at length and has some of the background about her son.'

'Why would I be interested in her son?' said Bux.

Mrs Batch put away her diary away and got to her feet.

'In that case,' she said, 'we will say goodbye and leave you to it.'

'You are going nowhere,' said Bux. 'So sit down.'

He needed a breathing space and time to think so he watched through the two-way mirror again and smoked and wondered. The thought of two foreign journalists chasing him around Stuttgart did not appeal. He could use the law to get any details he wanted, of course. He could put them on the next plane out of Stuttgart and throw them in a cell for a night. But he could use them – and he admired women with spunk, having been married to one for over thirty years.

The woman journalist was right about something else: to solve the Rückeran case – and Fiedler's, though they obviously knew nothing about that – meant solving the Lulu case first.

Bux knew how to handle journalists, and in the end he thought he got the better of the bargain. He wanted copies of the taped interviews with Mrs Cloutier, the army people and Mitchell and Myler. They could both attend his media briefings and Lang would act as the buffer between the two groups and supply them with all his work on the 7th Panzer Division. There seemed little point in mentioning the photograph of Lulu in Paris because, so far, there was no proof that it existed. At some stage the death of Fiedler might be mentioned, but they could make up their own minds if they bothered reading the local press.

'What you do in Stuttgart is up to you,' he said finally. 'But it goes without saying that there will be no access to the crime scenes.'

'*Scenes*, Kommissar?' said Mrs Batch.

Bux ignored her and continued, 'I will need the hotel room number and phone number,' he said.

'Do we get your number?' asked Mrs, Batch.

Bux thought for a second and said, 'You can get me through my direct line or the *Kripo* switchboard. If I am away another member of the detective team will let you know where I am.'

Mrs Batch thanked him politely and wrote down the details.

'May we have a number for your second-in-command, too?' she said just before they left. McKenna hadn't said a word.

CHAPTER 33.

Mrs Batch didn't appear for breakfast on the Sunday. Nor was she answering her room phone. He didn't have the guts to chap her door.

McKenna tried not to panic. In Batch's 'schedule' there was a press conference at noon in police headquarters on Hahnemannstraße, and he didn't know where it was and how to get there. Batch was the only driver in this party and had most of the cash. It struck McKenna as odd, too, that both she and the editor had warned against press conferences because cops just used them to point the press and the public in a direction that suited them. In Bloom's words, 'No one will get hard news in a room full of media wankers taking down the same quotes'.

He tried the girl on reception – another German with better English than most of the people he knew in Clydebank. 'The Beetle is still in the underground car park,' she said, after checking the hotel CCTV.

Had she seen her that morning? 'Very early,' said the receptionist. She was going out with her friend.

'*Her friend*?'

'The colleague of Kommissar Bux. Do I order you a taxi?'

This time McKenna walked all the way up to the fourth

floor, found his notes under the bed and walked back down and found a corner seat in the hotel bar.

He had read these a dozen times, from original notes to every transcript, but he started again, ticking off the clues. Nothing new. He asked the barman if he could find him a magnifying glass and he reappeared with one of those little plastic ones he had used as a kid, but it had to do.

He took a swig of his *Spezial*, cleaned his specs, rubbed his eyes and moved the magnifying glass over all three of the Cloutier photo albums: baby Lulu, the lovers of Lulu and the last weeks of Lulu. He peered at one, then the other and then back again. He held the albums up into the light, then upside down. Still nothing.

Then something did strike him, perhaps a memory of late nights inside *The Inquirer* library. Most files there, from people's names to photographs, were in chronological order, and the same must apply to family scrapbooks. But *two* of the images of Lulu, posing on Eagle Face and its rock that looked like a large bird, had been pasted in different collections.

He squinted at the pages of the yellow album, his eyes inches away from the photograph. Then the black album: it was definitely Lulu. It was the same smile and the same daft pose in both, but younger in the first one and with different clothes.

These were *not* taken on the same rock face. In the later version the rock face was slightly steeper and surrounded by tall trees; there was only empty sky in the background of the other.

Lulu, and whoever the photographer was, had found a rock face that mimicked another in a different place. The identical pose was her little joke, like a TV quiz show contestant who had to decide which image was Blackpool Tower and which was the Eiffel Tower.

McKenna sat back, stared up at the large fan on the ceiling and began to consider his options. Chapping Mrs Batch's door still didn't seem a good idea and, in any case, this was his discovery, not hers. In the end he opened his contacts book and found the name at the bottom of the Bs. The receptionist dialled the number for him and cancelled his taxi to Hahnemannstraße at the same time.

With his telling photos opened to the right pages, McKenna sat back to wait.

One hour later the polar bear figure shambled into the bar and headed for McKenna's little corner.

'This had better be worth it,' he griped. 'I have a radio interview in one hour. What the hell did you mean about Lulu and her photographs?'

'If I were you I'd forget your interview,' said McKenna.

'*If I were you* I would come straight to the point,' said Bux. 'I have more pressing matters. I remind you, I am midway through a difficult murder case.'

'If you are working on a murder case what are you doing here, then?' said McKenna, who was quite surprised at such directness.

'*I beg your pardon?*'

'If you weren't interested in this you wouldn't be wasting your time with a foreigner in a hotel bar, would you?'

Bux did not respond to that so McKenna lifted the three photo albums off the table and brandished them at Bux, like a courtier offering a king his crown.

Bux took a quick glance and demanded, 'What are these?'

'Lulu's family snaps.'

'And the meaning?'

'These are things we all missed,' McKenna said. 'That includes your mate Smilie on the day he went to see Mrs

Cloutier. That's Lulu's mother, I remind you.'

'Come to the point,' said Bux testily. 'You have five minutes.'

McKenna wasn't going to hurry for anyone and took his time.

'Look at these snaps,' he said. 'I bet a quid a police photographer is one of the first at a crime scene. Am I right? I also guarantee that if you look at a victim long enough you will see something different. They always say the camera never lies, but it does. Did you ever see a fillum called *Blowup*?'

'A fillum?'

'A movie.'

'I do *not* solve cases by watching old Antonioni movies.'

'So you *have* seen it? McKenna shouted delightedly. 'You see what I'm getting at, then: a photographer enlarges some frames and spots clues to a murder. The victim was lying in the grass and the killer was watching in the bushes.'

Bux grumbled, 'The photographer in the film was on drugs. Are you on drugs, Herr McKenna? Where exactly are you going with this?'

'I'm going to find Lulu. That's where I'm going.'

Bux checked his watch. 'Four minutes,' he said.

McKenna was not to be fazed.

'When we started on the story we spotted most things,' he said. 'We followed the SOE, Paris, the family history – but we *never* worked out the Eagle Rückeran was on about. At first we thought it was Hitler's mountain retreat.'

'Berchtesgaden,' said Bux still impatient. 'We dropped that idea early on. It would be highly implausible for a private in a Panzer division to be invited to Hitler's holiday resort. We tried a few others: the eagle as a Nazi symbol, an eagle on top of the swastika, and even the male surname Adler – German for eagle.'

'Have a look at these two snaps, then,' said McKenna.

Bux squinted at both photographs.

'I think I will have a drink,' he said. McKenna did the honours.

Out of habit, Bux tried not to appear too elated.

'These were definitely taken in two different places,' he agreed, pointing at both photographs again. 'These are different types of rock, too. I am not an expert on mineral formations, but the last one is definitely sandstone.'

'And the first one must be granite,' said McKenna, who made no attempt to hide his enthusiasm. 'Mrs Cloutier said it was taken near their home in the thirties; the Cairngorms, in other words. I don't think there's any sandstone up there.'

Bux was even more emphatic after he noticed something else.

'The last photograph was taken in France; the Forest of Fontainebleau, to be precise,' he said. 'As was her camping expedition. If you look carefully at the one of her close by a tent you can see the top of the chateau in the background. Fontainebleau is also famous for its odd-shaped boulders.'

'I should have spotted that from the start,' said McKenna. 'Family photos are usually framed in chorological order, aren't they?'

Bux agreed.

'Let's try it in order of events, then,' he said. 'The photographs in the yellow album may have been taken in the thirties, as you suggested, because Lulu does look much younger there – possibly still a teenager. Now let's move to the black album. There are photographs of her on a farm—'

'Nineteen thirty-nine: the day she joined the Land

251

Army.'

'Posing on the rock face.'

'Mrs Cloutier said both photographs had been taken on Eagle Face near Blair Lodge in the thirties, but obviously she made a mistake. There was another Eagle Face in the world.'

'Then the camping photographs?'

'Mrs Cloutier said they were taken before the war in Braemar, too.'

'Frau Cloutier is telling a fib,' said Bux decisively.

'Anyone could get dates wrong, and she is quite old,' McKenna insisted.

Bux simply scoffed,

'Do you think a mother who has been searching for her daughter for three decades will get the dates wrong? It seems fairly obvious to me that if family albums are in sequence, Lulu's camping holiday was between 1939 and 1944.'

'Hang on,' said McKenna. 'A spy who went camping in the middle of a war?'

'She must have had her reasons,' said Bux. 'Even spies do not spend their lives hiding under a table. She had a husband, did she not? Did Frau Cloutier tell you who took the photographs?'

'No. I'd have to take a guess. Like you say, the snaps in the forest had to be taken by her husband.'

'Any *guesses* on who took the Braemar photographs and *why* are there no images of children?'

McKenna didn't like where this was going.

'What the hell do you mean by "no images of children"?' he huffed. 'There was a son, and that was it.'

'But Smilie told me Mrs Cloutier had several evacuated children staying there,' said Bux. 'And why are you so upset?'

'I'm not upset.'

'You have gone red.'

'Because I'm pissed off,' said McKenna. 'You're leading us up the garden path here. First of all, the Cloutiers employed a Pole who did most of the work around the place, and still does. He probably took most of the photos at Blair Lodge. Now, Rückeran ranted on about an eagle – and he can't have been thinking of the one in Braemar, can he? He also said Lulu was murdered in Paris, remember? How far is it from Paris to Fontainebleau?'

'Fairly close,' Bux agreed. 'Fifty kilometres, or thirty miles to you.'

'It should be possible to find the location of that rock, then. There can't be many that look like a bloody great bird!'

'Perhaps,' said Bux, back in enigmatic mode.

'Wouldn't it be a good idea if we found some maps of Fontainebleau?'

'We?'

'Well, it's my tale, isn't it? It was me who found these snaps.'

'This is a police investigation into the murders of two citizens of West Germany,' said Bux rather pompously.

'*Two citizens?*'

Bux immediately moved the conversation on.

'You are a journalist, and a foreign journalist at that,' he said. 'You are here only at my acceptance. Perhaps you should remember that.'

McKenna slammed down his glass so violently his beer spilled on the table.

'I'll jump out of this window if I hear you say "perhaps" again,' he warned.

Bux sniggered and said, 'Perhaps you will.'

McKenna's venom took him aback. Then,

'I'm getting tired of your bullshit, Mister Bloody Detective,' he shouted, so loudly the barman looked over in alarm. 'Anyone would think getting in the way is part of your job. The way things are going I'll happily head off to Fontainebleau with Mrs Batch. I'm sure the French cops would be delighted to see those pics of Fontainebleau fuckin' Forest and then solve a WW2 murder case that involved Germans. So think about it: if we find Lulu you might get a herogram from the British government. If not, you can spend the rest of your life thinking of what a bollocks you made of your last case.'

Kommissar Bux replied with a smirk and a slow, sarcastic handclap.

'Well done, boy,' he said. Then his tone changed to something McKenna had not expected. 'Please, will you get me another glass of wine?' he asked politely. 'While you are at it I will think of where we can go with this.'

From their seat, by a window in the corner of the bar, Bux could just see the large square building that dominated one end of Heilbronner Straße. It was only mid afternoon, but the sky was so dark it was impossible to read the large sign on the roof of the building. But Bux did not need to: it was the middle entrance to the Bürgerhospital Klinikum, where ambulances always parked to ferry patients in and out. It was also where he first met Silke Müller.

In the most defined sense of the word the war did not end in 1945 for Bux. After the surrender he remained a member of *Feldjägerkommando III*, the Wehrmacht police force, although with subtle differences. Before 1945 it had been his uniformed job was to find battle-weary Wehrmacht deserters or stragglers. Some members of *Feldjägerkommando* would happily have had them shot;

Bux preferred to bend their ears about how wrong they had been, and persuade them back to war.

After the armistice the XIII US Army Corps did not have the numbers to maintain order at a Wehrmacht prisoner of war camp, close to the banks of Stuttgart's River Necker. Bux was paid only in food and crude accommodation, but the Americans were his new employers from then on.

On the evening of January 8, 1946, Bux was ordered to drive a young soldier to Bürgerhospital Klinikum, where the boy was to have his right leg amputated. The nurse, who showed the way to theatre, had been working for twelve hours and had already been involved in three operations. She was certainly not impressed by a pushy, outsize policeman with a makeshift badge on his shoulder. Bux himself did not like being ordered around by a girl his own age. It took some weeks before he began to notice the engaging smile and the quick wit.

Silke had suitors, of course. Beautiful girls usually preferred handsome men with a sense of humour, and certainly not cops or men of bulk. Bux, who had read his *Cyrano de Bergerac*, went into battle. He sent her poems and wrote letters which spoke of his 'pure deep love forever'. When peace and the recovery finally came to Germany, he took her to the theatre and the cinema.

On the day they walked out of the church hand in hand and friends and families (though not her parents) applauded he found out exactly why Silke had chosen an overweight cop with a notoriously low boiling point. It had little to do with poems, letters and trips to the movie house.

As the photographers clicked she whispered in his ear, so none could hear,

'My dear Bux,' she said, using his surname as she always did, 'how blessed I am to fall in love with a true man of

255

honour.'

Bux had never forgotten. He knew a detective's career could never be *entirely* honourable, but he had done his best. He also knew, like Silke had guessed, 'a true man of honour' would find injustice as abhorrent as murder itself.

So it was not McKenna and his ranting that had made up Markus Bux's mind, but something else.

'You can stop feigning indignation,' he said, even when McKenna arrived with the drink and even before he sat down.

McKenna grumbled on and tried not to smile. Bux looked him up and down and asked, 'Do you have a suit – and another tie?'

'What's wrong with these?'

'Detectives do not wear jeans and Three Stooges neckties,' said Bux, 'and I want you to play detective for me. Have you anything better?'

'What's going on? A detective, *me*? What about your mates?'

'Lang's mother is poorly and the others are finishing off a job in the Black Forest, which I might tell you about if you behave yourself. You've got ten minutes and *Mister Bloody Detective* will be waiting in that green Mercedes outside the front entrance. And make sure you bring *all* those photographs.'

CHAPTER 34.

Leopold Adler's family home was a sixteenth-century former hunting lodge on the edge of the town of Ludwigsburg, thirteen kilometres north of Stuttgart city centre.

It was said Napoleon had passed here on his way to Austerlitz in 1815 and the Duke of Württemberg once resided there. Modern-day locals loved to talk of their Daimler-Benz 'celebrity', who was always on television or on the radio and whose wife had once been a glamorous fashion model.

Fame had its drawbacks, however. After the first RAF murders in '71 Adler had invested in security guards, CCTV cameras and eight-foot high fences that were electrified at night.

Two muscular men carrying firearms were waiting in the rain outside the front gates of the estate. They checked the accreditation and looked under the car and only allowed them through after a telephone call to someone in the main house.

'Do you have German?' asked Bux as he pulled up outside the main door.

'I'm frae Clydebank,' said McKenna, which Bux took as a 'No'.

'Excellent,' Bux said, before quickly adding, 'I don't mean "excellent", of course. It is just that Adler has little English so he and I must speak in German.'

'What am I here for, then?' McKenna asked logically.

'I want you to *pretend* that you understand the conversation.'

'And how exactly do I do that?'

Bux had thought that through.

'Write notes, as if you were a detective working on a case. Nod your head and glower at him from time to time. I'll say something meaningful or give you a signal when I want you to pull out the photographs.'

'If it's all in German, what can I do for the words for my story?'

Bux said stoically, but avoiding eye contact, 'I will translate it for you later.'

Frau Adler, an attractive lady with a red, punkette hairstyle and with jeans ripped at the knees, was some twenty years younger than Adler, but knew how to play the good housewife. She offered them cheese dips and a choice of drinks and prattled on about the weather before Adler waved her away and she left them to it.

McKenna tried to keep his face straight when Bux introduced him as 'Detective Inspector McKenna from Scotland Yard'. Then the real-life detective went into full Billy Liar mode.

'Detective Inspector McKenna,' said Bux, brandishing McKenna's Manila document wallet, 'is in charge of a Scotland Yard squad that has been investigating Wehrmacht war crimes in France.'

'I have told you already,' said Adler to Bux. 'Members of the 7th Panzer division were not involved in war atrocities. You should concentrate on the SS or the Gestapo, Herr

Kommissar. I was not even a member of the Nazi party.'

Bux continued as if he had not heard,

'Herr McKenna has a special interest in Paris and the killing of members of the Special Operations Executive there. He has been examining the disappearance of one woman in particular. I have already mentioned the girl Lulu, do you remember?'

'The name means nothing to me,' Adler retorted. 'As I said, Rückeran may have mentioned it, but I do not see that as a reason to implicate me in whatever happened in Paris. I also told you I was *nowhere* near there in '44. I was on the Russian Front with my division.'

Adler was good, Bux thought. Chief executives of major companies did most of the talking and gave most of the orders. Adler knew how to hold a gaze when it came to telling fibs, and also knew the right time to become belligerent.

'If you are going to accuse me of something I suggest you do it now,' he warned. 'Anything else I say is best done in front of my solicitor. I do not think you and the *Kripo* would come out of that very well.'

Bux expected such threats. He was more interested to find that Adler could not take his eyes from McKenna's document wallet.

'Let's go back to the 7th Panzers and your time in Paris,' he began.

'We have discussed this several times.'

'Tell me again.'

Adler sighed and looked at McKenna again. The 'man from Scotland Yard' was busy with his notes.

'We were there for six days.'

'And what did you get up to?'

'What most soldiers got up to in Paris.'

'You mean girls, then?'

'I would think so, but we also went to the theatre and ate and drank a lot.'

'French girls?' Bux persisted.

'It was Paris.'

'A girl called Lulu?'

'I seem to recall that name, but it could have been any girl. Rückeran was always looking for the love of his life.'

A long silence, until Bux said, 'Do you think you would recognise her?'

'How can I recognise someone I never saw?' Adler blustered.

'I just thought that is we show you some images of her it might ring a bell,' said Bux. 'Old photographs often revive youthful memories.'

When Bux said that and pointed at the document wallet Adler blanched.

'Perhaps Herr McKenna can help?' said Bux.

McKenna took his cue like a professional. He opened the wallet and spread all the photographs across the table. Adler turned slowly, almost fearfully, like a family member who had just been asked to identify a body.

'Lulu,' whispered the deputy chairman of Daimler-Benz, as if addressing the woman in the photographs. 'I always knew you would come back and haunt us.'

Bux thought Adler looked quite relieved.

The routine from then on was uncannily predictable to Bux. The life story of an accused always came first, closely followed by the excuses and the justifications. A guilty party blames the upbringing, the family background or 'I was obeying orders' – a favourite during and after the war trials, though never before.

Adler was little different. He, Rückeran and Fiedler had been brought up by working-class, industrious, churchgoing parents and attended the same Stuttgart academy – Merz-Schule in Sigmaringer Straße. They volunteered for the 7th Panzer on the same day, not for a belief in Hitler and the Nazi party, but because they feared Stalin and his Reds. Adler was a driver in a Tiger I, Rückeran and Fiedler were in the motorcycle battalion.

Rommel's 7th, the Ghost Division, soon laid waste to Belgium and northern France, as Adler explained.

'We broke through in the late spring of 1940, crossed the Meuse through Belgium, went on to Cambrai and were in Arras by May 20. We were pulled out of the line after Paris fell and were rewarded with six days' leave. The choice was either to go home or remain in France. We chose Paris.'

Like many Wehrmacht soldiers they subscribed to *Der Deutsche Wegleiter für Paris*, which gave lists of where to go and what to do.

'That was fine,' said Adler, 'but not as good as meeting a beautiful French girl willing to act as a tour guide, and this on only the second day in Paris.'

'Did you approach her, or was it the other way round?' said Bux.

'Something of both, I think. Rückeran was fond of culture in those days. He preferred museums and art galleries to food and drink, but we talked him into some wine at La Belle Aurore, near the Pasteur Museum and close by the Eiffel Tower.'

'It was a beautiful summer's day,' said Adler, 'with the city at its most seductive, and many miles away from the reality of war.

'She was sitting on her own. Her head was back and her eyes were closed as if to feel the warmth of the sun on her

261

face. Naturally Rückeran, the big romantic, asked her over to our table. Then the damn music started.'

'"*Prix de Beauté*",' said Bux. 'The record we found in Rückeran's apartment."

'"*Prix de Beauté*",' agreed Adler. 'If someone mentions Paris now, I always think of that damn music: "*I will wait night and day. I will wait forever*". I swear to God the cafe owners turned that on deliberately every time he saw a Wehrmacht uniform. Do you understand, Herr Bux?'

'I understand,' said Bux. 'Music has often been a psychological weapon in war. Didn't Moscow use Shostakovich on the Russian Front?'

'Exactly,' said Adler. 'Some music was used to make the enemy afraid and other music to make the enemy homesick. Music and Lulu were a lethal combination.'

The flashbacks arrived quickly after that.

'She was beguiling: quite tiny, black-eyed and she had the duck walk of a ballet dancer. She always wore a beret – usually black, occasionally red. Her German was excellent, though we assumed she was French.'

'Fraulein Perfect, then?'

'*Frau* Perfect, Herr Bux. She told us from the start she was married and she wasn't my type, to be honest. She was attractive, but I had a girl at home, as did Fiedler. It did not concern Rückeran. He saw her as his perfect woman, the girl he would rescue from the horrors of war, and they would live happily ever after. Rückeran was a good friend but he was a fool and she was good at spotting fools.'

'Did that include his colleagues?'

'Fiedler and me? I suppose so. She had a gift for making men feel they were her best friend. She would look at us with those saucer eyes, all curiosity and sincerity, but impartial. She tried to keep all three of us happy.'

'Happy?

'She was not a whore, if that is what you mean. In terms of seducing silly soldiers she probably drew the line somewhere. But I understood why we liked her.'

'Nothing ever passed between you regarding her background?'

'It sounds silly, Herr Bux, but, with one exception we didn't want to get too close. You know the soldier's saying about war: never get attached to someone because you may never see that person again. We had six days in Paris, and it wasn't as if we were going to be friends for life.'

'What was the story of your second trip to Paris?'

'After Kursk and Kiev in late '43 the 7th Panzer Division had basically ceased to exist. We had twenty-three operational tanks and I thought that by Christmas we would either retreat or surrender. That was when the three of us were ordered to go and see our commanding officer. We were to travel to France at once, he said.'

'Were you told why?'

'I don't think he knew. We were very young and quite naïve and assumed we were being moved to another division. It could have been another rumour about the Allied invasion; there was a lot of hot air about that then. Whatever it was, a return to Paris seemed far more attractive than another year on the Eastern Front. I was lucky, too, because my Tiger I and my replacement came second best to a Russian T-34 at Memel.'

'Tell me about the journey to France. Where did you finish up?'

'There was a seventeen-hour drive to Warsaw and then a train through Germany and into France. We were to join the 3rd Panzer division quarters at Thomery, just south of Paris and on the banks of the Seine. On the second day we were ordered to drive to Rue de Saussaies in Paris.'

Adler sighed with a mixture of fear and disgust, and

added, 'Three members of the Gestapo, a *Kommissar* and two *Kriminalinspektors*, were waiting for us.'

The Gestapo began with the threats. Rückeran, Fielder and Adler had consorted with the enemy. They had given vital information to a British spy and they had damaged the Führer and the fatherland.

'They came up with all sorts of rubbish,' said Adler. 'There was one wild suggestion that she had targeted soldiers in the 7th Panzer Division and that if she got them to talk about Rommel and his whereabouts he could be assassinated.'

'And your opinion of that?

'Garbage. Absolute garbage.'

'But Rommel's staff car was strafed by the Royal Air Force several times. He was badly injured at one stage.'

'Well, if that was the case, she certainly didn't get it from us. The Gestapo were clutching at straws with that because there were other ludicrous accusations: we had passed on details of military bases and factories and even mentioned Daimler-Benz in Stuttgart. The Allies' precision bombing was our fault, too. The Porsche factory at Zuffenhausen had just finished the chassis for a new Tiger tank when it got bombed and that was no coincidence, they said. The way they carried on you would have thought Lulu was winning the war on her own. Anyway, it didn't matter what we thought: we were to go into Paris and find her. That was when we realised why the Gestapo were so desperate: they had no images of her.'

'One moment,' demanded Bux. 'Did they just pull you out of a hat?'

'I assumed the Gestapo got most of the details from her husband. I gather they got too heavy with the interrogation and he either died or swallowed a cyanide pill. They needed more, which was where we came in.'

In the end, said Adler, the friends from Stuttgart were given three days to find her.

'And after that?'

'At best a charge of aiding the enemy. At worst…'

It took only two days.

'We were walking down the Boulevard Garibaldi when Rückeran spotted her. "There she is. There's Lulu", or words to that effect. It was the first time we had seen her without her beret so Rückeran did well to recognise her. It didn't take long after that: the Gestapo had been tailing us. One of us had been ordered to raise a hand if we recognised her and then they made the arrest.'

'The whole of Paris and you walked straight to her?'

'It wasn't too far from where we saw her for the first time in '40. It was a bit like prostitutes, who always stick to their same little corner. The Gestapo thugs took photographs of all four of us before they moved in.'

'The photograph stolen from his apartment?'

'He persuaded them to give him a copy, like a damn holiday snap. He carried it around like some bizarre reward and even put it on his wall. I told him several times to burn it, or at least hide it somewhere, but no: he wanted to remember everything. He was like one of those friars who whip themselves for hours to atone. He wanted to go through life suffering.'

'And what happened next, Herr Adler?'

Adler had lost his colour and Bux had to ask him again.

'Two days later we were ordered to go back to Rue de Saussaies. We were the last resort.'

'And what were *you* supposed to do, Herr Adler?'

'The Gestapo wanted names of her controllers in London and Paris and fellow agents, code names and what she had found out. They must have thought we could talk her round, which really shows how desperate they

265

were. Scared, too: everyone knew the war was over. Paris was liberated within another six months and the Gestapo certainly didn't want to hang around.

'I remember everything. It was ten at night. We had all been drinking, apart from Rückeran, who wasn't a boozer in those days. There was a single ceiling lamp and a barred window just wide enough to see the shooting area on the other side of the courtyard. She was chained to a thick metal ring on a wall and the floor was covered in straw, presumably to hide the blood. Someone had scrawled *Frankreich uber alles* on the far wall and there was another one in English close to Lulu, which read *Life is Beautiful.*

'Most of her clothing had gone and she had been badly beaten. Both eyes were blackened and I think she may have lost one. Most of her nails, too. There was a female secretary in uniform in the next room to the cell and she had never got past the first page of her typewriter. She hadn't told them anything. It was obvious she would not last much longer. Rückeran had already made up his mind.'

'*Made up his mind about what?*' said Bux though he already knew. 'It was a mercy killing, was it not? You were going to shoot her.'

Adler shivered and stood to throw more wood on the fire.

'Originally, we were going to spin a coin, but the only one who had the guts was Rückeran. To be honest, even the drink didn't make Fiedler and me any braver.'

'So where did he find *his* courage?'

Adler had reached a conclusion long ago and didn't hesitate.

'Remember the story about that deer in the Schwaben Hills, Kommissar? The one he put out of her misery? He was going to do the same for Lulu. He told the Gestapo *Kommissar* that all he needed were a few minutes and, like fools, they agreed. They didn't even disarm him. We were a few metres away outside the cell. I am sure she recognised him. They whispered to each other, like damn lovers.'

'What were they talking about?'

'I don't know. What do people usually talk about when they are about to die?'

'Words that they think might save them,' said Bux. 'A mention of a family, perhaps. What good people they had been and which god they worship.'

'She never struck us as a type to ask for mercy,' said Adler, 'but in the end we never found out. We never asked Rückeran and I am sure he would never tell, even in his cups. Towards the end there was a horrible feeling of inevitability, like watching a car crash just before all the vehicles collide. He was in tears, but suddenly he got to his feet, pulled out his Luger, stepped back a pace and shot her in the head, just the once. There was total silence for a time. Then all hell broke loose.'

'What was the Gestapo reaction?'

'They were incensed. Rückeran had robbed them of their prey and there were all sorts of threats: he would pay, and things like that. Then they began to think about it: he had saved them a job and they were in a hurry. It was obvious she wasn't going to talk so their choice was putting her on a train to Dachau, or shooting her themselves. They ranted and railed for a time but there was nothing they could do. In the end they put "shot while trying to escape" in their killing book.'

Frau Adler knocked on the door to offer more coffee and food, if anyone was hungry. The men smiled and pretended they were discussing the football results.

'What became of the body?' Bux asked when Frau Adler had left.

'The Gestapo would never waste time getting rid of a corpse. They vanished as quickly as they had arrived so it was left to Rückeran. He chose Fontainebleau: a decent burial site, he said, as if that made any difference. But it was not too far from our base at Thomery. The opinion was that she would never be found.'

They hid the body inside some bedding in the back of a Type 40 Jeep. They took a shovel and a large wooden box. Rückeran, the sober one, did all the driving.

'It was a black night and bitterly cold. It took us over two hours to dig a hole deep enough because the ground was frozen. We made a pact on the way back that this story would be taken to our graves.'

'But you are telling me now.'

'Rückeran and Fiedler are not in a position to complain,' Adler said with a grim smile. 'At least they took it to their graves.'

'I assume you never went back?'

Adler agreed.

Bux pointed at McKenna's collection of photographs and asked, 'Would you remember it from these photographs?'

'I'm not sure,' said Adler. 'It was so dark it was hard to see anything. I do recall three large trees in a small circle around the place we dug.'

'So you never saw that rock face?'

'I remember Lulu and that smile of hers. I also recognise Fontainebleau, but as I said it was pitch-dark. I'm sure that if I went back there I would find it.'

'You will *certainly* be going back there,' said Bux explicitly. 'How did it all end?'

'We assumed we would go back East, but by then the Russians had got as far as Poland so we were sent to Berlin, with some of the remains of the 7th Panzer.'

'What about the medal?'

'The typical, twisted mind of the Gestapo,' said Adler. 'After the shooting, long after it, I heard one of them saying to Rückeran, "You will get an Iron Cross for this". And that's what happened. It was their revenge, you see. Something like that would scar him for life and they knew it. Fiedler and I talked about it later and we knew this was the onset of his madness. He didn't care whether he lived or died after that. He survived the war, but he was never the same man.

'There was a little ceremony in Berlin,' said Adler. 'Some bigwig – a general, I think … he obviously didn't know what had happened and probably wouldn't have cared anyway. The Russian guns were getting closer by then so he wasn't going to stay around long. Someone said Rückeran had performed an act of heroism and the general gave a little speech. Someone else took a few photographs and that was it.'

'Rückeran turned to drink after that?'

'He had never been a drinker but suddenly he went hard at it. He lost his good looks and he became very untrustworthy, particularly at work in Stammheim. I kept him in that job even though they wanted him out. It wasn't long before I started to agree with them.'

'Meaning?'

'He started coming out with these crazy ideas: he wanted to find Lulu's family and tell them what happened. He wanted to meet the boy and show him where the body was. Crazy; absolutely crazy.'

'So whoever killed him did you a favour?'

'Herr Bux?'

'You and Fielder must have thought he was going to be landing you in it?'

'I admit that,' Adler agreed. 'One night he phoned me, drunk as usual, and told me he was going to employ a private detective to find Lulu's family. Then he was going to phone all the Scottish newspapers to ask them if they knew the boy. Did you see all those newspapers in his flat?'

'I did,' said Bux.

'He read them all. He had little English, but it did not matter because he was looking for photographs and names he might recognise. Can you imagine the press if they found out about Lulu and Fontainebleau? The man was dangerous – so yes, I was quite relieved when he died. But it wasn't us, Herr Bux. The death of Fiedler proves that, and he was dying anyway, was he not?'

'Did you stay in touch with Fiedler?'

'I saw him at a couple of 7th Panzer reunions, until people started asking the usual questions, "Do you remember Paris? Were you at Kursk?" Things like that. We began to drift apart: family, divorce … he moved out to Ittersbach. The last time was just after Rückeran's murder. We met at an inn at Baden-Baden because no one would know us there. We tried to work out what happened and what to do about it.'

'Our public prosecutor also did his best to help?'

'Drescher? He knew I was a friend of Rückeran so he phoned me on the morning the body was found. There was nothing dubious about that. Drescher obviously thought he had been doing me a favour.'

'But you wanted to get rid of that photograph and its guilty little secret?'

'Drescher didn't know what it was, but I described it and asked him to lift it for me. By the time he arrived it had already gone, he said. We could put two and two together then. Someone somewhere knew about Paris '44.'

'What was your opinion on Fiedler's death?'

'It could have been an accident … there is always that doubt in one's mind.'

'Did it ever occur to you, Herr Adler, that this killer may have had help?'

'Help from whom?' said Adler. 'Are you suggesting Rückeran told him?'

'It was too much of a coincidence: the killer knew exactly the right time to find Rückeran alone and I am convinced that the killer spent some time in the apartment with him. Then Fiedler happened to be on the top of Ittersbach's castle walls on the first night of *Oktoberfest*, an occasion not noted for its sobriety.'

'You are suggesting I could be a target, too?' Adler said incredulously.

'Has that never occurred to you, Herr Adler? After all, did you not go into hiding here as soon as you hear about Fiedler?'

'I decided I should stay here until you got your finger out and managed to make an arrest,' retorted Adler. 'It is taking you some time, is it not, Kommissar? Can I remind you, too, that Rückeran did the shooting? I cannot be indicted for that.'

'Keitel and von Ribbentrop probably never raised a pistol in anger, but it didn't save them from hanging after Nuremberg. Some would argue that Rückeran had two accomplices, did he not?'

'We were *not* accomplices and we certainly didn't prompt him to do it. In any case, this woman was a spy; spies and their families know they could be shot.'

'It has not sunk in yet, Adler, has it?' said Bux who was losing his patience. 'All killings are taken personally by someone, particularly if it is a member of a family. Whether she was a spy, or the local cleaner, is immaterial. All that matters to an avenger is the name of the perpetrators.'

Adler sank slowly into his chair, seemingly exhausted.

'Would it help if I find the place in Fontainebleau?' he

asked, hopefully.

'Perhaps,' said Bux. 'This is a confession, of sorts, but so far we have no proof of your innocence. Did you find out what happened to the three Gestapo officers?'

'Apparently there were shot by the French Resistance, north of Paris.'

'Well, that has saved someone one job,' said Bux sarcastically. 'As things stand, it's five down, one to go. It's your word against the words of five dead men.'

'What happens if you do find her?'

'There will be an autopsy of whatever is left and a forensic team will be travelling with me. We should be able to set off tomorrow. Then we can find out if there is evidence of a war crime.'

'What happens tomorrow?'

'I will contact the *Sûreté Nationale* and work out the procedure of looking for a body in French soil and what to do when we find it. You must also come down to Hahnemannstraße first thing tomorrow. I will need this admission in writing.'

'But your colleague has been taking notes?' said Adler, pointing at McKenna.

'Herr McKenna is a field officer, not a pen and paper type,' said Bux. 'I suggest you be ready for an 8.30 a.m. meeting at the *Kripo* headquarters tomorrow. I can arrange a police escort if necessary. Do you take the same route into the city?'

'It varies,' said Adler. 'But I do not need a police escort. I have bodyguards.'

'Good,' said Bux. 'Telephone my office first thing and let us know when you are setting off. Hopefully, we can leave for Fontainebleau at about 11 a.m.'

'Why the hurry, Herr Bux? It's not as if she is going to disappear.'

'I have my reasons,' said Bux. 'Now make an excuse for Frau Adler. Tell her you have an urgent meeting. Make sure you bring enough for an overnight stay.'

'*Overnight*?'

'It is a six-hour drive to Fontainebleau. We have to deal with the French government and the *Sûreté Nationale*, and we are looking for a body that has been missing for more than three decades. I do not really see us getting there and back in a day.' Then in English, 'Come along, Herr McKenna. I will drop you at your hotel.'

'Are you staying in Stuttgart for long, Mister McKenna?' said Adler, politely, and in perfect English.

'That depends on the Minister of Propaganda here,' said McKenna.

He found a minibar hiding inside the wardrobe with a selection of cookies, peanuts, four small bottles of Gordon's and two packs of Durex.

Three bottles was enough, for McKenna was no gin drinker – but he didn't like unlucky numbers so he sat on his bed, stared at his reflection in the mirror and made a start on the fourth. When he began to feel light-headed but before he turned silly he rewound his new Sony Walkman and played the tape to the end.

He didn't need to be a translator to read anger, fear and sorrow, and Adler had been close to tears at times. Lulu and a few other words were the same in any language and Münchingerstraße was also mentioned on his original tape. Near the end Bux spoke of Fontainebleau and '*elf*', and '**elf**' was the time the Mercure bar opened in the morning, so the cop may just be leaving for Fontainebleau at 11 a.m. At some stage he would have to bite the bullet and ask for clarification from Batch.

His eyes were closing, so he clicked through the TV

channels until he found something to keep him awake long enough to finish the last of the gin.

It was a French movie he must have seen a dozen times, though never with German subtitles. And there was poor, pixie-haired Jean Seberg selling **New York Herald Tribunes** in the streets of Paris. He knew the ending, too: Seberg/Patricia betrays her small-time hood of a lover who happens to be a Bogart fan. It seemed symbolic of something, but McKenna was too tired to think of what. He was asleep long before the French cops arrived and the shooting started.

CHAPTER 35.

By next morning McKenna had decided he could manage without his driver/interpreter and didn't even bother to check if she was in her room or if she had been down for breakfast. Instead, he packed the leftovers from the minibar into his mini rucksack and asked the receptionist to change some pound notes to Deutschmarks and then order him a taxi to Hahnemannstraße for 9 a.m.

'*Bitte*, is there *ein* printing shop anywhere?' he asked her then.

She smiled politely and said, in her excellent English, 'For photographs?'

'Some photographs, but I wanna copy some tapes and words as well.'

'There is an InduPrint on Schellingstraße,' she said. 'That, the nearest would be. They will copy items two or three hours if you must hurry. The street outside, you turn right in and find in 300 metres. *Grüss Gott!*'

It must have been a quiet day for InduPrint because they were done within an hour. The shop assistant, who also had good English, told him which stamps he would need for *Inquirer* Newspapers Ltd, Albion Street, Glasgow, United Kingdom, and the whereabouts of the nearest post office.

Police headquarters was a long, four-storey building in a wooded area two miles north of the hotel. McKenna got past the twin barricades and four uniforms with weapons, but came to a full stop just past the front entrance.

'May I know what this is regarding?' asked the same aggressive cop, sitting on the same, Scrooge-like desk.

'I have an appointment with Mister Bux.'

'*Kommissar* Bux,' he amended. 'And your name … sir?'

'William McKenna. I'm expected.'

'William?'

'McKenna.'

The sergeant checked his clipboard and decided, 'I do not have your name here. Kommissar Bux is in a meeting. You may sit to wait.'

'I don't suppose Mister Lang is in?'

'Herr Lang will later come.'

McKenna tried not to smirk when he asked, 'Is that how you say it over here, too?'

'*Bitte?*'

'Is that the name for it over here?'

'*Bitte?*' and the face hardened.

'Forget it. My idea of a joke. Have you got a spare piece of paper I can leave for Mister Bux? And any chance of phoning me a taxi?'

Eleven kilometres to the north Leopold Adler kissed his wife and children goodbye and set off for his meeting with Kommissar Bux.

It would be a similar trip to the one from home to work, though it was rotated daily on the advice of his security guards. The E41 was the fastest, the Karlsruhe/Stuttgart Route 10 the slowest and the L1110, the choice for that day, the most scenic. The L1110 was ideal for Adler, as it gave him the chance to put his new Mercedes S-Class W162 through her paces.

The W162 was the company's successor to the old 770 beloved by Hitler and other senior members of the Axis. The W162 was for customers with the wherewithal to keep themselves alive: diplomats, Arab sheikhs and even West German industrialists. The safety measures included bulletproof windows, layers of armour plating and run-flat tyres. Adler likened to it to his old Tiger I.

Wagner's *Götterdämmerung* was on the car radio so he twiddled through the channels to find something more appropriate. The bodyguards' Mercedes and Adler's vehicle, which always followed some twenty metres behind, made a sharp turn left past Möglingen and gathered speed through the streets of Stammheim-Nord.

McKenna was dropped some distance away because the street was blocked to traffic on both sides. He asked the taxi driver to wait, but he either didn't understand or took no notice because he sped off as soon as he'd been paid.

McKenna thought Münchingerstraße wasn't much different from parts of Glasgow, though a bit posher, and there were no kids in the street and no gossiping locals here. But it had similar three- or four-storey stone-built tenements with a main front door and common stairways.

McKenna thought it would do no harm to have photos of the house of the man who had phoned him in the middle of the night and was later murdered, but he felt rather foolish when he pointed the Box Brownie at No. 3.

Close to Zuffenhausen-Im Raiser the sky suddenly blackened and a mist drifted slowly from the Necker River over the streets either side of the L1110. The visibility was soon so poor it was hard to see the Mercedes in front.

Nonetheless, he slowed down to sixteen kilometres an hour and turned on the vehicle's lights.

Adler's reaction was good, though not good enough. He saw the woman, who was heavily pregnant and pushing a pram into the middle of the road at once. He missed her, but the right-hand front wheel hit the pram and it and child were sent spiralling high into the air before landing in a nearby vineyard field.

The W162 had spun into a crash fence on the left side of the road and Adler immediately ran to help. Adler knew he was about to die when he finally realised that the body of a child was, in fact, a doll, and the pillow under the top of the 'expectant mother' had been hiding a Uzi sub-machine gun. He may have heard the first bullet – though not the eleven that followed, right to left, from stomach to neck. He was undoubtedly dead before he hit the ground.

The bodyguards did their best under the circumstances. When they first heard the power drill cackle of the Uzi the driver was forced to reverse because the road was too narrow for a U-turn. Both men had to dive for cover when the Uzi shredded all four tyres. The last they saw of the woman she was sprinting, at what they thought was remarkable speed, towards the narrow streets and woods of Zuffenhausen-Im Raiser. She was still carrying the pillow which, according to Adler's bodyguards later, demonstrated the professionalism of the operation.

McKenna thought it sounded like a roll of drums at first, but realised it was something else when he heard shouts and police sirens. They all seemed to be heading in his direction, so he bent under the yellow tapes guarding the entrance to 3 Münchingerstraße and hurried inside.

The name on the ground floor flat was *Huber*, but there was no response when he pressed the bell and thumped on the door. The door to the second-floor flat was blocked by more yellow tape so he made his way up to the third. He stomped on the stairs, coughed out loud and even called out 'Hello, anyone there?' like those halfwitted college kids in movies who always walked into darkened rooms on their own.

There was no response and the sirens were getting louder and the door at the top was open, so he went in.

He smelled the cigarette smoke before he saw a pair of boots, a parka and green trousers lying on the floor next to a sleeping bag and a rucksack the size of a door. The window had sheets for makeshift curtains. The main room was divided from a small kitchen by a glazed partition. The small bedroom had no bed and there was a bathroom/ toilet and a shower cubicle.

McKenna never saw, or heard, a thing. He bent down to see if there was a name on the rucksack when one arm was locked around his Adam's apple while the other pulled his head back so tightly he couldn't move.

Within seconds he began to lose the flow of blood to his brain and there were small dots in his eyes going smaller and smaller, like a TV being switched off. His head was pushed further downwards to the floor, but all he could see behind were a pair of flat shoes and a ladies' pleated skirt that looked oddly familiar.

Suddenly there were shouts and shots, an overpowering smell of cordite and the hot dribble of urine down his trousers. Then there was darkness.

CHAPTER 36.

McKenna knew he was still alive when he saw a light on the ceiling above him and felt the drench of sweat in the bed sheets.

It had been one of those maddening dreams in which you wake up just when things started to get interesting. He remembered some of it: he and Lucienne lightly dressed for a summer, walking hand in hand down a long, wide boulevard and smiling at each other, like new lovers. It was Paris because he could see, in the distance, the Tower with its pointy bit on the top. They seemed to walk for hours without getting anywhere until they stopped by a pavement cafe with an accordion playing and a woman singing somewhere inside. Then the sky darkened to a pitter-patter of rain and a roll of thunder. Batch spoke, he turned to listen, but someone with an infuriating, guttural voice kept interrupting and saying, over and over, 'Herr Mack-eener, Herr Mack-eener … wake up, Herr Mack-eener.'

He opened one eye and took stock.

It was definitely a hospital: all the walls were white and he was lying, flat as a corpse, on a bed with side rails – there to stop people falling off. A machine on the wall beeped every ten seconds and something was attached to his right arm. He seemed to have a ward to himself because all the other beds, a dozen or so, were empty, but with sheets made up smooth and tight.

The male voice from the dream asked, 'How are you feeling, Herr Mack-eener?' Carefully, because his head ached and there was a maddening ringing in his ears, McKenna turned to see who it was. He was sitting in the only chair next to the bed. He was probably in his fifties and a bit of a toff with his pinstripe suit and bow tie, though his shirt collar was dirty, as if he had slept in it overnight. McKenna didn't trust that insincere smile.

'How long have I been here?' he asked. 'God, my head aches.'

'You have a perforated eardrum and a bump on the head,' said the toff. 'You are at the United States army hospital of Bad Cannstadt in Stuttgart-Ost and have been here for four hours. My name is Hans Homann, by the way. Please call me Hans. I think you know the Kommissar.'

A grim-looking Bux, who had been forced to stand, nodded but said nothing. McKenna tried to sit up, but failed. He seemed to be drained of energy.

'I feel like shite,' he said. 'I feel like I just did ten rounds with Bruce Lee.'

'Ah, the English sense of humour, Herr Mack-eener,' said Homann.

'*Scottish* sense of humour,' said McKenna, 'and my name is *McKenna*.' He lay back, groaned and closed his eyes.

'I need a kip,' he said.

Suddenly Homann was no longer a caring hospital visitor. He pinched the nerves in McKenna's elbows so hard it made him cry out, and said, 'Stay awake!'

McKenna began to remember things then.

'Who were those cops in black uniforms and face masks?' he asked.

Homann frowned and became even more belligerent.

281

'You remember *something*, then.'

'It was Lulu's son, wasn't it?' said McKenna. 'That was the guy who got shot.'

'*That is not under discussion*,' Homann bellowed. Then, as if reading from a script, 'A notorious and well-armed member of the Red Army Faction was shot dead in a Stuttgart suburb after he attacked you. That is all you need to know.'

'*A notorious member of the Red Army Faction?*'

'Correct,' said Homann. 'Now you are going to listen, and you will drop all your silly theories. I also warn you that when you waltzed into the apartment at 3 Münchingerstraße you were entering the scene of a crime. That is an offence in this country. In fact, you could quite easily have been shot.'

'*I could have been shot*? I was just taking some snaps for the paper.'

Homann sighed wearily and turned to Bux.

'Will you explain, Kommissar? Or shall I?'

Bux replied in a disinterested monotone.

'Your taxi driver phoned for the police,' he said. 'You have a vague resemblance to someone else. The taxi driver had a police likeness in his vehicle.'

McKenna tried to sit up and pointed at the birthmark on his cheek.

'So it *was* Lulu's boy,' he said. 'The cops mistook me for him; right?'

'Be quiet,' spat Homann. Then, in a tone laced with menace, 'I warn you for the last time. If you continue to interrupt, things will, let us say, go badly for you. Now, I am going to ask you questions, you will reply and Herr Bux will take notes.'

Bux found him an extra pillow, lit him a cigarette and pulled out a notepad.

'Good,' said Homann. 'Then we can begin.'

McKenna had taken a taxi from the hotel to Hahnemannstraße for 9 a.m. 'as had been arranged', he said, with an accusing glare at Bux. 'You were in a meeting, or so it was said. Lang was otherwise engaged. I had some work to do so I took a taxi to Rückeran's apartment.'

'What sort of work?' asked Homann.

'Stuff for the newspaper; background, we call it. I don't think it would have been used, but you never know. The idea was to take photographs of the street and Rückeran's house – the murder scene, if you like. As soon as the taxi driver did a runner I heard what sounded like gunfire, then the sirens and more shots. I must have panicked. The door was open so I dived in.'

'And what did you find there?'

'There was no one in the bottom-floor flat. The door to the second was covered in police tape, but the front door to the top flat was open.'

'What struck you about the room?'

'He must have been there for a time because it smelled of fags and there were some of those army rations, half-eaten. There was a big rucksack, some men's clothes and a sleeping bag.'

'What else?'

'Like what?' McKenna asked.

'Did you notice any personal items; letters or photographs?

'There was no one living there.'

'No photographs, then?'

'His holiday snaps, you mean?'

Bux coughed and cleared his throat to stop himself smiling. Homann was not amused and huffed, 'Careful. You are in enough trouble. Did he speak?'

'Not a word.'

'Did you see his face?'

'He came from behind. All I saw was the skirt and the ladies' shoes. He started choking me, but all of a sudden he stopped and seemed to fall over on the floor. I heard shots, lots of them. I could see police in black wandering around and talking into what sounded like police radio traffic. Then I saw Mister Bux arriving and the others vanished. I went under and that's all I remember.'

'I imagine you thought it was a female?'

'You're joking! He had legs like Schwarzenegger. It was a bloke dressed as a woman.'

Homann took a long time to make up his mind. When he reached into his briefcase for two sheets of paper McKenna knew it was not good news.

'I want you to listen carefully,' said Homann. 'This is a copy of a note circulated to all newspapers, news agencies and television and radio stations in West Germany and much of Europe, including the United Kingdom.'

Homann read,

Andreas Fassbinder, a notorious Red Army Faction killer, has been shot dead in a police ambush in Zuffenhausen, Stuttgart-Nord. Fassbinder had played a key role in a number of RAF killings and has been on Bonn's most wanted list for some time. Parts of the police procedure are still ongoing and there will be further statements from the Ministry of the Interior at a later date.

McKenna stared at him nonplussed.

'You really think people will believe all this?'

'Everyone will believe it,' said Homann.

'Who the hell is *Andreas Fassbinder*?'

'That is the name on the passport of the man who attacked you.'

'*Fassbinder*? His name was James Rezin. I know who he

was and where he came from and what he did for a living. I also know his grandmother and I can't see her falling for this, either.'

Homann ignored that and went to his second sheet.

'I warn you that this document,' he said, 'is, how do they say' – he turned to Bux for support – '*es ist fur nationalen sicherheit?*'

'It is for national security,' said Bux.

'Thank you, Kommissar.' Then to McKenna, 'This document is extremely relevant to you, your female colleague, your editor and the owners of your newspaper. It is signed by the Lord Chancellor of the United Kingdom, so I advise you to take it seriously. It warns that all the people mentioned here could be charged under Section 2 of the Official Secrets Act concerning espionage; anything that may compromise military and intelligence operations in the United Kingdom. Are you with me so far?'

'I never signed the Official Secrets Act,' insisted McKenna. 'I'm just a bog-standard hack, not a bloody spy.'

'That may be so,' said Homann. 'But at least two of the people you interviewed recently were subject to the Official Secrets Act. You remember a gentleman called Myler? I have the original taped conversation.'

'You've lifted my tapes!' shouted McKenna.

'Of course,' said Homann smugly. 'We searched your hotel room.' Then, with a sneer, 'After all, it may have been necessary to contact your next of kin.'

Homann put his papers away and got to his feet.

'I have done with you,' he told McKenna. 'Herr Bux will give you a copy of all the paperwork when it is decided you are fit to leave hospital.'

McKenna didn't get very far with Bux, either.

He described the shooting of Adler, because that was

now 'a matter of public record' and the major media outlets already had a name and description of the killer.

'What about the inquest, though?'

'That is in the hands of Herr Homann.'

McKenna insisted.

'In our country, if someone is shot dead, whether he was a baddy or a goody, there's usually an inquiry.'

Bux thought for a few seconds before he replied, 'Governments everywhere prefer not to discuss certain people involved in sensitive assignments. So no, there will be no inquiry.'

'So Lucienne and I just imagined everything else?'

'I think that is a good way of describing it,' said Bux.

'Where is James Rezin now?'

'James?'

'Oh, all right … Fassbinder, or whatever you want to call him?'

'He is in the mortuary at *Kripo* headquarters. He will remain there until the Minister of the Interior decides what to do with him.'

'It would be nice to think he will end up back in Braemar.'

Bux sighed and stared out of the window.

'You can stop fishing,' he said. 'A RAF member has been shot dead in Stuttgart, and that is all I am going to say.'

'You sound like a tape recorder being rewound every few minutes,' McKenna said caustically. 'So you believe this story, too.'

'I believe in what I see and what I hear.'

McKenna persisted.

'If this was a well-known killer and you've been chasing him for yonks, how come he managed to live in that flat without anyone finding out?'

'The owners were away on holiday.'

'Aye, but how did *he* know that?'

'Coincidence,' said Bux.

There was a click of heels on the wooden flooring somewhere in the dark corridor outside the room. McKenna hoped it was Batch, but it was a man in army uniform with a pistol in his holster and a stethoscope round his neck.

'*Herr Homann sagt, kann der Patient nach Hause gehen,*' he told Bux after checking all the things doctors checked.

'Homann says you can go home now,' said Bux.

'Home?'

'I think he means your hotel, but perhaps this is a good time to check out the plane flights from Stuttgart to Glasgow; your friend, too.'

McKenna pulled a face.

'She's not a friend,' he said.

'Oh, is this your trial separation?' said Bux.

McKenna had been looking forward to his next question.

'What you are going to do about Fontainebleau now there's no Adler to show you the way?'

'Adler was to show me the way to Fontainebleau? I do not understand.'

'You can stop playing dumb,' said McKenna. 'I taped your interview.'

'*You did what?*'

'I taped your chat with Adler. It was on my knee under the coffee table.'

'Very clever,' said Bux, 'but there's not a lot you can do with that. Homann had your hotel room searched, remember?'

McKenna tried not to sound smug when he told him, 'I'd thought of that one, too. All the copies of my notes and tapes are on the way to Albion Street.'

'And the photographs? Homann said there was no sign of them.'

'Well, obviously he never looked in the minibar.'

Bux could not help smiling as McKenna continued,

'The tape of you and Adler are in German, but I've been through all this before. I'm sure Mrs Batch will be happy to translate.'

It occurred to Bux then. 'Where exactly is Mrs Batch?' he said.

'I don't know and don't really care. Colleagues usually go and see you in hospital, don't they? Some pal she is.' Then he thought and added, 'There again, she always has Lang.'

'*Explain.*'

'I can take a good guess where *they* are now.'

'What do you mean? Lang is visiting his mother in hospital.'

'I knew it wouldn't take *her* long,' said McKenna as if he hadn't heard. Then, peevishly, 'When do I get discharged from here?'

Bux tried to maintain a studied calm.

'*Take her long to do what?*'

'What do you think? She's been chasing a story, and usually that means getting information from men; a bit like that Lulu woman.'

'Lang and the girl? Together?'

'You've got it.'

'When was the last time you saw her?'

'A day ago, I would guess.'

'Did you have a hired vehicle?'

'A black Beetle; why, what are you thinking?'

Bux hurried towards the bell by the bed and the nurse appeared at once.

'Please bring Herr McKenna's clothing,' Bux told her.

'Will you sign him off?' said the nurse.

'*Just do it*,' said Bux. 'And hurry.'

CHAPTER 37.

The skies were beginning to lighten when the three identical green and white Mercedes sped west through Baden-Baden and on towards the French border.

Bux and McKenna, in the back seat of the lead vehicle, peered out of the window and wondered who would ask first about Mrs Batch and who had finished up the bigger mug.

The police vehicles lengthened into a convoy when they crossed the Rhine's Pont de l'Europe at Kehl and on to French soil.

'Members of the *Sûreté Nationale*,' said the driver, who also happened to be fluent in English. Then, again for McKenna's sake, he pointed in his rear-view mirror and said, 'The crime was on French soil so they are in charge of this part of the operation. There is also a representative of the French Ministry of the Interior.' McKenna nodded, but said nothing.

Bux had hardly spoken, either, though he did come to life as they passed a road sign for *D603, Verdun*.

'*All Quiet on the Western Front*,' said Bux.

'*Paths of Glory*,' McKenna responded, with a weak smile. 'Mrs Cloutier's husband is buried somewhere near here.' They looked at each other knowingly, like two trainspotter nerds sharing the same number.

Then they did begin to talk.

Bux approached it in a roundabout way and began with the trivia. The forensic team would probably have to work all night and most of next day, he said, assuming they did find Lulu close to the rock face that resembled an eagle. He thought it might be difficult to drive all the way because of the depth of the Fontainebleau Forest, and they might need a helicopter or even have to walk. Neither of the men liked the sound of that.

Detective Almerich Lang was 'on leave' so he could attend to his mother in hospital, which was half true, though by then most knew how a killer had found out the date, the time and the route Adler would take from Ludwigsburg to Hahnemannstraße. Bux thought it clever (though Rückeran had undoubtedly played a part in this) that he had chosen to hide in the *last* place a detective would look.

The Kommissar took a deep breath and said quietly, 'Frau Batch? I now know the details of her movements on the last morning.'

'She took off in the Beetle?' said McKenna who had already worked that out.

'That is correct. There is CCTV footage of her leaving the hotel underground car park at 7.08 a.m. A witness, a local builder, claims he saw a female sitting inside a black Volkswagen in Imkerstraße, which is less than a hundred metres from Rückeran's apartment. I assume the original intention was for the man to return to the top flat, change and collect his equipment, before they escaped together as husband and wife. The woman drove off when the first shots were heard.'

'It should be easy to trace the Beetle,' said McKenna.

Bux considered that for a tine then decided, 'It was indeed easy to trace. It was found abandoned close to Friedrichstraße – Checkpoint Charlie to you.'

'*Batch went over the Wall?*'

'It seems that way. According to two *Landespolizei* patrolmen the vehicle crossed the inner German border and into the East at Wartha, which is a five-hour drive from Stuttgart. The People's Police of the German Democratic Republic made no attempt to stop her, though there was a cursory passport check. There was a more thorough search by the Federal Border Guards in West Berlin, but at that stage there was no reason to stop a woman in a hire car. Clever, don't you think?'

'Clever?' asked McKenna.

'It would be difficult to find a more innocuous vehicle than a hired VW driven by an attractive female tourist.'

McKenna agreed.

'Yup; not exactly Bond and his Aston Martin, is it?'

'Créteil, said the driver. 'Not too far now.'

The closer they got to Fontainebleau the more officialdom: an investigating magistrate from Paris and a forensic archaeologist from Seine-et-Marne.

'Do you think the East Germans expected her?' McKenna asked.

'That is a rather stupid question, and one I can't answer,' Bux said irascibly. 'Perhaps you should telephone her and ask.'

McKenna did not respond and Bux decided such sarcasm was inappropriate.

'Look, Herr McKenna, I think all this was worked out in advance. She knew exactly where to go and what to do.'

McKenna remembered Batch in other ways then: a marriage to a member of the British Army of the Rhine, living in West Berlin and an excellent linguist. All that would certainly help.

'Did they find her husband?' he asked.

'Your Ministry of Defence will only admit to a Sergeant Frank Batch, a member of the Royal Corps of Signals. He has been based in Northern Ireland for the last three years. In other words, he has an alibi.'

'Where's the link between Batch and Rezin, though? Where does she fit in?'

'I don't know and I am not going to guess,' said Bux. McKenna decided he could do the guessing for them.

'I assume they were lovers,' he said. 'That might explain why I hardly saw her in Stuttgart: Lang apart, of course. Have you gone into her background?'

'Have *you*?' Bux bristled. 'Did no one in *your* office suspect she might have been a Communist?'

'You are joking, mate! Glasgow's full of them. My dad and half the shipyard were card-carrying members. Even I had a sniff. Anyway, if she's a Communist, I assume she'll be safe in the East?'

'Safe?'

'What happens to someone after they go over the Wall?'

'Your clever little friend would first speak to the DDR border guard, the border guard would telephone a superior and the superior would contact the Stasi, the Ministry for State Security. Then they will work out what to do with her.'

'And what *will* they do with her?'

'She would have plenty of job offers in the DDR,' said Bux grudgingly. 'The Stasi is full of devious types who know the best ways of misleading people. She may even have a future in their Foreign Intelligence group.'

Something else concerned McKenna.

'Are there newspapers in East Germany?'

Bux sniggered. 'You are fearful of being scooped; isn't that what it is called?'

'I suppose so.'

'I would not be too concerned. The DDR will take their time. One thing they *do* have in common with the West is never to make your enemy look too stupid because that will provoke him into retaliation. If she is going to work for them at some stage they certainly don't want her name and photograph in a newspaper. They might even drop it altogether. The public might never believe all of this, anyway.'

They were close. Bux opened a window and pointed at a small helicopter chopping in low circles overhead. It was carrying something large, held in a cradle by four thick ropes.

'I can't see my editor keeping the Batch stuff under the carpet,' McKenna continued. Bux was dismissive.

'You should join the real world, *Mister Newspaperman*. Think about it: your editor sent two of his staff to West Germany in the first place. Agreed? I am sure rival newspapers would be delighted to hear about that. If your editor has any sense he will throw his "scoop" in the bin. No one likes to be taken for a mug, particularly newspaper editors and their owners.'

'Well, you were taken for a mug, too,' McKenna responded. 'So was your boy Lang. I presume you will get a bollocking, too?'

'A bollocking?'

'Carry the can. Take the blame. There must be a superior somewhere working out exactly who made all the cock-ups.'

'There is not a lot they can do,' insisted Bux. 'We found a killer and I closed the investigation. I was about to retire, so while I might get a rap on the knuckles, they can hardly sack me.'

'When do you retire?' said McKenna with a sly grin.

'Midnight,' said Bux. 'Why do you ask, and *what* is so funny?'

'If it's midnight tonight we'd better get ready with the end titles.'

'I do not understand.'

'In movies there's always a grumpy cop about to retire who always get killed in the last scene. Tell you something else: the guy who shoots him is usually brought in by a government to shut him up. You know a lot about this case, don't you?'

'Very amusing,' said Bux, though he didn't find that funny at all.

The helicopter first flew out a little way, and then turned back before dropping its cargo of two large arc lights. Bux's driver pulled into a large car park with a sign for the Forêt de Fontainebleau and a large wooden hoarding fashioned into a map.

'We walk from here,' said Bux. 'There are too many trees and rocks for a vehicle. There should be a path part of the way.' Then they followed the guide into the terrible beauty of a forest night.

The local hadn't really been necessary, because it took less than twenty minutes to find it. The resemblance to a large bird was remarkable, even from a distance. The three large trees, formed into a V-sign, were unmistakeable, too.

The evening frost had hardened the ground and the digging was arduous, but ten-minute spells by beefy gendarmes made short work of it. After an hour one of the shovels hit something solid and a hand was raised high to warn the others.

Bux thought the wooden crate was a machine gun box because the ropes, used to carry heavy weights, were still intact. It took another hour of cautious digging before they could open the crate and look down on Lulu.

McKenna knew East End families often left the casket open, so newspaper death knocks had made him immune to corpses – possibly because they always looked as though they were sleeping. This was different.

It was nothing more than a collection of bones inside a wooden box, but first he felt guilty, as if he had been caught trespassing. Then he objected to Bux and his heavy-handed colleagues being there … the feeling that, after all, this Lulu was *his*.

Some of the cops may have felt the same, for no one wanted to reach down and lift the casket out. When two of them finally managed it some were in tears, though it might have been a strengthening wind and the cold, dry air in the forest.

Three cops clicked away with cameras the size of a suitcase. None took any notice of McKenna and his little Box Brownie, though he knew Bux was watching.

The anthropologist used a tape recorder and spoke loudly so everyone could hear: the body was still articulated and the bones were small and the frame light, with the wide pelvis and hips of a childbearer. The ribs had been broken and several of the teeth were missing, though the molars left were in good order. A woman in her late twenties or early thirties, the anthropologist decided, though most had already worked that out. There was a hole in the skull just above where the left eye had been, so whoever shot her had been right-handed. A wedding ring had refused to leave the fleshless finger and a silver charm amulet was still attached to the last cervical vertebrae of the neck. Someone had placed a black beret on top of the ribcage, like a Remembrance Day wreath.

McKenna looked away only when Bux tapped him on the shoulder.

'That is it for us,' he said. 'The French police and my team can finish off, and we will just get in the way if we stay.' Then, bizarrely, he slapped McKenna on the back and said, 'You have done a good job.'

The skies reddened into twilight and Bux had to use a flashlight to navigate the way back to the car park.

The detective could have been dead for all he knew, but for the red light of a cigarette every few seconds in the dark.

'*Are you OK?*' McKenna asked.

Bux remained silent and unmoving.

McKenna tried again. 'It's all over now. Isn't it?'

Then the vehicle's interior lights went on and a desperately grim Bux turned round and said, 'I don't think it's all over.'

McKenna wasn't in the mood for one of Bux's guessing games, but he asked patiently anyway, 'Meaning?'

'Remember that day at your hotel and those family photographs?'

'I remember; anything in particular?'

'Those of the old lady pushing a pram.'

'I know what you're on about. You mean there were no snaps of the kid? I mentioned that to Mrs Cloutier. It never struck me as a big deal.'

'*The pram,*' said Bux, this time more urgently.

'Still don't get it.'

'Obviously you have never had the privilege of bringing up children, Herr McKenna. Some prams are built to carry more than one.'

McKenna was hungry, thirsty and getting tired of Bux's

conundrums.

'Perhaps he was a big boy,' he retorted. 'It's just a bloody pram. Perhaps Lulu had planned more than one kid. I wish you'd come to the point.'

'I said at the time there was something odd about it,' said Bux. 'I couldn't quite nail it – then I saw Lulu's silver neck charm.'

'It was just a necklace. The sort you give to kids.'

'Not any kids and any necklace,' said Bux decisively. 'This particular neck charm is known in my country as *Brüderchen* und *Schwesterchen*, from an old Grimm's fairy tale. In English it would translate as "Little Brother and Sister".'

It was as if that arc light in the forest had suddenly been turned on again because suddenly it was all so obvious. McKenna stared askance at Bux and he simply nodded in confirmation.

'Twins,' said McKenna. 'Lucienne Batch and James Rezin were bloody twins!'

CHAPTER 38.

Bux and his *Kripo* team had bookings for the Hôtel Napoleon, close to the Château de Fontainebleau, a small, turn-of-the-century pile with log fires and candlelit tables. McKenna took the room allocated to the late Leopold Adler.

Bux joined him in the bar after lengthy telephone calls and a brief discussion with the investigating magistrate. McKenna was on his third glass of cold beer, and still trying to work out if this was a celebration, or a wake.

'Your colleague Mrs Batch,' Bux began as he sat down opposite and as close to the fire as he dared. 'Or do we call her Miss Rezin now?'

'Little Orphan Annie' was McKenna's suggestion, before he realised Bux was not in the mood for flippancy. So he asked instead, 'I suppose she was *born* in Braemar and adopted when she was just a few weeks old?'

'We have to assume that,' said Bux as he made a start on a glass of wine. 'There was only one Rezin registered on April 8, 1941.'

'How did she get away with that?' asked McKenna.

'I do not think it was her choice,' said Bux. 'In any case, a missing registering of a birth would hardly be a priority during a war. So far we know little about the early days of

Lucienne Batch. Most of it is conjecture.'

'Trust Batch,' said McKenna almost admiringly. 'An awkward cow to the end. What else have you heard?'

'I have conjectures,' said Bux enigmatically.

'*For Christ's Sake!*' McKenna cried. 'Don't go back into the Three Wise Monkeys routine. What harm will it do to tell me now? You know we can't publish and you're about to quit anyway, aren't you?'

Bux laboured to his feet so he could warm his backside on the fire.

'This is not on the record,' he warned.

'I'm clean,' promised McKenna.

'Remember Homann and his official warnings. And no secret taping.'

McKenna held up both hands in surrender.

'Swear to God and hope to die,' he said.

'I see all the pieces now and how they might fit,' Bux began. 'Let's start in April 1941. I think it was your contact who mentioned the fate of mothers of illegitimate children, particularly in the Scottish Highlands.'

'That was Myler,' said McKenna.

'Mrs Cloutier also mentioned her daughter's adventurous nature, the travel, the mountaineering and the SOE operations. She must have decided that children would get in the way. It might also explain why there are no family photographs. The girl left there immediately; the boy a year or so later.'

'Why the wait?' asked McKenna. 'And where did she go?'

'I do not know. You will have to find that out for yourself.'

'Well, you have heard all my tapes, so what's your opinion?' asked McKenna.

'I have no opinion on that,' said Bux.

'What about Rückeran and his first telephone call to me?'

'Think back to Myler's tape,' suggested Bux. 'And the mention of Rückeran approaching the Braemar registry office. That was some weeks before he phoned you. When the family heard from the registrar they could take things on from there. The phone call to you was a setback, of sorts, because others knew about Rückeran by then. In the end that family used you quite cleverly.'

'I think they did a good job on the Stuttgart cops, too,' McKenna responded.

'I have to agree,' admitted Bux.

McKenna checked his watch.

'At some stage I am going to have to go and see Mrs Cloutier,' he said. 'We found Lulu for her, but she lost two other members of the family. It's only fair to tell me what happened with the boy. That will be the first thing she asks.'

'There's not a lot to tell you,' said Bux.

'*Tell me.*'

'He was still alive when I arrived,' said Bux.

McKenna leaned forward urgently and said, 'So it wasn't over. He could have been saved?'

'He was dying, Herr McKenna.'

'They wanted to take him out,' cried McKenna. 'They had to stop shooting when you arrived. Otherwise it would have looked like murder.'

'You have seen too many gangster movies,' said Bux. 'If it is any help I sat down on the floor and held his hand for the last few seconds. His mouth was moving as if talking to someone. Then there was a final, last sigh and an exhalation.'

'Was anything left for his granny? Were there any belongings?'

'There was a large watch that can go back and some clothing, but little else. There were some local maps in an inside pocket; Stuttgart and the Black Forest and a cigarette lighter. Some pills, but I don't think Mrs Cloutier expects those back.'

'What sort of pills? Was it something to do with the epilepsy?'

'They were phenobarbital tablets,' said Bux. 'I gather they are used to control seizures. So you are probably right.'

'Yes, but what sort of seizures?'

'I am not a damn doctor,' said Bux. 'A killer evaded the West German police forces for some time, so it must have been a mild form of epilepsy.'

Then he remembered the shooting, the angle of the gunshot and the English cigarette so he added, 'In a mild case a sufferer may have to lie down for a short time. I don't think he was a driver.'

'If you're not a doctor, how do you know that?'

'Epileptics are seldom allowed to drive.'

'So that was where Batch came into it?' McKenna suggested.

Bux stared into the fire as if he might find the answer in there but said nothing. McKenna did not press him further.

'Mother's ruin?' he asked instead.

'*Mother's what?*'

'Gin,' said McKenna.

CHAPTER 39.

'It happens, sir,' said the sassy blonde on the flight from Paris-Orly to Heathrow, as she helped clear up the sick with a wipe that smelled of lemon. She showed him a spare paper bag, in case it happened again, and added, 'Have a good flight.' The other passengers pretended they hadn't noticed. McKenna, who had a window seat this time, stared at the clouds outside and thought of the night before.

Bux had been in a sociable mood from the start. At midnight he asked McKenna and three of his *Kripo* colleagues to stand and join him in a toast.

'I am pleased to announce that Markus Bux is no longer a *Kripo* detective,' he said. '*Prost!*' McKenna hadn't known his first name until then.

Then the serious drinking began.

McKenna, of course, wanted to talk about the case but, sociable or not, Bux kept it tight. He spoke of his life during and after the war when he had been the German equivalent of a Red Cap, a military policeman. He mentioned Silke a lot, and that they may visit Scotland during their planned tour of Europe. There was a ridiculous games session to finish. McKenna won the film quiz and Bux the best at getting a wine glass to whistle the loudest. At the end Bux gave him a bear hug that took all his breath away and they shook hands. Then, more seriously, his farewell words: 'someone official' would be waiting for him when he landed at Heathrow.

By the time McKenna surfaced Bux had gone and had sorted out the bills.

'This for you, too,' the girl receptionist said. 'A gift from *gentilhomme friend*,' which turned out to be four large bottles of schnapps and a Lonely Planet travel guide. McKenna was going to miss him.

He stored the booze in the suitcase and kept the travel guide in a pocket to read on the flight. It was a nice gesture, though he couldn't see what he would do with a guide to Fontainebleau in German, except perhaps give it to someone for Christmas. It might have been Bux's idea of what passed for a joke in Germany.

He opened the book. There was a short message on the inside cover, in English but in that odd German script, '*Good luck. Enjoy your flight home. Some day we may meet again in Scotland. I hope my gifts make it through customs!*'

The last five words were in German, so he called over the air hostess to ask if she could translate.

'*Im Nachhinein sind alle kluge,*' she said. 'I think that means "in hindsight everyone is wiser". Please fasten seat belt now.'

McKenna's ears popped painfully and suddenly the plane lurched, so sharply he dropped the travel guide. He reached down to pick it up and the piece of paper that had been hiding inside. There was no message this time, but it wasn't necessary.

When the plane landed and began to taxi McKenna was still staring out of the window at nothing at all.

It was easy to spot the suits: two men in their thirties with hands behind their backs, confident and aggressive among families and friends waiting at arrivals.

They escorted him through a door that said 'Customs Only', where three men in short-sleeved white shirts spent an hour checking his suitcase and all his clothing, though he was allowed to keep on his socks. They took away his notes and the Box Brownie, but left the Cloutier family album.

The suits took over from there: first an official caution and then more papers with the relevant details of the Official Secrets Act, all of which was more or less a repeat of what Homann had told him in hospital.

'Anything to say?' asked the senior suit. McKenna was too tired and too homesick so he just shook his head. The three customs men reappeared: he could pay duty for two of his bottles of schnapps or have them confiscated. He paid up.

It started to rain as soon as he stepped outside the airport and it took half an hour for a taxi. He had never been so happy to see the Dear Green Place again.

Things had changed at *The Inquirer*. The commissionaire with the army medals had given way to two attractive females in their twenties in charge of a front desk the length of a cricket field. There was an arty-farty mural on the wall behind them and as many flowers and plants as there were in the Botanic Gardens.

Editorial had new arrivals, notably a bespectacled lady in her fifties hard at work in what had once been the office of the editorial administrator. The name on the door had been painted over.

'Welcome home,' said Bloom unsmilingly as they shook hands. 'Sorry there's no red carpet for you.'

Three Americans in their late forties were waiting inside Bloom's office. They wore identical black, Brooks Brothers suits with trews that didn't quite reach the shoes. Steven Stotz, the legal adviser to *Inquirer* Newspapers Ltd, was based in Fleet Street but was originally from Texas.

'Guddaseeya,' he said to McKenna.

The other two were lawyers: the one with scary, Christopher Walken eyes was Mister Butler from Los Angeles and the one who kept his shades on throughout was Mister Fry from Boston. They addressed each other by their surnames, as a lot of Americans did, and were fond of talking while looking out of the office window, presumably for dramatic effect. They had a language of their own: 'Active Shooting Situation, A Crisis Dispensation, Covert Aggression' – and, their favourite – 'Plausible Deniability'. They used that one a lot.

Stotz began by handing out copies of the letter from the office of the Attorney General warning of the perils of contravening the Official Secrets Act and another from the Press and Broadcasting D-notice Committee.

This was a new one on McKenna, so he read it carefully. *'You are requested not to publish anything about the identity, whereabouts and tasks of persons of whatever status or rank, employed by any of the British services and listed in our notes below.'*

The names in the notes below were *Inquirer* Newspapers Ltd, Bloom, McKenna and the two surviving member of the Cloutier family, Mrs Cloutier and Mrs Lucienne Batch.

Stotz, Fry and Butler went straight into plausible deniability mode and how the British and Bonn governments and *Inquirer* Newspapers Ltd would use it.

Stotz's guess was that, 'Both governments were withholding information about events that were probably illegal, but their response is plausible.' In other words the governments admit that a Briton served both Bonn and Britain and was involved in operations in West Germany during the recent past, but nothing more.

There were two ways for a government to enforce that, said Stotz. 'One is the pay-off and the other is the frighten-off, and the governments are going for the latter.'

Butler didn't sound positive, either.

'I would guess both governments know we would never print this story. D-notices are only advisory requests so are not legally enforceable, but we certainly don't want to provoke the Attorney General into an Official Secrets Act case. That might finish with someone in the glasshouse.'

'A possible two-year stretch,' added Fry. 'The guilty ones would be whoever suggested the story in the first place and the man who wrote it.'

The three Americans looked at Bloom and then McKenna.

McKenna spoke for the first time.

'Did James Rezin have to sign the Official Secrets Act?'

'Of course,' said Stotz.

'But he wasn't employed by the British government. He had been booted out of the SAS. He was in the pay of Bonn.'

The three Americans looked at each other for an answer.

'Good point,' said Fry, as he checked his notes, 'but I don't think that will help. It says here the newspaper will not publish anything about persons "employed by any of the armed services". It doesn't say where, when and with whom.'

'In other words, we can't publish anything?' said Bloom.

'As things stand, no,' said Stotz, 'apart from the story of Lulu being found in the Forest of Fontainebleau.'

'Is that all?' asked McKenna.

307

'I don't think you have a choice,' said Fry, who had suddenly started to use 'you' instead of 'us'.

'Even if we took a risk every other newspaper will say your story is a fabrication. It will be easy to get quotes from the governments to prove it.'

Butler agreed. 'You have to think about the Batch case, too. Her involvement might be a bit embarrassing. The rival papers will have a field day with that. In fact, you are in a similar position to Bonn and Downing Street.'

'Which is?' said McKenna.

Bloom replied for all. 'No one likes admitting they were taken for mugs.'

McKenna still had a few questions of his own so he asked, of no one in particular, 'What do we say if someone asks where Mrs Batch is?'

Fry was convinced he had thought this one through.

'She went to West Germany on holiday,' he said without hesitation.

'Half true,' said Bloom. 'She had time owing.'

'Then she stayed out there for journalistic experience,' suggested Stotz.

'We might get away with that, too,' said Bloom.

Butler was convinced.

'After a month no one will remember her anyway,' he said. 'If they do you can play the plausible deniability game. If it's good enough for the government it's good enough for newspapers. It just leaves you without a story.'

Lots of nods and sips of tea and coffee.

'Oh, I have a story,' said McKenna.

'Come again?' said Bloom.

'We still have a story,' McKenna said.

'Where?'

'Right here,' said McKenna. He bent down, took off his

shoes and socks and pulled out the *pièce de résistance*.

The photo was in black and white and of poor quality. It had been folded into quarters and was soiled and muddied, like something rescued from a rubbish bin. The Eiffel Tower in the background was obvious, as was the deep snow on the ground. In the foreground three soldiers and a woman seemed to be in conversation. The men were wearing field caps; two were in lighter uniforms than the other, who was in deep black. The woman's head was bare.

The words on the front of the photograph were only just readable – *Lulu and Friends* – but the caption on the back in a copybook, Germanic script was more recent and quite clear: *Adele Cloutier mitt Lukas Rückeran, Manfred Fiedler und Leopold Adler. Paris, February 24, 1944.*

The three Americans left two hours later, in what McKenna thought was a mixture of incredulity and elation. Bloom, whose boyish smile had also returned, asked him to stay on.

'I assume someone gave you that photograph?' he asked. 'Someone with a grudge against the Bonn government?'

'I'd like to protect my sources,' said McKenna.

'Fair dos; none of my business. I was just concerned that whoever gave us the snap might finish up in bother?'

'I don't think so,' said McKenna. 'I would think Bonn might have trouble proving who handed it over anyway. I was more worried about my other sources.'

'You mean the Official Secrets Act duo – the two retired army men?'

'Mitchell's not bothered. All he did was tell a few stories about the war. We can use Myler's words, but can't quote him. He has one request, though.'

'Which is?' asked Bloom suspiciously.

'He wants to meet you.'

'Do you know why?'

'I'd rather leave that for now,' said McKenna diplomatically. 'I was thinking more of Lulu's mother. Could she be charged with something?'

'What would they charge her with?' said Bloom. 'Guilty for being the mother of an SOE agent? Granny of a lad who left home when he was a kid? She's ninety, anyway, isn't she? I can't see her appearing in a Tory Star Chamber, can you?'

'And Batch?'

Bloom got to his feet and walked to the window looking onto Albion Street.

'She is not a source of ours,' he said quietly with his back to McKenna. Then louder and as if composing a reference to a new employer, 'Lucienne Batch will be greatly missed and I wish her all the luck in the world.'

'So you don't think she'll face charges?'

'As far as I know she never committed a crime,' said Bloom, 'though some people may regard being a member of the Communist Party a crime. She did dump a hire vehicle in the middle of Berlin, but so what? Anyway, *Inquirer* Newspapers Ltd has sorted that out with the vehicle hire company.'

'But she did use us,' McKenna pointed out.

Bloom turned round purposefully.

'Everyone uses everyone else, particularly in the newspaper business. That's why we've got the best hard news story since Watergate. We owe a huge debt to Lucienne Batch – and whoever gave you that snap, of course.'

Chapter 40.

After prolonged discussions between senior staff and lawyers, a copy of the Paris photograph, its caption and the first 3,000 words of the Lulu story went by registered letter to an address in London's Victoria Street.

Ten days later, November 27, the first of a four-part series duly rolled off *The Inquirer* presses.

Bloom had chosen a Saturday initially because it was up to the Sundays to try to follow it up, and they were not very good at that. Come the Monday there was a feeding frenzy, but the rivals never caught up. How could they? An *Inquirer* reporter had not only been there when the remains of a British war hero was found after four decades but, in front page vernacular, the reporter had also had 'a brush with death the day he met a killer in pursuit of his story'.

Bloom thought the photo was the real reason the Attorney General had not responded to the registered letter, though he would never find out. All *The Inquirer* had done, after all, was to publish a picture of a girl called Lulu and three German soldiers caught for posterity in a snowy Paris street. Readers could then make up their own minds on the significance of the murder of the three men and the discovery of the woman's body in the same week.

The grainy, black-and-white image on the front page,

said Bloom, would soon be 'as famous as Capa's "The Falling Soldier" or "Raising the Flag on Iwo Jima".'

The main headline *Looking for Lulu*, above a sub-deck of *How We Uncovered the Truth of the Murder of a British War Hero* were also over the top for some, but reasonably accurate. McKenna was amazed to find that the basics of one story could be told in sixteen words. Bloom had insisted on joint bylines – *By William H McKenna and Lucienne Batch* – which made sense, given that Mrs Batch was supposedly still working for *The Inquirer* and she had done a lot of the paperwork.

A marketing company sold the serial rights in Germany, France and the United States. McKenna got his contract, a title and *Chief Investigative Reporter* on an engraved business card.

Lulu hadn't quite finished with him.

The consular staff in London had looked after everything, from organising the death certificates to coping with the various coroners in France and Germany. It was rumoured they had also paid for the two caskets and the cost of the flights, though Bloom insisted that the owners of T*he Inquirer* had forked out for that.

Either way, Lulu and son duly arrived home on December 1. There was a nasty incident the day before when the Tory candidate for Kincardine and Deeside (a new constituency that replaced Aberdeenshire West), his PR people and a photographer turned up at Blair Lodge. No one got past Janek on the main gate. Mrs Cloutier had already refused an MBE, on behalf of her daughter.

McKenna had no such problems. The letter had arrived, via a solicitor's office in Aberdeen, on November 29, asking if he would take part in a brief ceremony at midday on the day Lulu came home. There was no objection if the occasion was covered by an *Inquirer* photographer, although 'it is wise if visitors wear stout walking shoes on the day in question'. McKenna assumed that was because of the bad weather up north and the poor condition of the track to the house, but that was not the case.

'We should have borrowed a Land Rover,' said Chadwick, the photographer, as he carefully negotiated the Ford along the snow-covered Blair Lodge lanes. 'Everyone living in the country should have one of them.'

Chadwick was from somewhere in the North of England and a tad outspoken, like Bloom, and McKenna thought at first he was being facetious. Then he realised Chadwick had only just joined the staff and wouldn't know anything of Lucienne Batch, and certainly not her preferred mode of transport.

'Is this it?' Chadwick asked.

'This is it,' said McKenna.

McKenna thought later there had been a sense of déjà vu about the whole afternoon. Little had changed, at least not on the surface. It had snowed, it had been difficult to get up the drive – and Janek was still waiting outside the front door with Bruce the dog alongside. McKenna assumed this was to be a cremation because there were no fresh holes in the family plot and no sign of a vicar or a priest. The two journalists, Mrs Cloutier, Janek and the dog were the only mourners.

Mrs Cloutier did seem more outwardly frail. Her hands shook, and when she spoke the voice was so weak it was as if she was talking from a long distance away. She seemed oddly disinterested when McKenna spoke to her, as if she was discussing the local weather or a traditional family holiday. She laughed mordantly when she described the visit of two members of Aberdeen City police force to tell

313

her that James was in a Stuttgart morgue and Lulu in an undertaker's casket in Fontainebleau.

'They didn't know where to start,' said Mrs Cloutier. 'The retrieval or another family death?' She had decided then on cremations, assuming James ever came home, and the ashes would be scattered outside Blair Lodge. She wasn't into church ceremonies, she pointed out.

McKenna did his best and asked the obvious questions, of course; probably too obvious, because Mrs Cloutier was careful and still slyly watchful.

Lucienne was adopted within a month of her birth in 1941, she said, using the surname for the first time. She had been brought up 'somewhere, possibly abroad'.

'America?' guessed McKenna, who remembered the odd twang.

The old lady just shrugged. When it suited her after that she simply suffered an acute loss of memory because every other personal question was met with the same frustrating response, as if that explained everything: 'It was wartime.'

'That's interesting,' she said when Stuttgart and her grandchildren were mentioned, and, 'I can't explain that,' to everything else. McKenna would have loved to have known if she had heard from Lucienne, 'off the record', he said, but she ignored that, too.

In the end McKenna decided *The Inquirer* had enough words for a month of stories already. It was snowing, and Chadwick wanted his snaps before dark.

McKenna watched from a distance as Janek carefully pushed Mrs Cloutier and wheelchair out of the house, down the grassy slope and into what remained of the garden. The old lady did well: posing and looking meaningfully at the camera at the right time and in the right place. She even suggested a few changes and Chadwick never complained. When he had finished McKenna was called over and handed one large urn, and the Pole took the other so the ashes could be scattered together in the family plot.

At the end Mrs Cloutier held out a translucent hand and McKenna bent down and pecked her on the cheek. She smiled and whispered, 'Thank you, Mister McKenna. Thank you for everything.'

That should have been that, but it wasn't, because the great film director in the sky wanted one last take.

They had reached the gate on the way out when Chadwick suddenly braked, turned off the engine and dived into the car boot to find his camera just as a dozen geese flew west over the house in a long, V-shaped formation.

'By gum, mate, did you see that?' said Chadwick.

'I did,' said McKenna.

'Them ducks?' said Chadwick as he finally drove off. 'Do you ever watch them wildlife things on telly?'

'Occasionally,' said McKenna impatiently. 'They were geese, anyway.'

Chadwick was quite unfazed and wanted his answer.

'Do you ever wonder if it's the same bird that leads the way?' he asked.

McKenna smiled grimly and said, 'Don't know, but I bet it's always a female.'

McKenna began to relax when they passed Glenshee on the road south.

'What did you make of Mrs Cloutier?' he asked his driver.

'A bit dotty, but a nice old dear,' Chadwick replied. 'Incredible story, isn't it?'

'You seemed to get on with her. What were you talking about?'

'She kept going on about cameras; the size of the lens,

the best makes and how long it took to get a snap into a newspaper. She asked me to send her some. Poor old dear; quite sad, in't it?'

'Very sad,' McKenna agreed. 'Did she mention the family?'

'She rambled on about this and that. She mentioned her daughter and the twins. It got quite confusing in the end.'

'That's the trouble with a family spread all over the place,' said McKenna. 'Mrs Cloutier's husband and her son-in-law are both buried abroad.' He paused and then added, 'Lucienne's away in Germany now.'

Chadwick pipped his horn and shouted abuse at the elderly couple in a camper van in front. 'I heard all about that Lucienne,' he said when he got past. 'The picture desk just *loved* her.'

'Did Mrs Cloutier mention her?'

'Just summat about her dad's grave.' Then, out of his window, '*Bloody Kraut!*'

'Say that again.'

'Them Volkswagen camper vans are always getting in the way.'

'Not that bit: the one about Lucienne's dad and his grave.'

'All she said was that Lucienne was on holiday in Germany and might be able to take flowers to the grave. Are we stopping anywhere for nosh?'

McKenna tried not to sound concerned when he asked, 'Are you sure she said Germany? Her father is buried in Paris. He was in the French Resistance.'

'*Stuttgart*,' said Chadwick enthusiastically, as if he had just remembered a clue for a quiz. 'I remember now; she was talking about Stuttgart. That's in West Germany, isn't it? I wouldn't worry. She probably meant France. Old folk are always forgetting things.'

316

McKenna stared out of the window and didn't speak at all for some time and only until they passed a sign for 'Glasgow 32', when he told Chadwick to pull in at the Little Chef by Dunblane.

He left Chadwick to order while he went to use the public phone by the pay desk. He got as far as putting in the 10ps and lifting the receiver but then decided he wouldn't bother.

EPILOGUE

Janek trod carefully down the steep steps, holding firewood and kindling in one hand and searching for the light switch with the other.

It had always been a cold house, this, but there was a chill shudder of dread every time he went down into the cellar. It reminded Janek of the images of the ovens in the death camps and the Nazi boast that 340 corpses could be incinerated in a single day. The sooner he finished here the better.

The snow had arrived before he had managed to stack the wood under the eaves, and it was still wet. So he poured a small amount of petrol on the kindling and took the box of matches out of his pocket.

Then he stopped, scratched his head and wondered if there had been a mistake.

Forty years at Blair Lodge had made him immune to the family eccentricities, but he was baffled by Mrs Cloutier's insistence that the family photographs, scrapbooks and even Lulu's diary were to be torched.

'To ashes,' she had told him, and had even repeated it in Polish.

The family albums and the scrapbooks were ablaze at once, but he hesitated at the last. There was no sound from within the house and Mrs Cloutier would never be able to get down the stairs unaided so he blew out the match, picked up Lulu's diary and held it up to the light so he could see it better.

The Pole had enough English to understand the large letters in red, the words a child might write on the cover of her first diary – *The Life of Lulu* – and below that, in smaller letters, 'By Eugenie Cloutier'.

It seemed such a waste, but a job was a job and Mrs Cloutier would know by looking at him if he had finished it. But he must have used too much petrol and had to step back from the oven so, hurriedly, he dropped the diary on the concrete floor.

A number of photographs, six or seven in all, fell out.

Janek bent to pick them up and realised at once they had not been taken by him, though most of those in the albums were his. There was one of Lulu reaching down to gather up a doll that had fallen off that silly pram with the wire wheels, and another of daughter and mother together. There was one of the twins in the pram, staring at the camera and frowning, as if someone had just given them bad news.

Janek shivered, despite the heat, when he saw the final photographs, which were in colour.

A boy with butter-coloured hair was smiling into the camera in the same forest and atop the same rock face that Lulu had once posed on. Remarkable, too, how the rock resembled an eagle, like the one across the valley here. The boy was probably still in his late teens and it must have been a warm summer because his Panzer tunic had been discarded for his field-grey undershirt, and he had even taken the standard Luger from his hip holster.

Janek was not a stupid man. The history of the Cloutier family would always involve secrecy and things best kept that way, but now he understood why for the first time. He knew why the twins had been discarded and why there were few photographs of them. He wondered if they had come to know their own history, though he doubted that.

He stared fixedly at the photographs for a little time longer until, without further hesitation, he flung the diary into the oven and closed the doors.

Mrs Cloutier was waiting at the top of the stairs. She did not speak, but questioned with her eyes, and when he nodded to confirm she smiled.

He took that as approval of an operation well done.

THE END

Lightning Source UK Ltd.
Milton Keynes UK
UKOW06f1604130915

258529UK00001BA/1/P